Embroidered Truths

Needlecraft Mysteries by Monica Ferris

CREWEL WORLD
FRAMED IN LACE
A STITCH IN TIME
UNRAVELED SLEEVE
A MURDEROUS YARN
HANGING BY A THREAD
CUTWORK
CREWEL YULE

Embroidered Truths

Monica Ferris

BERKLEY PRIME CRIME, NEW YORK

THE BERKLEY PUBLISHING GROUP
Published by the Penguin Group
Penguin Group (USA) Inc.
375 Hudson Street, New York, New York 10014, USA
Penguin Group (Canada), 10 Alcorn Avenue, Toronto, Ontario M4V 3B2, Canada
(a division of Pearson Penguin Canada Inc.)
Penguin Books Ltd., 80 Strand, London WC2R 0RL, England
Penguin Group Ireland, 25 St. Stephen's Green, Dublin 2, Ireland (a division of Penguin Books Ltd.)
Penguin Group (Australia), 250 Camberwell Road, Camberwell, Victoria 3124, Australia
(a division of Pearson Australia Group Pty. Ltd.)
Penguin Books India Pvt. Ltd., 11 Community Centre, Panchsheel Park, New Delhi—110 017, India
Penguin Group (NZ), Cnr. Airborne and Rosedale Roads, Albany, Auckland 1310, New Zealand
(a division of Pearson New Zealand Ltd.)
Penguin Books (South Africa) (Pty.) Ltd., 24 Sturdee Avenue, Rosebank, Johannesburg 2196,
South Africa

Penguin Books Ltd., Registered Offices: 80 Strand, London WC2R 0RL, England

This book is an original publication of The Berkley Publishing Group.

This is a work of fiction. Names, characters, places, and incidents either are the product of the author's imagination or are used fictitiously, and any resemblance to actual persons, living or dead, business establishments, events, or locales is entirely coincidental.

First edition: June 2005

Berkley hardcover ISBN: 0-425-20301-8

Library of Congress Cataloging-in-Publication Data

Ferris, Monica.
    Embroidered truths / Monica Ferris.—1st ed.
        p. cm.
    ISBN 0-425-20301-8
    1. Devonshire, Betsy (Fictitious character)—Fiction. 2. Women detectives—Minnesota—
Fiction. 3. Needleworkers—Fiction. 4. Needlework—Fiction. 5. Minnesota—Fiction. I. Title.

PS3566.U47E44 2005
813'.6—dc22

                                                                    2005041037

PRINTED IN THE UNITED STATES OF AMERICA

10 9 8 7 6 5 4 3 2 1

Acknowledgments

Mexico City is wonderful. Godwin is right, John is wrong, it's a great place to vacation. The places I mention down there are real, except for the night club—I was privileged to see and hear a flamenco guitar performance in a private home. Maru is real, she designed the tlattoli pattern in the back of this book. The places described in Excelsior and Minneapolis are real, except that a sushi bar has replaced The Waterfront Café. I wish to thank Ellen Kuhfeld, my own private editor, sounding board, and idea person. Also Berkley Prime Crime and my agent, Nancy Yost. Needleworkers everywhere: I am more grateful than I can say.

Toda es segun el color del cristal con que se mira.

Everything depends on the color of the glass you see through.

—Spanish saying

One

✤ ✤ ✤

IT was a glorious spring morning in Excelsior. Trees were showing off their bright new leaves, and while tulips were dropping their petals, lilacs and lily of the valley were sweetening air already throbbing with the call of robins. Betsy would have left the door of Crewel World open if her shop manager Godwin had been there.

Uncharacteristically, he was late, so she had to keep it closed so its *Bing!* would warn her of a customer's entrance—she was busily rearranging the back of the shop. The idea came from Susan Greening Davis, whose newsletter had become Betsy's Great Guide. The layout of a shop should be changed at intervals of, say, six months, suggested Ms. Davis. Regular customers typically went to the same spot to look at familiar stock, and moving merchandize to a new spot would make them hunt around, and perhaps discover a new designer or even a new skill. One of the happiest things a shop owner can hear is a customer crying, "I didn't know you had these!"

Interestingly, rearranging the layout would often bring a similar cry from an employee—occasionally even a shop owner. Of course, if something has been on a shelf so long even the owner has forgotten it, it should go into the deep-discount basket by the cash register forthwith.

On the other hand, there is, or should be, a pattern to a shop layout, a way of drawing the customer in, teasing with a spinner rack of cute and inexpensive charts, then another one of new flosses, and yet another of the familiar and popular, and so on, building desire, until the customer finds herself standing before a display of expensive kits, the hunger to buy at a peak.

Or so Betsy hoped. She was standing on a little ladder, reaching to rearrange one of the track lights so it shone on the lovely new Kreinik silks when she heard, "Betsy? Betsy, are you in here?"

The voice came as something of a shock, because she hadn't heard the door make its annoying *Bing!*

Betsy jumped down and hurried out between the two stacks of box shelves that divided the needlepoint-knitting area from the counted cross-stitch area. "Here I am! Oh, hello, Mrs. Wells. How—I mean, when did you come in? I didn't hear the door."

Mrs. Wells, a regular customer, turned to look at it. "You know, I didn't either. Do you suppose . . . ?" She went to the door, opened and closed it again. It did not emit its harsh ring. "How about that?" she said, then, "I'm here to pick up my Spectrum canvas."

"Oh, wait til you see it, it looks wonderful!"

Mrs. Wells had recently finished stitching a needlepoint canvas using a chart rather than stitching over a canvas with the pattern already painted on it. Painted canvases cost hundreds of dollars, while the chart was a mere twenty-five dollars. Plus materials, of course. Betsy had seen an ad for the Amybear chart in an issue of *Needlework Retailer* and ordered it on spec. Mrs. Wells's glad cry on seeing it on Betsy's shelf prompted Betsy to order two more.

Now, Betsy went behind the big desk that was her checkout counter and picked up a fourteen-inch square wrapped in brown paper. She carefully picked the tape away from one end of the package to disclose a framed circle of twelve segments, each segment a different color done in squares and rectangles of different stitches. Like a proper color wheel, the colors ranged from cool purple and blue to hot red and orange.

It was the stretching, matting, and framing Mrs. Wells was here to pay for today; she had selected an antique gold frame that was a perfect choice.

"Wow!" said Mrs. Wells, reaching for her checkbook.

"You did a great job," agreed Betsy. "And so did Heidi." Heidi was Betsy's finisher.

"Where's Godwin this morning?" asked Mrs. Wells a few minutes later, as she stood at the door looking around, the retaped needlepoint piece under one arm.

"He's a bit late this morning," said Betsy. "I expect him any minute." She tried to keep the concern out of her voice. Godwin was rarely more than a few minutes late, and then he always called to say what had happened and when he'd be in. But today the shop had been open an hour with no sign or signal.

Mrs. Wells left, and Betsy went back to the track lighting.

"Betsy!" Again she was startled by the voice of someone in her shop without the warning *Bing!* But it was Godwin's voice, and it sounded distraught.

"Goddy?" Betsy hurried out to the front of her shop to find her store manager leaning on the library table that stood in the middle of the floor. He was unshaven and wearing the same clothes he'd had on yesterday, now badly rumpled—and Godwin was a very fastidious dresser.

"What on earth's the matter?" she said.

"It's John. He's thrown me out." John was Godwin's lover.

"Again?" Betsy regretted the query the instant it came out of her mouth. Godwin was a good man, but very sensitive.

Still, John had thrown Godwin out on several other occasions—and they had always made up after a few days or a week.

"It's different this time, this time he really means it," said Godwin in a low voice.

It was always "different this time," but this time Betsy held her tongue.

He fell into a chair and rested his forehead in his hands. "He wouldn't take two minutes to explain what the problem was, he wouldn't even let me take a change of clothes, just tossed me out on my ear. I drove around for awhile, then I went back home and thought I'd park in front with the top down so he'd look out the window and feel sorry for me. But he didn't, so I slept the whole night in my car."

That explained his appearance.

"At least he didn't throw your clothes out into the street this time," Betsy pointed out.

"Yes," agreed Godwin. "But you know something? The time he did that, he was mad for a *reason*. I don't know *why* he's mad this time. He's been getting crankier and crankier all week. *Nothing I do* suits him. And last night was the final straw. He yelled at me for doing the dishes—I am *serious,* for doing the dishes! He *hates* coming into the kitchen in the morning and seeing dishes in the *sink*, but last night he didn't want me to do them. That was the *last thing* in a *string* of things he didn't like. He didn't like the *shirt* I wore to work yesterday, he didn't like the *music* I put on for dinner— and it was one of our *favorite* albums!—and then he stomped in to shout about the *dishes*. It's like he was *looking* for a fight! So I thought *fine,* and gave him one. And he ordered me to leave. 'Out!' he said, just like that. And I don't know why, I just don't know *why*."

"Poor fellow," said Betsy, and meant it. She came to put a hand on his shoulder.

"What am I going to *do*?" he cried, grabbing her hand and wetting it with his tears.

Betsy thought about it. "First of all," she said, "you are going upstairs to wash your hands and face, then borrow a razor and clean yourself up. Then you are going out to buy a change of clothes. You know you always think more clearly when you look good, and besides, our customers expect it of you. Possibly by the time you get back down here, John will have come to his senses and phoned looking for you. It will be a good lesson to him if you aren't waiting for that call."

Godwin stopped sniveling to think about that. "I think you may be right," he said.

"Of course I'm right."

Heartened, Godwin stood and hugged her. "You are the *best* friend I've ever had! Where do you keep your razor?"

"Take a fresh one out of the linen closet in the bathroom."

"Thanks." He took the spare key to her apartment out of the checkout desk drawer, and went out the back door of the shop, which opened into a back hall leading to the entrance hall to the upstairs apartments.

Betsy went back to work rearranging the aim of her track lights, but her mind was only half on her work. Godwin was a good friend as well as a first-class employee, and she was sad to see him this unhappy over a break-up with a person she personally thought not worth one of Godwin's tears. Every time one of these rifts happened, she would secretly hope Godwin would realize he had outgrown John—and every time they'd end up back together. It was a lot like watching a woman friend unable to dig in and divorce her awful husband.

One reason Godwin stayed with John was that John was lavish with money. He often took Godwin on weekend trips to New York or San Francisco, and, every February or March, on a week's vacation to Cancun. A senior associate in a prestigious Minneapolis law firm, John earned a generous salary, and these trips were first class all the way. Godwin always came home from Cancun tanned, sated, and sporting a new piece of jewelry.

But this year had been different. Because of a complex case he was working on, John kept putting off his vacation. And when the case was over, March had just turned to April, and John declared it was too late to go, because, he said, Cancun was an oven in April.

Godwin had been sad about that. He had come in to work the next morning out of an early April snowfall, sighing that Cancun in a heat wave was surely better than Minnesota in early April. "Someone famous said, 'April is the cruelest month,'" he said, turning to look out the window. "Was he from Minnesota?"

Betsy laughed. "Though he was born in America, I don't think T. S. Eliot ever even visited Minnesota," she said.

That was the same day Godwin cut out a color ad from

the Sunday paper. He'd been clipping coupons—he adored any kind of shopping, even for groceries—but this was not just a twenty-five cent coupon for salsa. Attached to the coupon was an ad announcing a chance to win a week in Cancun. The entry blank, which featured a rectangle in a bright-colored cubist design, was not to be mailed in, but brought to a local grocery store and put behind a decoding screen where, more than likely, the word *Sorry* would appear.

But not this time. Later that evening Betsy was taken from an interesting article on Elizabethan Blackwork to answer the phone.

"I won, I won, I *won!*" a voice shrieked in her ear.

Godwin.

"Won what?"

"A trip to *Mexico!* I will never in my whole life eat any salsa but Mexicali Rose!"

"You mean that coupon you cut out was the winner? That's *wonderful!* Congratulations! This is so great! You get to go to Cancun after all!"

"Well . . . no," he said, turning down the volume a notch or two. "What I won was third prize, a pair of return plane tickets to Mexico City. But you see," he hastened to add, "that's actually *better*. Mexico City is up *high,* even higher than *Denver,* so it's not terribly hot there. And we've *done* Cancun about to death, this will be a *whole different place.* Besides," he added, more pragmatically, "this will be *my* treat, and I couldn't *afford* Cancun, not the places *John* is used to staying at."

"Your treat?"

"Yes, I've been really good about my credit cards lately, so I can *actually afford* to do this."

The next day, Betsy had asked, "How does John feel about you taking him instead of him taking you?"

Godwin chuckled. "He *likes* it. He was surprised, of course, but I said, 'It's about my turn, isn't it?' and he said, 'Well, why not?' So I think he's pleased."

"Good for you, Goddy," said Betsy. "It's especially nice of you to offer to pay for everything."

"Yes, well, I'll have to get on-line and see what rates I can get for a hotel. But it *is* past the season, so I should be able to get something decent for not very much money. I mean, I know Mexico City isn't Cancun, but there should be at least one nice hotel."

Soon Godwin reported that Mexico City, in fact, offered some spectacular hotels, well up to John's standards— but, sadly, their rates were outside his budget, even in the off-season. John, by Godwin's report, was amused and touched by Godwin's efforts to please him, and said he was willing to come down a step or two, so long as he didn't have to wrestle with a *cucaracha* for his pillow. So Godwin consulted with Travelocity, and found a terrific price at the three-star Hotel del Prado and booked it for five nights. "I'd go for a week, but if I did, we couldn't afford to go sightseeing." By then he had acquired a book on Mexico City and was thrilled to discover there were Aztec ruins nearby—"With actual pyramids! I *adore* pyramids!"—plus the world-famous Museum of Anthropology—"John *adores* museums!" And, of course, lots of night life and plenty of places to shop, which both of them adored.

It took a little while for the tickets to arrive and the flight to be scheduled, so it was not until April 22 that Betsy had driven the two of them to the airport and wished them *bon voyage*.

Godwin had come back six days later jubilant and showing off a tan acquired on a jaunt to Teotihuacan, the ancient pyramid complex outside Mexico City. "I climbed all the way to the *top* of the *Pyramid of the Sun!*" he proclaimed, then staggered around panting heavily to demonstrate how hard the task had been in the thin air. Customers were amused. One who'd been there was definitely impressed. "Those steps are steep and it's a hard climb!" she'd said.

Among the gifts he had brought home was a clay statue of a high-nosed standing woman spinning wool by hand, a replica of an Aztec piece in the Museum of Anthropology. "It's for the shop," he'd said, and put it on a shelf near the knitting yarns. About the famous Museum of Anthropology, he told everyone, "*That* place is *fantastic,* but it just wore us *out!* It's bigger than any other museum *I've* ever been in." He told Betsy over a lunchtime sandwich, "I learned a lot about the different kinds of nations they had in ancient times down there. The Maya were all right if you like conquest, the Olmecs had a thing for conjoined twins, but those Aztecs were *nasty!* I didn't know until we went to the museum what 'flay' *really* means. Do you know, their priests would actually walk around *wearing* someone else's *skin?*" He gave a dramatic shudder.

Betsy put her sandwich down. "Oh, ick, Goddy!" she said. "Who told you that? Does John speak Spanish?"

"Oh, no, he makes a point of not learning the language. They had guides in lots of languages, but it didn't take a guide to tell us about the flaying, they made *statues* of it!"

"Enough, enough!" said Betsy, pushing her sandwich away. "How was the rest of the trip?"

"It was *nice.* In fact, everywhere we went there were usually people who spoke enough English so we got along fine.

And when there weren't we had this taxi driver, he became like a friend, he took us everywhere, and translated for us. Once we got used to his accent, he was great. We sometimes brought him into the hotel, because that was the one place where *no one* spoke any English. On the other hand, their breakfast buffet was *superb!*" He waxed so lyrical on the *huevos aporreados* and *orejas chilaquiles verdes* that her appetite came back.

At a *Sabado Mercado*—Saturday Market—John had bought a semi-abstract iron sculpture of a man on a horse. "We think it's a man on a horse," amended Godwin, "but whatever it is, John liked it, and *I* bought it for him." And after some spirited bargaining, Godwin also bought himself a beautiful bracelet of heavy silver links and, for Betsy, a necklace and earrings of white shell and red coral. He'd even bought a gift for Sophie, the sweet and lazy shop cat. It was a chicken made of slices of colored sponges—the body was a simple cylinder, the head and tail silhouettes. Hidden in its underside was a small disposable plastic cup that had a long string hanging from it. Sophie had sniffed the chicken eagerly, possibly picking up strange smells but more likely hoping it was something good to eat. Godwin lifted it out of her reach, wrapped a small square of sponge around the string, and slid it downward. A loud squawk came from the chicken and Sophie fell off her chair in surprise. Godwin laughed and showed how a more careful tugging of the sponge down the string produced a sound like a rooster's crow. He continued to play with the toy, not noticing that Sophie had fled to the back storage room of the shop, where she remained hidden until Godwin tired of making it squawk.

That evening, Betsy had taken the foam rubber chicken upstairs to be put into a drawer, and was probably almost as glad as Sophie that Godwin never asked where it had gone.

Remembering that, Betsy sighed. Godwin was sensitive, but not always about others.

She was reaching rather far forward to nudge the last track light into place when she heard the front door to the shop open. But still no *Bing!*

She climbed down the little ladder and went into the front to find a tall, very slender woman with bright red hair running long white fingers through the desperate-sale charts on the checkout desk.

"Hello, Ms. Lavery," said Betsy. Susan Lavery was a relatively new customer.

"Hi, Betsy. Your doorbell's broken."

"Yes, I know."

"I bet half your customers are pleased about that."

"Me, too, mostly." Indeed, the raucous note the thing sounded whenever the door was opened was at least as much annoyance as aid. But estimates to replace it were high enough to make her decide to put up with it. Until now, of course.

Susan laughed. "I've got a friend at work who just announced she's pregnant. She's about six weeks along, and I figure if I start now, maybe I can have a baby sampler done for her in time for the baby's first birthday."

Betsy smiled and said, "Well, in that case, you'll be ahead of the game. Lots of children get their stitched birth announcements about the time they start kindergarten. But if I may offer a suggestion?"

"Certainly," Susan said in her pleasant, dry drawl.

"Godwin came back from Mexico City with some charts from a new designer he met down there. She does an interesting mix, some are exotic little symbols from the Aztec language and some are cute teddy bears and blocks that would look darling on a birth announcement."

"Who's Godwin?"

For a moment Betsy looked as blankly at Susan as Susan was looking at her. Then Betsy said, "That is amazing, but I think it's true: You've never met my store manager, Godwin DuLac."

Susan frowned. "I think I've heard that name before, but I'm sure I've never met him. But I've only come into your store, what, six or seven times?"

"Well, Godwin works at least as many hours as I do, so it's odd you haven't met him. But that's not the point. Here, let me show you some of her designs." Betsy led the way to a spinner rack devoted to baby and toddler charts.

"I have some pastel pink or blue aida cloth you can work these on," said Betsy, handing Susan three charts. One was of a trio of ducklings, one a trio of baby bluebirds, one a laughing Teddy bear. "You can use the alphabet chart I sold you last week. What I suggest you do is work one or two of these on the cloth now, plus a border from that kit you bought the first time you came in—"

"My word, how do you do that?" demanded Susan.

"Do what?"

"Remember what I bought here!"

"I don't know. I can't do it all the time, just once in awhile." Betsy didn't want to say that Susan, with her height, beauty, and that improbable hair, was a memorable person.

"Anyway," Betsy continued, "Do the border and the figures

now. If the mother decides to name the baby ahead of time, you can put that on—and then all you'll have left to do is fill in the date."

"Okay, I like that. Say, what's that?" She reached for another counted chart. "Hey, it's a tlatolli!"

"A what? What's a 'tlatolli'?"

"This is," said Susan, holding out the chart. It was another of Maru's designs, a strange device that looked like a J outlined on one side with crenellations.

"Oh, that. Godwin brought it back from Mexico. It's Aztec."

"You bet it is! It means 'talk.' You see it in Aztec paintings in front of figures who are lecturing or talking."

"You do? How interesting." Betsy looked more closely at the chart. "Like a speech balloon in comic strips, I guess."

"Sort of, except it doesn't say what they're talking about. Here, I want this one, too."

Betsy hoped Godwin would come down while Susan was still here, but she kept her record intact by going out the front door just about one minute before he came in the back.

He found Betsy selecting some yarn for a new knitting project she wanted to try.

"Betsy, I was thinking, I just about maxed out my credit cards in Mexico City, so how am I supposed to shop for clothes?"

"Get just one pair of slacks and two shirts. There's a K-Mart and a Target right up Highway Seven at one-oh-one."

"K-Mart?" He stared at her in surprise. "You want me to buy work clothes at *K-Mart*?"

"Or Target," she said, nodding. With John, Godwin had become accustomed to far, far more upscale stores than these. But she wasn't going to continue the custom. "You have such a great sense of style, I'm sure you can find something affordable that will look terrific."

He smiled, if faintly. "I hope you're right." He sighed and took himself off.

Two

G ODWIN came in with a big white bag marked with a
red bull's eye, and a smaller plastic Walgreen's bag.
Betsy gave him the key to her upstairs apartment, and he
went away, to return about forty minutes later wearing
manufacturer-faded blue jeans and a pastel-plaid shirt in
yellow, green, and blue. His penny loafers were worn on
bare feet—the skin on his feet was so sensitive to fabric
dyes, Godwin wore only white cotton socks he knit himself.
Since those were at home, where he was forbidden entrance,
he wore none.

"I sometimes have trouble with leather on my feet, too,"
he said, "So I washed my socks out and used your hair dryer to
reduce them to merely damp," he said. "They'll probably be
dry enough to wear right after lunch." He raised both hands.
"Not that I'll be going out to lunch," he said hastily. "But if
you could bring me back something when you go out, I'd appreciate it. All I had for breakfast was a pair of Tic Tacs."

"I'm planning on going next door to the deli," said Betsy. "Let me know what you want. My treat, of course."

"Thank you twice over!" said Godwin. "I held my breath when I bought this outfit, because I know my credit card's close to being maxed out." He leaned forward and mouthed quietly, "Cheap underwear, too."

Betsy chuckled. "Was it worth it? I mean, the trip to Mexico City?"

"Oh, my God, *yes!* Even if it takes a year—*two* years—to pay it off, it was too wonderful to miss! That's why I don't understand why John is being such a pissant now."

"Maybe . . ." Betsy hesitated, then finished the thought. "Maybe it's because John resented you paying for everything, instead of him."

Godwin smiled in surprise. "Now why on earth would John *not* want to have a free ride for a change?" He shrugged to show he hadn't any idea why, and continued, still smiling, "You know, I think this is the first time, the actual *first time,* I ever paid not just my own way but his, too? He kept saying he didn't think I should do it. But I showed him the tickets I won, and said I had almost no charges on my card, so why not? And he finally said, 'You're right, why not?' "

"I see. Well, maybe he's got another difficult case to work on, and it's made him touchy."

"I'd agree, except he's always been too fair to take work problems out on me. At least without first warning me he's in a bad mood because of some problem at the office."

"Well, what did he say when he threw you out? I mean, did he say something like, 'I don't want any more of your . . .' what? Your pride, your mouth, your dumb sense of humor, your silliness?"

"Thank you so much for that list of my faults," Goddy said with a hurt sniff.

"Oh, you know what I mean."

"Okay, yes, I guess I do." Godwin thought a few moments. "Here's what he said: 'It's gone, the sweet boy is gone, it's all over, get out, just get out. Out! *Out!*'" Godwin made sweeping motions with both arms. "Like that."

Betsy had a sudden notion, but she hesitated to present it. Godwin noted the hesitation and leaped on it. "You know something, don't you? What *is* it? Have *you* talked to John? He called here, didn't he? What did he *say*? Did he tell you not to *tell me*?" His voice showed rising panic.

"No, no, nothing like that. I was just wondering. Goddy, could he be seeing someone else? Someone . . . younger?"

Godwin had been engaged in a fight with the calendar for as long as she'd known him. Combining dieting, exercise, light tanning, hair brightening, tooth whitening, and a bit of botox, Godwin followed a complex regimen to make himself look barely twenty, when in fact he could reach out and touch thirty.

Godwin's mouth formed a small O, as he tried and tried to say, "No," or "Nonsense!" Finally he managed, "He wouldn't!"

"Why wouldn't he?"

"Because he loves *me*!"

"Goddy . . ."

He burst into tears. "I know, I know! Then why am I homeless?"

She took him into her arms as he wept helplessly on her shoulder.

"Oh, dear, what's the matter?" asked a strange voice, and

they jumped apart like clandestine lovers caught in an embrace.

"Well, hello, Mrs. Sowinski!" said Godwin.

"Hello, Goddy. What's got you so upset?"

"Nothing much, really. You know how I am, I cry over every little thing. And it has nothing to do with the shop, really. Anyway—" He sniffed deeply and forced a smile. "I'm all over it now. What can I get for you?"

"I'd like a fat quarter of fourteen-count gridded aida in ivory, please."

Mrs. Sowinski was a heavyset woman with short red hair and a liking for big floral prints. Even her spring coat was a deep green with enormous yellow flowers splashed all over it. She used to do simple counted cross-stitch pieces—the big, complex charts intimidated her—until she discovered Zweigart's gridded aida cloth. She knew about gridding—marking fabric into five-thread segments with a single thread—but claimed that she routinely messed up even that simple task on a large piece of cloth. So when Betsy discovered that Zweigart put out aida cloth already gridded, she ordered some with Mrs. Sowinski in mind. As it turned out, other customers liked it, too. Gridding could be tedious and time-consuming; buying cloth already gridded was a blessing for many stitchers. Their only complaint was that Zweigart didn't also offer linen already gridded.

But now the news was even worse: "I'm afraid Zweigart has discontinued its gridded cloth," Godwin said. "And we're already out of the fourteen count. I have some eighteen count in a stunning shade of ivory, would you like to try some of that?"

"Hmmm, eighteen count. Do you think I'm ready for eighteen count?"

Evenweave fabrics were designated by the number of threads per inch. The bigger the number, the finer the weave.

"Eighteen's not any more difficult than fourteen—and you've turned out some wonderful pieces in fourteen. Actually, I've been wondering why you haven't moved up to eighteen." This last sentence was spoken in a confidential tone.

Mrs. Sowinski smiled and raised a hand against that statement. "Oh, you have not!" she said. "But do you really think I could handle eighteen count?"

"Absolutely! Now, are you going to need a new pattern, or do you already have one?"

"Oh, I don't know. Do you still have that chart Wild Wonders? I've been thinking it would look nice on the wall of our cabin up on the lake."

"I'm pretty sure we do, but let's go take a look."

The two of them passed through the twin sets of box shelves, into the part of the shop where the counted cross-stitch charts and materials were kept.

"*Arrrrrgggghhhh!!*" came a cry a few seconds later. "What *happened* back here?"

"What? What?" cried Betsy, rushing to the back. She looked around. Everything looked fine to her. "What's the matter?" she asked.

"Everything's been moved!" said Goddy. "I can't find *anything!*" He was waving his arms in a helpless way over his head.

"I just did what you and Ms. Davis suggested, for heaven's sake!" said Betsy.

"Oh?" said Godwin. For a moment his face was blank, then he nodded as he took in the rearranged area. "That's right. Okay. I get it now."

Mrs. Sowinski began to laugh. "You scared me for a minute there, Godwin," she said. Turning to Betsy, she said, "Do you know where to look for the chart called Wild Wonders?"

"Of course," said Betsy. "It's right over here." She shook her head at Godwin, who was looking a trifle embarrassed at his outburst.

Mrs. Sowinski bought the chart and half a yard of the eighteen-count aida, saying the part she didn't use would go into her stash. She also bought a skein each of three shades of green floss because she wasn't sure if she had enough of it at home.

After Mrs. Sowinski left, Betsy said to Godwin, "You are the most amazing man!" and hugged him.

He squirmed out of her embrace, saying, "Don't make fun of me, I'm too fragile to handle that."

"Who's making fun? I'm serious! You were in the middle of a real emotional storm when a customer walked in, and you pulled yourself together faster than . . . than a speeding bullet." She smiled at herself for that limp simile, but Godwin simply bloomed.

"Do you really think so? I thought I lost it again when I walked in back and everything was changed around. It was like my whole life, everything changed around, so I don't know where I am. . . ." His courage began to falter again.

"Here, now, buck up," she said. "Everything is going to be all right. I promise. Okay?" She put it strongly, hoping it was true. "Now, how about some lunch? What would you like?"

He thought for a few moments. "A great big sandwich, double beef on whole wheat with horseradish sauce and a thick slice of tomato. And potato chips. And a kosher dill pickle—not a spear, the whole thing. Large iced tea to drink."

When Betsy brought it back for him, he ate every crumb. He even put real sugar into his iced tea.

In consequence, that evening he decided they needed to eat light. "Let me make something I had in Mexico City," he said. He searched the refrigerator and cupboards and gave Betsy a short list. "Here, run to the grocery store and get these," he ordered crisply. "By the time you get back the soup should be ready."

He prepared a simple soup of boiled chicken and rice, then served it with a plate on which were avocado, sweet onion, green chilies, cilantro, and tomato, chopped and heaped into little piles. He showed Betsy how to strew a little of each over the soup to flavor a few bites, then strew again, so the add-ons never sank into the soup but remained bright stars of flavor in the firmament of chicken and rice.

"I had this for supper every night at the hotel," said Godwin. "The city is over seven thousand feet in the air, and your metabolism changes at that altitude, so you have your main meal at noon and then a light supper at night. Otherwise you wake up at three A.M. sick as a dog." He smiled. "A man on the plane told me that, and I told John, but he thought I was just trying to save money, and he ate a Big Mac—yes, you can buy them in Mexico City; in fact, there was a Mickey D's in the mall attached to the back of our hotel—and fries, super sized, the first evening we were there. And sure enough, he was up a couple of hours after we went to bed, groaning and complaining. He wanted lots of sympathy, which I gave him, along with a lecture on listening to me—sometimes I really do know what I'm talking about, you know."

After dinner, Betsy said, "Well, what do you want to do? Go to a movie? Watch TV? Maybe do a little stitching?"

Godwin sighed. "I suppose I could work on a model of that symbol, the thing that means 'speaking' that I got from Maru."

"You mean the tlatolli?"

He stared at her. "That sounds like what she said it's called. But it's not written on the chart, so how do you know that?"

"Susan Lavery told me."

"Who's she?"

"A tall woman with the reddest hair you've ever seen. She bought the chart, and the teddy bears one, too. Looks like we have a hit on our hands. You be sure and tell Ms. Maru, okay?"

"Sure, I'd be glad—oh, wait a second. My laptop's at John's."

"Do you have her e-mail address? I can tell her."

"No, I put it into the laptop and threw away the paper she wrote it on." He heaved a discouraged sigh.

"Well, do you want to go down into the shop and pick out something else? Maybe some white cotton yarn to start a new pair of socks?"

"Later, maybe." He sighed again and curled up on the couch.

"Tell me more about how you met this designer." Betsy was still looking for clues that something happened in Mexico that precipitated this quarrel.

"Well . . . okay. We were in the Polaco district, which is

about the nicest—we had our private guide with us, he was a lot of fun—anyway, he took us to the Polaco District and turned us loose for a couple of hours. John bought dinner at the Konditori restaurant—would you believe it's Swedish?—Scandinavian food with Mexican spices, strange and delicious! Afterwards we went for a walk and I saw this home decorator shop and went in because I saw it had needlework supplies. I wanted to see what they had, maybe something different from here at home. They didn't, and they didn't have anything like the variety of things we carry. It was worse even than Michael's. But I met Maru in there, looking for floss in pastel colors for that pattern of a teddy bear."

"Where was John all this while?"

"Looking at furniture. They had some nice armchairs with an interesting fabric on the seats. So Maru and I got to talking—she was so interested that I'm Vice President in Charge of Operations of Crewel World, Inc.! and she showed me another Aztec pattern she's working on, kind of a weird-looking bird. She said it's from a seal the Aztecs used."

"Where is she getting these designs?"

"She's taking classes at the Museum of Anthropology."

"Goddy, you don't think John will do something like erase your hard drive, do you?"

"No, I don't think so. I mean, he saw how excited I was about meeting Maru and buying her designs, so he knows they're important. He's angry at me, not at the work I do. Now, if you don't mind, I think I would like to go down to the shop for a ball of sock-weight yarn and a pair of knitting needles. If John does take it into his head to throw my clothes away, it behooves me to get started on a spare pair of socks."

Betsy frowned after him as he slouched out the door.

There had been serious quarrels before between Godwin and John, and John had even expelled Godwin a time or two. But this felt different. She remembered her promise that all would be well, and hoped again that she would be able to keep it.

Three

❖ ❖ ❖

A T 6:40 the next morning, Betsy's clock radio gently clicked on and began playing an old rock song, Sonny and Cher's "I Got You Babe." She woke feeling slightly panicky, because that was how the weatherman woke, over and over, in *Groundhog Day.* It was one of her favorite movies, and she and Godwin had ended up watching it last night while working on stitching projects.

Once she realized she was not in Punxatawney, PA, but in her own bedroom, she smiled and nearly went back to sleep while indulging in amused recollections of scenes from the movie. But feline footfalls coming up the mattress roused her again. Sophie, Betsy's cat, normally slept in her own basket in the living room, but last night she moved into Betsy's room. Sophie knew and liked Godwin, but Godwin belonged down in the shop. Now he was up here and not just for a visit; he hadn't gone home at bedtime. Like most cats, Sophie was deeply traditional and looked on any change in the routine with suspicion. She walked heavily up the bed to Betsy's shoulder, gave her high-pitched cry, and looked toward the door, calling Betsy's attention to the anomaly that was still going on this morning.

Sophie was a very large cat, mostly white, with tan and gray patches on her head and back. Her enormous fluffy tail was a mix of tan and gray, currently twitching erratically. Sophie had been on a diet since Betsy inherited her at an obese twenty-two pounds. And despite Betsy's best efforts, her cat's current weight was twenty-three pounds. She was a beautiful cat nevertheless, lazy but sweet, whose one exercise was asking everyone she met if they had something for her to eat.

Her reaction to Godwin's occupation of the guest bedroom was thus an anxious look at the door, followed by her special breakfast cry. "A-rew?" she asked. "A-rew?" Betsy laughed and pulled her in for a snuggle. Sophie obediently began to purr, but she continued to look toward the door at intervals.

When Betsy finally got out of bed and reached for her robe, Sophie tried to lead her to the kitchen.

"First things first," said Betsy, heading for the bathroom.

But soon Sophie was crouched over her morning serving of Science Diet dry cat food, the one formulated for fat, old, lazy cats—though they didn't put it that baldly on the label—while Betsy made herself a cup of English Breakfast tea.

Normally, she drank her tea while checking her e-mail and reading her RCTN and INRG newsgroups—but her computer lived in the guest bedroom, and there'd been no sign that Godwin was up and about. She didn't want to wake him, poor thing. They'd stayed up late last night, and while he'd gone to bed first, she was sure she'd heard him crying in the guest room just as she was falling asleep.

She wished he weren't so fastened on John. In Betsy's opinion, it was an unhealthy relationship, with all the power on John's side. Well, most of it. When Betsy had promoted Godwin to store manager—Godwin preferred to call himself Vice President in Charge of Operations and Editor in Chief of *Hasta la Stitches,* the shop's newsletter—she had nearly doubled his salary and offered him the same benefits program she had for herself. It wasn't nearly enough to make him John's fiscal equal, but it made Godwin less of a total dependent. Godwin had been thrilled, and later said it made John treat him with more respect.

Her smile had a hint of triumph in it as she went to put her empty cup in the sink. She decided oatmeal would be breakfast this morning. It could sit on the stove until Godwin was ready for it.

She went to the cabinet where she kept her pots and selected one the right size that was heavy enough to simmer without burning.

Her smile faded as she considered whether it had been a good idea to take a bite out of John by promoting Godwin. John was the type of gay man who liked his boyfriends immature. He had a record of taking in young men for a year or two, and then turning them out when they became too sophisticated. While Godwin had been very naïve at nineteen, that was no longer true—and an even more mature Godwin had emerged under the burden of more responsibility.

It was interesting, Betsy reflected, that John hadn't discarded Godwin. Perhaps John had done some growing in the past few years, too. Or maybe it was that Godwin remained incurably silly and fun even as he became more hard-working and reliable.

She half-filled the pot with water, added salt, and put it on a burner to heat.

Not that Godwin hadn't occupied the position of store manager practically from the start. Betsy had inherited the shop when her sister died, and, having no experience in owning her own business and little knowledge of needle-work, had quickly come to rely heavily on the young man to guide her through the learning process. His promotion had been only recognition of a status he had from the start. Still, now he was making more of the decisions about employees and sales, had begun publishing a shop newsletter, and was building a Crewel World Website.

The pot began to steam. She went to a different cabinet and got out the round canister of oatmeal, the old-fashioned kind that has to cook for awhile but has a nuttier taste, and a package of raisins.

So maybe there was more to this relationship between John and Godwin than a sophisticated man indulging a naïve boyfriend, she thought. And why not? Godwin was not just an amusing, charming boy. He was a creative soul, kind, loyal, and intelligent, with flashes of mature insight. Maybe John was ready for a more mature relationship. Betsy sure hoped so.

She measured the oats into the boiling water and turned the heat down. If that was the case, then this was just a lover's quarrel. Which meant that probably some time to-day John would call the shop to talk to Godwin and start the process of making up.

Having talked herself out of her worry over her manager,

she decided to have a couple of sausages to go with the oatmeal—Betsy tended to celebrate good feelings by eating something nice. She got out the brown sugar to sprinkle on her oatmeal along with the raisins.

She had eaten her share, showered, and dressed before Godwin wandered vaguely out, his blond hair all pushed to one side on his head, his chin whiskery, and his eyes red-rimmed.

"Good morning, Glory!" Betsy said cheerfully.

"Whatever," he mumbled. "Is there coffee?"

"No, but the water's still hot for tea. Or if you can wait awhile, I can perk a pot."

"Can't wait, my heart needs a jump-start."

So Betsy made him an extra-strong cup of black India tea, put a bowl and spoon on the table in front of him, pointed out the oatmeal simmering on the stove and the sausages keeping warm in the oven, and went to do her morning commune with the Internet.

It took three cups of strong tea, but Godwin was looking a lot more cheerful as they went down the stairs at nine-thirty to start the opening-up process. Sophie trundled ahead, eager to begin her daily chore of cadging treats from the customers.

Betsy went through the back door, through the back room, through the twin set of box shelves that divided the front of the shop from the back, heading for the desk that served as a checkout counter—and stopped short.

"Goddy," she called, "are we expecting a really big order from somewhere?"

"No," he called from the back room where he was start-ing the coffee—the shop offered a free cup to its customers. "Why?"

"Because there is a really huge box by our front door."

Goddy came trotting through, to stop short himself and stare. It was one of those cardboard boxes refrigerators come in. "Wow!"

Betsy dodged around him, heading to the front door with the keys. "It's a mistake, it must be. I bet it's books for ISBNs." Next door to Betsy was a used-book store of that name.

She unlocked the door and looked for a label. There was none, only a single word written with a thick-nubbed marking pen: GODWIN. Her heart sank.

"It's for you," she said. "From John."

It was a struggle, but the two of them managed to push the box into the shop. Godwin got a box opener from a desk drawer and slit open the top.

"My *clothes!*" cried Godwin. The box was full to the top with clothing, pushed in any old way. "Oh, *look* at them!" He pulled out a pair of trousers, badly wrinkled. "My Versace suit!" he cried, and began to dig for the coat.

"Hold it, hold it!" Betsy ordered. "Look at what you're doing, for heaven's sake!"

Godwin glanced around, the floor near the box was like a teenager's bedroom, knee-deep in shirts, slacks, underwear, and socks, lots of white socks. And some not so white.

"Oh, my God, he put the dirty in with the *clean!*"

He dropped the shirt in his hand and went to sit at the library table and put his head into his arms.

Betsy came around behind him and rested her hands on his shoulders. "I'm so sorry," she said.

"If only I knew what I did wrong, I could apologize."

"You didn't do anything wrong. Because if you had done

something so wrong he'd throw you out and send your clothes after you, you'd be pretty sure what it might be."

"I can't think, I just can't think," he said thickly, his face muffled in the arm of his shirt.

"Sometimes," said Betsy, looking at the strew of clothing around the big box, "a bit of physical exercise gets the blood flowing and ideas come to you."

"What does that mean?"

"It means you can't leave that mess in the middle of the shop."

He raised his head and looked around. "Oh, for heaven's sake, why didn't you stop me sooner! Let's get this cleared away!" He rose and hurried to begin stuffing clothes back into the box.

Betsy came to stop him. "Wait a minute," she said, and he obediently stopped, a fistful of socks in either hand. "How are we going to get this box upstairs?"

"In stages, of course," said Godwin. "First we get the stuff back in the box, then the box into the entrance hall. We'll go through the front door, it's shorter. I can carry armloads up the stairs, it'll only take a few minutes."

It took more like half an hour, which was fine. Betsy hadn't been kidding about the exercise and, besides, Godwin needed a few minutes to pull himself together. Meanwhile, Betsy continued opening up alone, knowing Godwin wanted time to himself to mourn the sad condition of his precious designer suits and silk shirts and hand-tooled Italian shoes.

He came back into Crewel World even more depressed than she feared. "I was hoping he'd call, but instead he throws my clothes out after me," he said.

"But not into the street like that one time," she reminded him.

"Yes, but that time he yelled at me, called me names, called me on the phone to yell some more. This time, nothing, just silence." He pulled his shoulders up and twisted his head from side to side. "My muscles are all clenched," he reported. "It's like my whole body knows this is different from the other times."

"Oh, Goddy," she sighed sympathetically.

"But at least he didn't tear things or cut them to ribbons like some people do when they break up. Nothing's damaged, an iron will put most of it right. But for the rest, where do you keep your washing machine?"

"In the basement—they're pay machines for my tenants but I use them, too. Do you have change?"

"I dunno." He began to search his jeans pockets. "Not much," he reported after a minute, looking at a small collection of coins.

"Here," she said, and went for her purse. She had some change but had to break two dollars from the cash register to make sure he had enough.

"Do you have to put your own money in?" he asked.

"Of course. Work's work, this is personal."

"Even though I'm an employee?"

"I'm not doing this for an employee, I'm doing this for a friend."

"Oh, *Betsy!*" He came at a trot to embrace her and they stood that way in a silent embrace—until they sniffed simultaneously, which made them laugh and break apart.

"John also put my computer and my briefcase in the box, but not my good gold and diamond jewelry. Why would he be so mean?"

"Perhaps he's not being mean, he's giving you an excuse to get in touch with him about them."

Godwin stared at her, then bloomed so gloriously at that possibility that she was forced to say, "Now, maybe not. Maybe he is being mean. You know him best, what do you think?"

He faded while he thought a few moments, then shrugged. "I have no idea. Sometimes he is a mystery wrapped in an enigma. What's an enigma?"

"Something hard to understand."

"Yes, that's John all right."

That afternoon, he spent the minutes between customers dashing down to the washer and dryer in the basement, and left work a few minutes early to take a suit and a jacket to the cleaners. But he insisted again on cooking supper, and this time poached two whitefish fillets which he covered with steamed crab and shrimp, and chopped asparagus in a white sauce.

After supper he declared himself exhausted and went into the guest room. But he came out half an hour later, complaining he was too overwrought to sleep. "I'm going to a movie," he said. "Want to come?"

But Betsy was tired herself. And she had to get up very early in the morning for her water aerobics class, so she sent him off alone.

She worked on a model she was making for her shop— Laura J. Perin's splendid "Independence Day," a colorful counted needlepoint canvas. It was an abstract pattern of fireworks, with flowing and jagged lines indicating movement and glass "gems" dotting it.

It had seemed intimidating at first, with its variety of stitches. Now that it was underway, Betsy decided it wasn't all that hard. It was beautiful, and she was enjoying the use of so many different kinds of fibers.

Still, she was tired. It didn't take long for her brain to call a halt, so she went to bed early. She didn't hear Godwin come in.

Four

Betsy was wakened early the next morning by the clock radio. Thanks to daylight savings time, it was now dark at 5:30 A.M. again. Bummer. Sophie, sleeping at the foot of the bed, raised her head when Betsy turned on the bedside lamp.

"A-rew?" she inquired.

"Water aerobics," explained Betsy, as if the cat understood—perhaps she did. It was hard to tell just how intelligent Sophie was. It was in the cat's interest to feign stupidity; it made for fewer demands.

Betsy pulled on her swimsuit, crawled into a pair of jeans and a sweatshirt, and crept quietly down the stairs with her dressing bag over one shoulder. She didn't know what time Godwin had come in, but he had or Sophie wouldn't have slept at the foot of her bed.

Three mornings a week Betsy went to the Courage Center in Golden Valley, with its Olympic-size pool filled with very warm water. Though the Courage Center was primarily for rehab and therapy, nonhandicapped people could use it, too. And this very early session meant she would be back home almost as early as her day normally began.

Today, Friday, Renée was running the session. A tall, sturdy blonde with a drill sergeant's voice, Renée put the class of about a dozen women, mostly seniors, through their movements. While some whined at the pace she set, all obediently jumping-jacked, grapevined, and cross-country-skied across the pool, and most thanked her at the end of the hour, proud of not being treated like fragile antiques.

Betsy was climbing the stairs to her apartment soon after eight. She walked in to the scent of coffee. Godwin, resplendent in midnight blue slacks and royal blue shirt, was setting the table. "Good, you're home," he said. "The water's boiling, we'll have soft-boiled eggs in four minutes."

"Wow, thanks!"

"A-rew!" demanded Sophie, determinedly underfoot, and Betsy went to the cabinet under the sink to open the large tin full of Sophie's Science Diet dry food for obese cats. She had switched from Iams on the recommendation of her pet shop owner, but it was proving even less effective at making Sophie svelte.

Betsy had instructed Godwin not to feed Sophie, as the animal had long ago learned that by lying about who had or had not fed her, she could get two or even three breakfasts or suppers.

By the time Betsy had measured out a modest scoop of food, and washed and filled Sophie's water dish, breakfast was ready.

Over the last few bites of toast, Betsy asked, "Where were you last night?"

"I went to the Dock, to see *Harry Potter and the Goblet of Fire*. I told you I was going."

"Yes, but you didn't come home after. I tried to wait up, but I finally got tired and went to bed. Did you meet some friends at the theater?"

He smiled. "No, I went for a drive alone. I drove all over the place, up fifteen to Wayzata, then up one-oh-one to five and—I don't know, just around. At first, I wanted to think how to get John to take me back, then later I wanted to think what it would be like to never go back to him even if he asked me to. I actually kind of came to like the idea. Then I came home."

At 9:15, Betsy was changing into her work clothes and Godwin was washing dishes when the phone rang. He picked up the receiver before she could. "Hello? Well, *hello* Tasha!" Hope was in his voice, Betsy could hear it clear over into her bedroom, where she was trying to decide whether to go for comfort or good looks in her footwear today. She was wearing a knit dress in a shade of deep pink, and the shoes would tell her what earrings to put on, the fancy blue crystals or the cute pink bunnies. She came to the door, comfortable pink shoe in one hand, handsome blue shoe on one foot. She stood there listening to Godwin talk. Who was Tasha?

"No, I haven't heard from him. He's not at home? How strange. How did you know to call here?" A lengthy pause. "I see. No, she's here, and I *know* she would have told me if John had called her." Godwin stepped out of the kitchen to glance at Betsy, who nodded agreement vigorously. "I'm sorry I can't help you. Yes, all right, if he does, I will, right away. And if he comes in, have him call me here or at Crewel World. 'Cause now I'm worried, too. 'Kay? Thanks, Tasha. Bye."

He hung up and said to Betsy, "John didn't come in to

work today, and he's got a couple of appointments. He's not answering his phone at home. That was his secretary calling you, she thought maybe you knew where I was. She was surprised but happy when I answered. She asked me where John is."

"He didn't call here last night," said Betsy. "What do you think? Does he do things like this?"

"Oh, gosh, no, *especially* not standing up a client. Besides, he's up for partner in the firm, so he's being very puck—no, punk—punk-something. What's the word?"

"Punctilious?"

"Yes. He's being that right now. So I don't understand this at all."

"Do you have a phone number for John that the law firm doesn't have?"

"I have his cell phone number. But I should think they have that, too."

"Still. Call it and see if you get an answer."

Godwin turned back to the phone, thought a moment, then punched ten numbers. He waited, and waited, apparently listening to a ring. Then he punched a number and said, "John, this is Godwin. Your office called and they wonder where you are. Where are you?" Then he hung up. "How *very* odd," he said.

Betsy absently put the shoe in her hand onto her foot and came across the living room toward the kitchen limping because the shoes had unequal heels. She looked down at her feet. "Gosh, look what I did."

Godwin did and said, "I don't think that's a look that will catch on, boss." He hung the dishtowel over the handle of the oven door and said, "It's funny about John. I mean, it seriously *isn't like him* to miss appointments."

"Could he be at home, sleeping off a hangover, with the phones turned off?"

Godwin started to shake his head no, then thought about it. "You know, last time we broke up, he said afterwards that he was a mess. He said he missed me *so much* he was screwing up at work."

"There, see? But you know him better than I do. Is it possible he's worse this time?"

Godwin brightened at the idea, then thought about it and shook his head. "My broken heart wishes it was true, but my brain says no." He came to sit across from her. "Still, I think we should go over there."

"What's this 'we,' white man?" she said, quoting the punchline of an old joke.

"Seriously. I've got a funny feeling about this."

"Well, then maybe you should go over there." She looked at her watch. "It's just past nine-thirty. If you leave now, you can be back by ten-thirty, can't you?"

She looked up to see him smiling in a pleading way at her, eyebrows lifted really high.

"No," she said. "I'm not going with you."

"Please? Oh, please, please, *please*? I'm scared to go alone!"

"What are you afraid of?"

"I don't know. Yes, I do. I'm afraid I'll find him drunk or drugged—and . . . with someone else." He bit his lower lip, ashamed at expressing that thought.

"Oh, Goddy," she sighed.

"I know, I'm terrible for even thinking it. But if I walked in and found him with . . . someone, I'd do something really stupid, like scream and break things, and it would be just too horrible. But if you were with me, I could be brave and only cry a little." He already looked on the edge of tears.

"Oh, all right, all right. But when we get there, you go in first. Oh, and we have to find someone to watch the shop."

"Yes, okay, no problem. Nikki Marquez has been begging for extra hours. She's going back to college in the fall, and is already working two other part-time jobs. She told me to call her any time."

"Well, if she's working two other jobs, she probably won't be available. But call her, call someone. I'm going to go put on a matching pair of shoes."

By the time she got back, Godwin was just hanging up the phone. "Nikki will come in at ten. I told her we'd pay her for half a day even if we don't need her that long."

"Fine."

Nikki was waiting at the front door when they went down. She was a tall, slim, beautiful girl with dark, curly hair and blue eyes in a square face. She didn't look particularly Hispanic, probably because the last person to speak Spanish in her family was her great-grandfather and he, like his son and grandson, didn't marry a Hispanic woman.

She brought along a small red cooler. "Snacks, if that's all right," she explained. Nikki was diabetic and preferred fresh fruit and chilled fruit juices to the coffee, tea, and secret stash of cookies the shop offered.

"We probably won't be gone long enough for you to need a snack," said Betsy, going swiftly through the opening-up procedure, "but you can work as much of the morning as you like. I really want to thank you for coming in on such terribly short notice."

"I was glad to, Ms. Devonshire." Nikki was a very polite young woman, and a little in awe of a wealthy business-woman like Betsy.

"Come *on,* Betsy," said Godwin, now impatient to have it over with.

"All right, I'm coming," said Betsy, stooping to turn on the radio hidden behind a row of books in the box shelves. She looked around, picked up her purse, and said to Nikki, "I've got my cell phone if you have any problems." Nikki had only worked a few times before in the shop, and Betsy felt a little anxious about leaving her all alone.

"Yes, ma'am, but I'm sure I'll be just fine. You take your time." She looked from Betsy to Godwin, obviously won-dering what this was all about.

Betsy chose not to enlighten her. "I'll call if we're going to be more than an hour," she promised and went out the door being held open by Godwin.

"I'm too nervous, you drive," said Godwin, so they went around back to Betsy's new midnight-blue Buick. The park-ing lot had been resurfaced last year and yellow lines marked the reserved spaces for Betsy's tenants. The Dump-ster in its corner of the small lot was brimming over again, its lid lifted by bags of trash. Betsy made a mental note to call the company about getting a bigger one.

She unlocked the doors and Godwin swung into the pas-senger seat, fumbling for the seat belt. "I wonder what we'll find," he muttered.

"We'll find him sitting at the breakfast table in a litter of toast crumbs, drinking his third cup of coffee and wondering why you haven't called him this bright Sunday morning."

Godwin started to point out that today was, in fact,

Friday, then got the joke and hooted with laughter instead. "Maybe you're right," he said and was comforted by the thought the rest of the ride.

John's house was a one-level ranch-style house built of orange brick with dark brown trim. It sat in a shallow but beautifully landscaped front yard. A big picture window in the front was underlined by a built-in flower box currently featuring deep yellow hyacinths. A modest front porch protected a wide front door with glass lights on either side of it. Though it was broad daylight, the front porch lights were on.

Godwin went slowly up the curving walk, Betsy not far behind. The porch was a thick cement slab under a flat roof supported on slender wooden pillars painted gray. The door was deep green, its hardware highly polished brass. The thin curtains covering the tall, narrow lights on either side of the door were yellow. Betsy noted all this as she came up the walk and while Godwin pushed the doorbell over and over. She was thinking how attractive it was, and how like a photograph in a magazine. She realized she had never been inside the place. When there was no answer to the doorbell, which Betsy could hear pealing faintly, Godwin sighed and went into his trouser pocket for a key ring. "He forgot to take my spare key away from me," he murmured, and turned back to the door, which he took his time unlocking. He opened it, and looked back at Betsy, who gestured at him to go in.

"I said you had to go in first," she reminded him. "You know he doesn't like me." That was true; on the few occasions when they'd met, John had made clear his contempt and resentment. He had tried at least once before to make Godwin give up his job at Crewel World. In Betsy's opinion, that was because John was a control freak afraid Betsy's trust in Godwin was causing him to become too independent.

"All right," he said, and went on into the house, calling, "John? John, are you here?"

He left the door open behind him, and Betsy could see into a small reception area with gray, textured paper on the walls and a beautiful oriental rug in shades of gray and light yellow on the hardwood floor.

"John?" Godwin called again.

There was a small, long-legged table against the wall just big enough to hold a bronze statue of two nude wrestlers.

Betsy could hear Godwin's footfalls. Evidently the hardwood floor continued into the living room. They cut off abruptly, and Betsy wondered if there was another rug.

"Oh, *John!*" she heard him shout. "Are you—oh, my God, oh my *God! Nooooooooo!*"

Betsy ran into the house. Godwin was in fact standing on a larger version of the entry's oriental rug, this one in a beautiful living room sparsely furnished with a gray leather couch, a glass and pewter coffee table, and a yellow leather chair so oddly shaped it had to be a costly designer piece. On the far wall was a magnificent fieldstone fireplace, and stretched on the floor in front of it was the body of a man.

"Goddy?" said Betsy, coming to take him by the arm. He was trembling violently, and turned to clutch at her, breathing in odd gasps. She put her arms around him.

After a few seconds he got enough control of himself to mutter, "I think he's dead. What do you think, is he dead?"

Without letting go, Betsy looked over at the body, that of a tall man with graying hair matted darkly at the back. His face was turned away. He was wearing a cream-colored sweater, straight-leg blue jeans, and brown sandals with a complicated arrangement of narrow straps. Betsy recognized the sweater: Godwin had one just like it, one he had knit himself.

She looked at the man's chest, which was not moving. She waited a very long time for it to move, but it didn't.

"Yes, I think he's dead, Goddy. Are you sure it's John?"

"It must be. I can't look. Will you go look? Wait, don't leave me."

"We'll look together."

The two approached the body, still holding onto one another, stepping sideways until they could look down and see the face.

It was John. His eyes were closed, he might be asleep. Except he still wasn't breathing. On the floor against his stomach was a statue made of iron in some abstract pattern that might be a man on a horse. There was a dark stain on the horse's rump, and from this angle they could see that the shape of John's skull was wrong.

Betsy broke away from Godwin to stoop and touch the face. It was cold and stiff.

Godwin began making a peculiar noise, like a siren, "Rrrrrrrrrrrrr," getting higher and louder, until Betsy rose to take hold of him again.

"Easy, easy, Goddy," she said, and stroked the back of his head and neck. "Steady, now. Where's the phone? We need to call nine-one-one."

"K-k-kitchen. No, don't leave me! Oh God, oh God, oh God."

"Come on, then." She put an arm around his shoulder and led him into the kitchen, which was in the back, separated by a counter from the living room. He had fallen silent, though he was still trembling. She stroked his back, a gesture she repeated while she lifted the receiver of the cordless wall phone with her other hand and punched 9-1-1.

"Nine-one-one, what is your emergency?" asked an operator very promptly.

"My name is Betsy Devonshire and we're at seven-twelve Larkspur in Excelsior, where there is a dead man in the living room."

"Are you sure he's dead?"

"Yes, he's cold and stiff and not breathing."

"Do you know who the dead man is?" she asked.

"Yes, he's the owner of the house, his name is John Nye. He didn't come to work this morning and we came to see if something was wrong."

"Who's this 'we'? asked the operator. "Is someone else there as well?"

"Godwin DuLac. Godwin has the key to the house. He is a friend of the deceased."

It seemed to take forever for a squad car to arrive, though it was only a few minutes. Siren blaring, it roared up Third Street, slowing when it saw them on the porch, waving at it. The driver was Lars Larson, whom they both knew. He got out quickly for a very tall, broad man encumbered with a utility belt and bulletproof vest, and came trotting up the walk.

"What's the problem here?" he asked.

"John Nye is dead," Betsy said, opening the door for him. "It looks as if something hit him on the head." She and Godwin followed him into the house, Betsy still talking. "There's a metal statue in front of the body."

Lars went to kneel beside the body. He felt the face and

neck, and tried to move the top arm, which resisted. He looked at the statue but did not touch it. "Cold," he remarked. "And stiff." He looked at Godwin and asked, "Who was here last night?"

"We don't know," said Betsy.

A frown formed. "What do you mean, you don't know? Godwin, don't you live here?"

"I used to," Godwin confessed, head down. "He threw me out four days ago. He sent my clothes and things over to Crewel World yesterday in a big box." The young man gestured to show the dimensions of the box.

Another siren became audible, growing louder.

"This probably happened last night," said Lars. He looked at Godwin. "Where were you last night?"

"Huh?" Talking of the box seemed to have sent Godwin from near hysteria into a deep gloom.

"He was with me," said Betsy quickly. "He's been staying with me." When Lars moved his pale blue gaze from Godwin to her and raised his golden eyebrows in surprise, she said, "In the guest room, for heaven's sake!"

Godwin made a barking sound and then began to laugh. The laughter quickly became hysterical and Betsy wrapped her arms around him and said, "Hush, hush, hush," over and over.

The siren cut off and seconds later another police officer came into the house—Lars had left the door open, anticipating. He was shorter than Lars—but of course, almost everyone was shorter than Lars—with dark hair and eyes. "Whatcha got?" he asked.

"DOA. One John Nye, attorney at law. This is his house. A homicide, looks like."

The man came over for a look and made a face of distaste. "Holy cripes!"

Another siren approached. "That'll be the ambulance," noted Lars. "I'll go flag it down. Nobody touch anything, all right?"

"All right," agreed Betsy, and took Godwin to the other side of the room, where she spent the next minute bringing Godwin down to a semblance of self-control.

"You don't say anything to anyone, nothing at all," she murmured in his ear, when he settled down enough to listen.

"Why not—oh. Is that why you lied and said I was with you last night?"

"Yes. What time was it when you came in, anyway?"

"I don't remember. Pretty late."

"Worse and worse. Well, they'll figure this out pretty quick, I hope. No need to worry."

"Okay," he said, and they both stood there, waiting and worrying.

Five

LARS opened the front door—the other cop had closed it. A new siren's cry was suddenly very loud, then cut off into silence. A sound like car doors slamming, the slap of feet on sidewalk, a hesitation in the sound as they stepped onto the porch. Then a whole herd of people came rushing into the living room. The "herd" quickly sorted itself into two young men, a young woman, and a big black case, with Lars coming behind.

The emergency techs looked awfully young, the girl especially—she appeared sixteen. All three wore earrings, and two had visible tattoos. But they seemed to know what they were doing, swooping down over John's body, opening the case, searching for a pulse, testing the stiffness of a hand, a foot, lifting an eyelid, frowning over its coolness—and suddenly relaxing, all anxious competence melting in a trio of sighs.

One of the men said to Lars, "Better contact the ME."

Godwin asked, "That's medical examiner, right?" And the trio turned to look at him and Betsy, surprised at their presence. When the surprise turned to compassion, Godwin burst into tears.

Lars reached for the microphone fastened to his shoulder, and Betsy took Godwin by the arm and retreated farther away, into the kitchen. She pulled a paper cup from a holder beside the sink and filled it with water from the special little faucet that was doubtless attached to a filter under the sink.

"Here, drink this," she said. "And try to get hold of yourself. I don't want you blurting things out, okay? Just keep silent, or you'll have us in a pickle."

Goddy obediently took a sip, nearly choking over it. He took a calming breath and tried again, more successfully. Then, frowning, he said, "What are you so worried about? For all we know, this was an accident. That statue is *heavy*."

"Yes, but there is no mantle on that fireplace, so where did that statue come from? I hardly think he threw it up in the air and let it fall down on his head."

Goddy stared at her. "Oh."

Betsy nodded. "Now, you did go to the movies last night, right?"

"Yes."

"Did you see anyone you know there?"

"No, no one." He hung his head. "As a matter of fact, as soon as the lights went out, I fell asleep."

"You fell asleep at a *Harry Potter* movie?"

He shrugged. "I was tired."

"Did someone wake you up when it was over?"

"No, the lights coming back on after the movie did, and it was like after a nap, I was fresh and wide awake. And worried. So I went for that drive. I drove all around the lake."

"Did you stop anywhere along the way?"

"A couple places. Boat landings, mostly. I pulled off the road where I could see the water—I think better when I can sit and look at water."

"I mean, did you stop where there were people?"

"Oh, you mean go into a bar or something? No, I didn't want to talk to anyone, I wanted to think." He turned to the sink, opening the cabinet door under it, reaching to put the cup into a trash container there.

"Don't do that," said Betsy. "Put it in your pocket."

"Why?"

"Because it has your fingerprints on it."

"Honey, my fingerprints are all over this house!"

"If John has emptied the trash between the day you left and yesterday, that cup is proof you've been in the house since he threw you out."

Goddy looked down at the wadded paper in his hand. "Oh, yeah," he said, and closed his fingers over it. Then he looked up at her. "You don't think anyone could really believe—" he began.

"When they start looking for suspects, they'll find you."

"Lars knows me better than that!"

"I wouldn't count on that, and, anyway, it won't be Lars, it'll be Mike Malloy," she said. "And what he thinks, we know too well."

Sergeant Malloy, the lead investigator of Excelsior's small police department, wouldn't dream of harassing gays, but he most sincerely believed that those who yielded to the temptation of their sexual orientation were susceptible to other kinds of wickedness as well. And of course he was, or soon would be, aware of the young man's problems with John. Certainly Godwin had told Jill about it when she came in yesterday—and Jill Cross Larson was married to Lars.

Godwin's eyes grew very large as he began to realize all this. "Oh, how I *wish* I'd stayed in last night!" he groaned. "I could've done my thinking in the *tub*!"

They heard footsteps and turned to see Lars approaching.

"Is there anything missing from the house?" he asked Godwin. "Maybe this was a burglary gone wrong."

"We haven't looked," said Godwin.

"Well, come on, I'll come with you. And don't touch anything if you can help it."

"Let's check the back door first," suggested Betsy, since they were in the kitchen. "To see if there was a break-in. Oh, gosh! Nikki! Looks like we'll be here awhile. I'll call her."

While she did that, Lars and Godwin went through the laundry room to look at the back door.

She had barely hung up when they came back, Godwin looking downcast. "Not a scratch," he reported. "And it's locked."

"Maybe we'll find a window open."

The house was all on one level. On the other side of the kitchen was the master bedroom, which jutted out behind, making the house form an L. It was very large, probably an addition. It looked in perfect order. The furniture was dark wood, the carpet a dense plush of dark green, the walls a faint peach. Godwin, his arms folded against temptation to touch or fondle, walked around, sighing and sniffing. Betsy resisted an urge to comfort him, fearful of starting him crying again. Lars waited patiently.

Beyond the bedroom, the bathroom was as large as an ordinary bedroom. The floor was purple tile and there were a lot of marbled mirrors. There were twin lavender sinks, and a lavender whirlpool bath sat on a dais three steps up. All had gold fixtures shaped like dolphins. There were bottles of scented oils set beside the bath, which was draped in purple veiling, and everywhere there were fat candles and stacks of thick white and purple towels. One wall was covered with a mosaic from naughty old Pompeii. It was like something out of a DeMille movie, and Betsy wanted to giggle. Then she saw Godwin's nostalgic expression and managed not to. But Lars cleared his throat repeatedly.

She opened a capacious wicker hamper and found it full of used towels and a deep purple robe. Godwin came to look and frowned. "John always wears white."

"So is it yours?" she asked.

"No. It's for guests." He sat down on the lowest step of the dais and put his face in his hands.

She sat down beside him and put a hand on his shoulder.

"I take it this means Mr. Nye had a visitor?" asked Lars.

"Well, he threw me out," Godwin said, "so what else could I expect?"

Betsy said angrily, "He could've waited, oh, I don't know, a week, maybe?"

Godwin snorted into his hands and coughed, then raised his head. "He wasn't a patient man." A single tear came down his cheek, but he brushed it away impatiently. "He always said he loved me, but he wasn't always kind."

Lars said, "I guess you shouldn't give the eulogy."

That made him laugh, if harshly, and they continued to tour the house.

On the other side of the living room were three rooms. The one facing the front was a den or library, its many shelves full of a wide variety of books from legal tomes to modern novels. The front window had old-fashioned venetian blinds. It and the side window were locked—Betsy checked. There was a big potted ficus, and an antique desk with an up-to-date computer on it. The desk chair was high-backed, upholstered in leather, and a comfortable club chair invited a visitor to sit in front of it. Everything looked in good order, here, too; no strew of papers or open drawers. A wooden file cabinet blended in with the bookshelves. Betsy reached to open a desk drawer, but Lars made a warning noise, so she didn't.

"Did Mr. Nye do much work at home?" Lars asked.

"Some," nodded Godwin. "He almost never had clients come to the house. But he gave great parties." He gestured toward the computer. "He loved the Internet. He had weblogs he read every day, and a lot of Internet friends he'd never met face-to-face."

"Did you use this computer, too?"

"Oh, no. I have my own, with my own account. We *never* read each other's mail. That was one thing I really liked about John, he gave me my own space and never came in uninvited." Godwin hung onto his composure with agonized effort.

"May we see your room?" asked Betsy.

"Sure, it's back here."

A bathroom was between the den and Godwin's bedroom. It was much more utilitarian than the lavender paradise, with a sky-blue tile floor, blue and cream wallpaper, a skylight, and etched-glass doors on the tub-shower.

Godwin's bedroom was larger than John's den, and it overlooked a garden ablaze with flowers and a small pond with a tiny waterfall. "A man comes by every week to take care of the yard," said Godwin. "In June he puts koi in the water. They're greedy things, always sticking their heads out to beg for treats."

"Scaly versions of Sophie?" said Betsy.

Godwin smiled. "Yes. We should introduce them." He waved that thought away. "Maybe not, one or the other would get eaten."

Betsy laughed and looked around. Godwin had a sleigh bed in what looked like maple, heaped with pillows. An upholstered chair sat by a window, with a wooden frame on wheels beside it, a Dazor light bending over from the other side. In the far corner was a small desk, its top empty. The two windows in the room, half covered with Roman blinds, were also closed and locked. Betsy looked around, wishing she could open drawers.

"Where's your computer?" she asked.

"It was in the box he sent over."

"Weren't you working on a project?" Betsy asked, noting that the frame was empty.

"John sent over my needlework projects." He asked Lars, "Can I take the stand? And the light? They're mine, I bought them with my own money."

"Not right now. This house is a crime scene, remember. You can claim all your things when they settle the estate."

"Estate? Yes, that's right, John was rich, so he had an estate. And he had a will, I know he had a will, he mentioned it once. I wonder if he left me anything?"

Betsy asked, "Did he say he did?"

"No, just that he had a will. That was a couple of years ago. He said I should make one, too. But I said I intended to die broke and so I didn't need a will."

The closet door was ajar, Betsy went to open it with the toe of her shoe. Inside was a riot of hangers, some on the floor. A pink straw hat with a crushed crown was on a shelf. Godwin reached around Betsy and took it before she could stop him. "We bought this in Mexico City," he said. "I was going to leave it behind, but it was such a great trip I couldn't leave anything behind. John stepped on it when he came to talk to me in here while I was unpacking. He was in a bad mood, but I don't think he stepped on it on purpose." He put it on and went to look at himself in the mirror over his dresser. He tipped it a bit to the side, made a funny face, then took it off and broke down completely.

Betsy led him to the beautiful bed, sat him down and went into the bathroom to look for tissues. She found a box of Kleenex pop-ups encased in a needlepoint holder designed to look like a box of Kleenex—Godwin had an interesting sense of humor—and pulled out four, which she took back to him. Lars had gone away.

"Thangs," he mumbled and blew his nose.

Betsy sat down beside him and thought. She went back over the house in her head, looking with her memory at everything.

"Did John wear a watch?"

"Sure, he had a Rolex, a nice fat one."

"He isn't wearing one now."

"He isn't? Are you sure?" Godwin twisted up his face, trying to remember. "I didn't notice it was gone. He wore it all the time."

"I'm going back to look again," said Betsy. "You wait here."

She went back into the living room and found Lars all by himself with John's body. "What's going on?" she asked.

"We're waiting for someone from the Medical Examiner's office," he said. "Phil's out on the porch, and I sent the ambulance away. No need to tie them up. The BCA is on its way, this place will be pretty busy in a little while."

Betsy went to stoop beside the body.

"Don't move him!" barked Lars.

"I won't, I won't. I'm just trying to see if he's wearing a watch. Goddy says he has a Rolex but I don't see anything on either wrist." The body's arms were drawn up close to the chest, but Betsy was pretty sure both wrists were empty.

Lars came to lean over her. "Huh," he said, and pulled a flashlight from his belt. He shone it at various angles. "Nothing, and it didn't fall off," he noted, probing the shadows with his light.

"That's funny, because it didn't look as if anything was disturbed in the bedrooms," said Betsy. "We should look in the basement next, I suppose—" She was interrupted by a yell from Godwin's bedroom.

"Godwin? What's wrong?" She had barely straightened when the young man came running out toward her. In both hands he was holding a small, cedar-wood chest.

"Gone!" he shouted. "My jewelry's gone!"

Betsy put out a hand to stop him. "What are you talking about? I thought John sent all your things!"

"Not my diamond studs! And my gold ring, my beautiful gold and emerald ring!" He held out the box. "He sent my silver bracelets and the amethyst ring, but my *good* stuff, he kept that. My gold chain, gone! Even my beautiful ormolu birdcage, *gone*!"

"What the hell's an ormolu birdcage?" demanded Lars, notebook in hand. "And I thought I told you not to touch anything!"

Godwin sank to the floor with a groan. "This's my jewelry box, I can look in it if I want to! And it's empty! All my good pieces, gone, gone, *gone*!"

"I didn't see a birdcage in your room, Goddy," said Betsy.

"Not a *big* one, a little, little one," said Godwin, holding up a thumb and finger about an inch apart. "Ormolu is gold plated, gold over silver," he explained to Lars. "Like gilding, only better. It was a tiny, little bird cage with a weentsy wee bird made of two diamonds in it. A bird in a gilded cage, like the song, like me. It was our own little joke—and now it's *gone*!"

"Maybe he sold the stuff," suggested Lars.

"No, no, *no*!" raged Godwin. "He *wouldn't,* especially not the ormulu bird!" His face was wretched, streaked with tears. Betsy's heart went out to him; it wasn't just the jewelry, it was what the jewelry meant.

She turned to Lars. "Perhaps it *was* a robbery. If so, there are other things missing. If we could open drawers and closets, I bet we'd find more nice little things gone."

Six

❈ ❈ ❈

THE Medical Examiner's representative was a short, gray-haired woman in a dark brown pant suit. For a doctor, she had no bedside manner—perhaps, Betsy reflected later, this was why she went into the autopsy line. She was taciturn to the point of rudeness, and cast so chill an eye on Betsy and Godwin that they stood quietly against a wall, too intimidated to speak and afraid to walk away. Officer Phil Ott, the dark cop who'd come in after Lars, picked up on her suspicious glances, and came to stand next to them with an air of keeping custody. Even Lars, normally at ease with anyone of any rank, simply stood to one side and didn't ask any questions.

Of course, there being no hope of life in John Nye, and the probable cause of his death both apparent and present, there weren't many questions to ask.

Mike Malloy was investigating another crime and so arrived after she did; minutes later a crew from the state's

Bureau of Criminal Apprehension came in. The Medical Examiner became distracted by the investigators, so Betsy raised a hand to draw Lars's eye and indicate she was taking Godwin into the den. When he nodded permission, they slipped away.

There was some kind of rumpus going on out front; Betsy heard the noise coming through the front window of the den. She went to look out and saw a small crowd gathering, talking to one another and on their cell phones, gesturing vehemently at others to come where the action was—though there wasn't any outside the house.

This part of Excelsior had no sidewalks, so they stood in the street or on the broad driveway to the garage, and two even ventured close to the picture window to try to peer inside. This last move evidently drew the attention of the people in the living room. Betsy heard an exclamation from someone, and watched as Lars and Phil went out to do a little crowd control, waving people off the property. A new uniformed officer enforced the retreat by running a yellow plastic tape from tree to lamp post to tree along the edge of the lawn and across the driveway.

Betsy went to half-sit on the desk and put a comforting hand on Godwin's shoulder as he sat slumped in the office chair.

After about a quarter of an hour, Mike Malloy looked into the den and asked, "What were you two doing here?"

"We found the body," said Betsy.

"I figured that," said Mike, sounding a little aggravated. "How did you come to be here in the first place?"

"John's secretary called me to ask if I knew where he was, because he hadn't come to work," answered Godwin. "I didn't want to come alone, so Betsy came with. We came in and . . . and here he was." Godwin put a trembling hand in front of his mouth.

"Did you move him?" asked Mike, coming in and shutting the door.

Godwin shook his head emphatically. "No."

"I touched him," said Betsy, "which made me realize he really was dead. Lars took us to look around to see if anything's been taken, and so far there's jewelry missing. Lars said not to disturb anything, leave fingerprints or smudge them, so we didn't open any drawers."

"And we haven't been down in the basement, yet," said Godwin. "Because the door is closed and we didn't want to touch the doorknob."

"What kind of jewelry's missing?" asked Mike, pulling out his notebook.

"Well, Godwin said John always wore his Rolex, but there's no watch on his arm," said Betsy.

"And I had some nice diamond stud earrings and a ring with a big emerald and two small diamonds, and a gold chain—twenty-two carat—and a gold necklace with a little . . . diamond bird in . . . in an ormolu cage." Godwin was tearing up under this recital, so Betsy reached for his hand and began to rub it gently. He gulped and regained control. "John has some nice pieces, too, but his jewelry box is in a drawer in his dresser, so we couldn't look. Nothing else seems to be missing—I mean like television sets and cordless phones and all."

"Was the door locked when you got here?"

"Yes." Betsy nodded. "Godwin has a key, so he unlocked it. And the back door was locked, too, right?" She looked at Godwin.

"Yes," he confirmed. "Oh, I did touch that doorknob,

sorry. But I didn't unlock it. We didn't see any windows broken, and they all seem to be locked." He looked at Betsy, who nodded confirmation.

"Who else has a key to the house?" asked Mike.

"The Molly Maid," said Godwin after a moment's thought. "She comes once a week while we're at work."

"Anyone else?"

Godwin's forehead crinkled. "Not that I know of."

Betsy said, "I looked in the laundry hamper in the master bath, and there's evidence John had . . . company recently."

Godwin explained, "There's a robe he keeps for guests— like for when we go swimming, if someone didn't bring one." His mouth twisted up, but Betsy squeezed his hand hard and he sniffed lengthily, then sighed and nodded that he had himself back under control.

"But the towels were damp, like from a bath or shower," Betsy said to Mike. "I'd add 'or swimming,' but it's a little early for swimming." Spring-fed Lake Minnetonka didn't get warm enough for swimming until mid-June.

Mike had some more questions, and then a tall, very slender blond investigator from BCA also questioned them, and had them fingerprinted before they were allowed to leave.

Godwin again came close to losing his composure when they came into the living room to find two sturdy young men zipping John's body into a blue bag. But he only sobbed once as they crossed the living room and went out the door.

Someone must have called in a tip because there was a professional-size television camera perched on a man's shoulder, and another man with a beautiful haircut and a light blue shirt moved into their path to ask questions. "Are you the ones who discovered the body?" he demanded. When they kept going, he followed, pushing a microphone into their faces while a cameraman hurried backwards down the driveway so he could keep his camera aimed at them. "What brought you to the house? Do you know who murdered Mr. Nye? Are you relatives?" And as Betsy brought out her keys and made her Buick chirp its locks open, he hurtled a final question. "Are you Mr. Nye's gay lover?"

Betsy shoved Godwin into the passenger seat, gave the inquiring reporter an icy stare, then stalked around to get into the driver's seat, start the car, and drive off with a little squeak of tires. "Jackals!" she growled.

Beside her, Godwin wept.

B ACK at the shop, she hustled Godwin through the entrance to the apartments on the second floor, then into her apartment, then into the guest bedroom. The room was light and airy, painted in mottled shades of blue, with an iron-gray four-poster bed set at an angle in one corner. Godwin went right to it and curled into the fetal position on top of the blue and gray quilt. Betsy spoke soothingly to him while pulling off his shoes. She went to the closet and got a lightweight blanket from the top shelf and floated it over him.

"Do you want me to sit with you?" she asked.

"No," he muttered.

"Would you like something to drink? Cocoa? Scotch? Orange juice?"

"No. Can I be alone for awhile?"

"Sure. I'll go down to the shop. But I'll come up as often as I can to see how you're doing. And of course you can call down there if you want anything."

"Thanks."

"You're sure you're all right?"

"I'll never be all right again."

"Oh, Goddy, of course you will. You are so surrounded by people who love you, you can't be anything else."

He sniffed but did not reply.

She paused at the door, a hand on the knob. "Let me predict something. If you thought it was ridiculous the number of hot dishes I was gifted with after I got out of the hospital, wait til you see our kitchen by tomorrow afternoon."

"Huh," he said, but something in his tone said he was comforted by the prediction.

Betsy went downstairs, and down the back hall to her shop. It was nearly noon, and she found Nikki Marquez nibbling on a bunch of red grapes.

"Oh, I'm glad you're back!" Nikki said. "I thought I saw you and Godwin going in the door to the upstairs, but when you didn't come back, I thought I was mistaken."

"Godwin's up in my apartment," said Betsy. "He's very upset and won't be coming down."

Nikki put the grapes down. "Why, what happened?"

Betsy sat down behind the desk. "Well, we went over to Godwin's partner's house to see why he hadn't gone to work, and I'm afraid we found him dead."

Nikki just stared for a few moments. "Dead? What, some kind of accident?"

"No. And not suicide, either. Someone came into the house, probably last night, and struck Mr. Nye on the head. The police are there now."

"Why, that's *horrible*! Poor Godwin! He . . . he was in love with John, wasn't he?"

"Yes, but what makes it worse is that they quarreled recently."

"Oh, dear. But they made up?" She saw Betsy's mute expression of denial and said, "That *is* worse! How dreadful for him! He must be just sick!"

Betsy nodded. "Yes, he is. I put him to bed, but I want to go up and check on him every so often. Will you be able to stay until I find someone else?"

"Oh, of course. In fact, I can stay all day, if you need me to."

"Well, thank you, that would be very helpful."

"Only thing is, I need some lunch, and I need it pretty soon." Her brow wrinkled with concern at adding to Betsy's burden.

"Would something from the deli next door be all right? They've got soups, salads, and sandwiches at the deli."

"Sure. I'll get something and bring it right back."

"No, I meant, how about I buy us both something."

"Well, gee, you don't have to do that. But thank you!" Betsy gave Nikki some money and asked for half a turkey sandwich and a cup of tomato soup for herself.

"Oh, wait, let me give you more money," she said. "Get a bowl of chicken soup for Godwin. Whole wheat crackers, he likes those."

Nikki took the additional five and went out. The silent door reminded Betsy of that failing, and she wrote a note to herself to find a workman to replace it—she'd never liked the obnoxious sound it made, and now was the perfect opportunity to select something more musical. A tune? No, not a tune. Hearing "Carolina Moon" might be amusing the first few times, but the fiftieth repetition in a day might be a bit tedious. A single musical note would be fine. Or maybe two, like a doorbell.

When Nikki came back, Betsy took the chicken soup upstairs. She found Godwin asleep on the bed. She put the soup and crackers down on the computer desk and went to wake him.

"Goddy," she said gently. He didn't stir. "Goddy? It's me, Betsy. I brought you some lunch."

"Huh?" he murmured, then sat bolt upright, looking around in terror. "What? What?"

"Easy, Goddy, it's me, Betsy."

"What? Oh, hi. What's wrong?" He looked around, rubbing his eyes with one hand. "Say, what time is it?" He looked down at himself, surprised to find he was dressed. Then his face changed, sagging into despair. "Oh, my God, it's not a bad dream, is it?"

"No, baby, I'm afraid not."

He coughed violently, moved to dangle his legs over the edge of the bed. "What's going on?"

"Nikki's staying in the shop all day. I've brought some chicken soup up for you. I want you to eat some of it. There's bottled water in the refrigerator, also milk, grapefruit, and cran-apple juice. Eat, then change into your pajamas and go back to bed. Everything's all right downstairs, so you just rest."

"I feel awful," he said. And he looked awful, with brown shadows under his eyes and lines around his mouth. He stared at the floor, and his eyes widened as if he were seeing John's body spread there. His hands clutched the blanket around his waist.

"Do you want me to stay with you?" she asked. "Or call someone, a friend, to stay with you?"

"No," he said, but absently, still staring.

"Godwin," she called, drawing out the sound, and he looked up at her. "It's going to be all right. It's terribly, terribly hard right now, but it will get better."

"I don't see how."

"I didn't either, when I lost Margot. But it does. Time passes, and wounds heal. You have a lot of friends, and their love will help."

"All right." This time he didn't sound convinced.

"I've got to go back downstairs. Nikki's been a great help. Thank you for calling her."

"Yes? All right. You're welcome."

"Will you eat the soup? It's chicken soup, the universal medicine."

He smiled faintly. "All right."

She turned to leave.

"Betsy?"

"Yes?"

"Are you going to try to find out who murdered John?"

"Do you want me to do that?"

"Yes. Yes, please. We never got a chance to make up, and that's what makes this like the end of the world." He sniffed, and two big tears rolled from his eyes. He blotted them with the sleeves of his shirt.

"I'll see what I can do. But if this is a burglary, then Mike will probably solve it before I can even get started. He's good at that kind of crime."

"Come on! Everyone knows he's not the swiftest boat on the river."

"That's when it's about amateur criminals. When it comes to the pros, he's very, very swift."

"Okay, we'll let him have a shot at it. But if he doesn't arrest someone in the next day or two, then it's your turn."

"All right." Betsy did leave then.

On her way back downstairs she reflected on Godwin's simple trust in her sleuthing abilities. It was a strange thing, this ability of hers to solve crimes. She had no training in investigation, and she never sought out opportunities to sleuth. It was as if crime came looking for her, usually in the person of a customer who had a relative falsely accused—sometimes by Mike Malloy. And to her mind, when she solved a case, it was more luck than skill or talent.

Of course, this time there would be no relative anxious to clear a brother or cousin. Betsy was pretty sure Mike was at this moment bending over a dusty fingerprint and nodding sagely. A burglar who hadn't realized John was home, who had been surprised and frightened when confronted by John, and struck out with the first thing to hand, then run off with only a few pieces of jewelry. And who would pay very dearly for what he'd done.

Betsy came in the back door of the shop, where she took out the little three-step stool, opened it, and climbed up to reach for the shop's Christmas decorations in the large box high on a shelf.

Nikki, hearing the sounds of effort, came to help. In the box, near the bottom—of course—was a small wreath made of golden sleigh bells. Betsy had bought it at a post-Christmas sale, intending to cut the thing apart and sell the bells in Christmas kits. She still might, but meanwhile she would hang it on her door to use as an announcement of a customer's entry.

She hung it by its loop over the doorknob and opened and closed the door to try its effect. "Good enough," she pronounced. Then she noticed she had slammed the door in Bershada Reynolds's face. "Oh, I'm *so* sorry!" she exclaimed, opening it again.

Bershada, a slim black woman, was a retired librarian made eloquent from years of nonverbal expression. She paused a moment to take in the apology, then, eyebrows raised in gentle rebuke, entered the shop.

"What can we do for you?" asked Betsy.

"I came for a knitting pattern. I want to try that kind that looks like strips of color woven together." Bershada looked around the shop. "Where's Godwin?"

"Upstairs. He won't be in today."

"Then it's true?"

"What's true?"

"John Nye was found dead at home?"

"Has it been on the news already?" asked Betsy.

"Not that I know of. I stopped at the Waterfront Café—do you know they're doing the coffee house thing, with lattés and chai and all? They've even put some computer connections in the back. Anyway, I just stopped for a chai, and Jimmy Folsom was there and he said Leecia Millhouse, who lives practically next door to John, watched while they brought him out in a *body bag*. Girl, there's crime scene tape all around the house. It looks like *murder*." Bershada stopped to draw a breath, and her expression changed. "Wait a minute, you already *know* about this, don't you?" She reared back and looked at Betsy sideways. "Who told you?"

"No one. We were there."

"Where—at the *house*?"

"Yes." Betsy explained how she and Godwin had gone over to see why John hadn't gone to work and found him.

"Oh, the *poor baby*!" said Bershada, meaning Godwin. "Is he all right?"

"I think he will be. He's badly shaken up, of course. I put him to bed and told him to stay there."

"Well, of course, and I hope he does. He and John hadn't made up?"

"No, and that's what's making it so hard."

"Yes, of course. Is there anything I can do?"

"No, I don't think so. But thank you. I'll tell him you asked after him. Now, this pattern, would it be entrelac you're looking for?"

"Yes, I think that's the name of it. You use circular needles to make a purse." She gestured a round shape.

"Yes, I just got a very nice pattern in, so I don't have a model yet. I'm going to try it myself, or maybe a sweater, I like the look of it. I have a nice yarn for the purse, it's from Japan, all wool, and overdyed. Do you know how to back knit?"

"No, what's that?"

"Well, the pattern calls for knit and purl, but sometimes as few as two stitches. Having to turn the needles around every two stitches is a nuisance, so there's this thing called back knitting, where you knit backwards, off the lefthand needle. Godwin showed me how to do it. Let me see if I can remember."

She pulled two knitting needles out of the vase of accessories on the library table, picked up a small ball of yarn and swiftly cast on ten stitches, then knit a row. "See, here's how it works." Bershada came to stand looking over her shoulder. "Knit two," Betsy said, doing so. "Now, put the left needle *behind* the stitch, throw your yarn around it counterclockwise, and pull it through. And again. See?"

"Well, I'll be. That doesn't look hard at all."

"It's not. Well, it's a bit clumsy at first, but it's not hard to do."

Bershada bought the pattern, and two skeins of the Japanese wool in shades of purple, green, and blue, and a pair of number-five knitting needles. "I have circular needles in that size already," she said.

As she prepared to leave, she asked again, "You're sure there's nothing I can do for Goddy?"

"A card would be—oh, for heaven's sake, I *am* an idiot. He's feeling abandoned, of course, so I remembered what happened when I got that dose of poison and came home to a flock of hot dishes. So if it's not a huge imposition . . ."

Bershada smiled. "Not at all. Just let me get myself home and I'll start cooking."

Seven

THE next day, the hot dishes started to arrive. Bershada must have told everyone she knew, and each of them spread the word even further. Customers Betsy hadn't seen in months came in, bearing Corning Ware and Pyrex, wrapped in newspaper to keep it warm—or frozen, some women apparently keeping something always ready to bring to a bereavement.

At first Betsy brought them upstairs. Later, she trusted Nikki, who was threatening to become full time, to bring them up. By the end of the day, she was waving them through. Still, by the time she closed at five, her legs ached from all the climbing.

They continued to come all evening. Touching at first, it became amazing, then silly, finally ridiculous.

The last one arrived around nine. Godwin, hearing laughter, came out of his room to see what was going on. Jill Cross Larson, who rarely laughed, stood in the midst of outrageous abundance, every flat surface in the apartment covered with ceramic and glass bowls full of a wide assortment of meats (or tuna), vegetables, and cream of mushroom soup, with yet another hot dish in her hand, laughing. "Coals to Newcastle!" she crowed.

Godwin, who had not so much as peeped out all day, looked around. Slowly a smile formed, and then he, too, began to laugh.

Betsy rejoiced to see it, but said, "What on earth are we going to do with all this?"

Godwin, leaning against the door frame, only shook his head and laughed some more.

It was Jill who came up with a solution. She was herself a police officer—a sergeant—tall, very fair, with a beautiful Gibson-girl face normally displaying only the Gibson Girl's cool aloofness. Yet behind that stolid face was a keen intelligence and a gentle heart, the latter evidenced by the package in her hands. "You can send most of it to homeless shelters, churches that feed the homeless, and a shelter for abused women," she said.

Betsy asked Godwin, "What do you think? After all, this is yours."

Godwin shook his head, "Even if we gave up eating any other kind of food, we could never eat all this." He looked at Jill. "I bet you have a list of phone numbers we could call about donating."

"I sure do. All police departments do. I'll send you the list by e-mail tomorrow from work." She handed her hot dish to Betsy, who found it warm to the touch through the layers of newspaper around it, and went to take Godwin by the shoulders in a firm grip. "Are you going to be all right?" she asked.

"Yes," he replied, nodding, looking around. "I think I will be. Thank you."

And the next morning he insisted on coming back to work.

Word flashed around the town that Godwin was at work— e-mail and cell phones had made the gossip grapevine in Excelsior stunningly efficient—so at one in the afternoon there was a special session of the Monday Bunch. Its purpose was to lend aid and comfort.

Godwin soaked it up in bucketfuls. The Monday Bunch was emphatic. "How dare they!" was the sum of opinion about the media, though they put it variously. Needles flashed, scissors snipped sharply, and hearty sniffs and the occasional "Hah!" underlined their remarks.

"Don't these reporters have anything better to do than harass our good citizens?" asked Alice, who a minute earlier had pinned verbal medals on Godwin and Betsy for taking the time to go see if something was wrong at John Nye's house.

"Those reporters are like vultures, only worse," grumbled Bershada, clipping off a new length of DMC 457 and separating the strands before threading her needle with two of them. "Vultures can't help doing what they were designed to do, while reporters actually go to college to learn how to circle in on trouble."

"What I don't like," said Alice, "is the way they ask a question they don't expect an answer to, just to get themselves on the news. 'Are you guilty of kidnapping that child?' they shout at someone. What do they expect that person to do? Stop and give a long, complex defense? When the policemen are pulling him by the elbows?"

"That's the perp walk," contributed Godwin, bringing a fresh cup of hot water and a tea bag to the table for Doris.

"What's a perp walk?" demanded Alice.

"A 'perp walk' is when the police take someone in hand-cuffs on foot along a route lined with photographers. John told me about it. He said it's kind of a humiliation for the prisoner and it gets the police some air time, showing them doing their job."

"Oh, I've seen their pictures in the paper," nodded Martha, her crochet needle flying in and out as she built a brown and yellow afghan square. "They look funny trying to pretend they always carry their coats over their two wrists."

"Or over their heads," said Bershada dryly.

"What are you working on, Doris?" asked Alice, leaning sideways for a look.

"It's something I just bought." She handed around the chart, which was Maru's Aztec design of a tlattoli, which looked like a J with square projections around its outside.

"Goddy brought it back from Mexico," explained Betsy. "It's a word in the Aztec language—tattle-tot, or something like that. It means speech or talk."

Godwin sat down, picked up his knitting, and launched into his story of meeting the designer in a store in Mexico City.

"She sounds nice," commented Emily.

"She's very nice," said Godwin.

"This means talk, huh?" said Bershada, looking the chart over. "I think we should adopt this as the official emblem for the Monday Bunch. Talk, talk, talk; that's what we do." There was laughter and agreement.

"This is interesting," said Emily, taking it next. "Two sets of instructions. In this first one, you do the backstitch-ing first, then fill in the color. That's different." "That's different" is Minnesota Nice for "That's weird." She handed it to Alice.

"What did you say the designer's name was?" asked Alice.

"Maru—it's a nickname for Maria Eugenia."

"Never heard of her," declared Alice in her bluff way.

"No, she's only been published in Spanish-language magazines so far," said Godwin. "Here, let me show you something else she did." He went to a spinner rack in the back and returned with a chart in a small zip-loc bag. From a distance it looked like a pair of fat, red, lumpy Xs, but on closer examination it was a pair of red frogs with their legs extended.

"Her daughter likes frogs, so she designed this to decorate a dress or pinafore." He turned the bag over to show a white dress with a row of red frogs around the hem and waist.

"Too *cute*!" exclaimed Emily.

"No, it's too *icky*!" said Martha, an elderly woman with a brisk air. "Slimy frogs, ugh!"

"I bet a boy would love to have a Sunday shirt with a frog on the pocket," said Alice in her deep voice.

"A knit shirt with a row of these across the chest," amended Bershada. "He'd be the hit of his kindergarten class. All the girls would scream and pretend to be horrified."

"Except one," nodded Doris, shyly. "And she'd catch him at recess and kiss him." Some of the women gave knowing chuckles.

"What, hoping he'd turn into a *prince*?" said Godwin, and there was laughter.

"I'll take one of those charts," declared Emily. "But I also want Anchor 229. Frogs are green, not red."

"One skein enough?" asked Godwin, starting for the back again.

"Yes, thanks."

Godwin came back with the skein—and another plastic bag. "How about this Maru pattern?" he said, handing Alice a chart of stacked alphabet blocks in pastel colors.

"The same person did that Aztec thing, those frogs, and *this*?" she said, eyebrows raised high.

"That's right; you won't find *her* in a rut," said Godwin.

Betsy, conferring with a customer over a scarf pattern only ten stitches wide to be knit on enormous needles, smiled at Godwin's enthusiasm. He enjoyed pushing new designers, and evidently this Maru had made quite an impression.

Godwin stayed all day, buoyed by a steady stream of customers who came in to wish him well.

So he was in the shop when, near closing, a man, tall and seriously graying, with a somehow-familiar face, came into Crewel World.

Godwin simply stared, so Betsy said, "May we help you?"

"Yes, I think so," he replied, looking not at her but at Godwin. "I'm Charlie Nye, John's brother."

Eight

❖ ❖ ❖

Now it was Betsy's turn to stare.

Godwin, his face now stern, had come forward and stood with his feet apart and one hand in a pocket. "I'm Godwin DuLac. I'm very sorry about your brother." He spoke in a low, even register Betsy had never heard before.

"Thank you." Charlie Nye's face was sad.

"How did you find out about—" For an instant the façade broke, but was immediately restored—"about what happened?"

"The Excelsior police department called our parents," replied Charlie, "who called my sisters and me. Then Johnny's secretary called me directly—I was listed as next of kin at his office. I asked her if there was someone local I could talk to, and she gave me your name and said you worked here. I'd like to talk to you. Please?" There was a world of pain in his voice.

"Okay. I don't know if you know how well . . . I knew him."

The man smiled crookedly. "You two were lovers, right?"

For an instant Godwin looked frightened, then he blushed to the roots of his blond hair. Then he lifted his chin and growled, "Well, I don't know if I like—that is—what makes you think that?"

And suddenly Betsy understood what Godwin was doing. He was pretending to be straight.

Charlie looked around, his attitude uncomfortable. "Look, is there somewhere private we can talk?"

Godwin looked at Betsy, who said, "Why don't you take Mr. Nye upstairs?"

"All right," said Godwin. He explained to Charlie, "I'm staying with Betsy—Ms. Devonshire—temporarily. She owns this whole building and lives upstairs. Come on, this way. I can make you a cup of—of coffee."

Of course, thought Betsy. Straight men don't drink tea. She was sorry she couldn't go watch Godwin try to climb the stairs like a straight man. Trying to imagine it made her giggle, so it was just as well.

They were gone about forty minutes, and when they came down, Godwin's swish was back. "He knows, but he doesn't care!" Godwin murmured to Betsy as he sashayed by. He stopped by the knitting yarn to turn and say to Charlie, "Would you like to look around the shop?"

"No, I don't think so. I've got a lot to do, a number of people to connect with. It was good of you to take time from your day to speak with me. Thank you." He smiled thinly at both of them and left the shop.

"Well!" said Betsy as the jingle of golden sleigh bells died away. "That wasn't what I expected!"

"Me, either!" said Godwin. "He is a *nice* man!" He sat down in a chair at the table. "I wish John had been more like him," he added quietly.

"What did he say?" A thought struck. "Goddy, do you mean that *he's* gay, too?"

Godwin chuckled. "Oh, no, he's straight. Got a wife and kiddies and is very happy about it. But he's nice. John . . . John could be nice, when he *wanted* something or needed to *please* someone. But Charlie's just *nice*. He's like I wish John was. Oh, Betsy!" Godwin put both hands over his face.

She went to sit down next to him. "Poor Godwin," she said, putting a hand on his shoulder, and they fell silent for a minute while he pulled himself together.

"He wanted to know what kind of funeral John might want, and I had to say that we never talked about things like that, except like as a joke. You know, scatter my ashes on Cary Grant's grave. Charlie said his family was all raised Presbyterians, so since I don't have a better idea, he's going to take John home to Fargo for the funeral, and have him buried in the family plot there. But he says it's fine if I organize a memorial service, or see if I can get a role in the memorial service where John worked. Because I'm sure not going to be welcome at the funeral. Charlie says the rest of his family wouldn't stand for any—how did he put it?— '*acknowledgment* of John's sexual practices.' Funny word, 'practice,' isn't it? Like doctors and lawyers are always practicing. When do they do it for real?"

Betsy pulled him gently back on topic. "You told me John told you his family wanted John to pretend he wasn't gay when he was at home. But Charlie knew, he walked in here knowing—and knowing you were John's partner. And he wasn't cruel to you."

"It seems Charlie was an exception, John could talk to him."

"Then how do you know the rest of his family aren't all exceptions? I mean—you know what I mean."

"Yes, I know, but Charlie said the family was pretty set against John—he calls him 'Johnny,' did you notice that?" Betsy nodded. "Anyway, his family absolutely wouldn't let him come home unless he let them pretend he was just a confirmed bachelor."

"Yes, and leave you here alone."

"Yes, well, what else could he do?"

He could have stood up to them, she thought angrily. Or, he could have stayed away and shared his Christmas with poor Godwin, whose family wouldn't let him come home under any circumstances; and they'd both have had a merry Christmas with someone they loved. But, of course, John might have been one of those people who were loyal to their families no matter how flawed, who went home for holidays that were nightmares, because those ties were stronger than the pain. So she said, "I don't know, Goddy, I don't know."

He stood. "Me either. I wonder what kind of memorial service Wellborn, Hanson, and Smith will put on? I should find out—Tasha will know, I can ask her. There will probably be a lot of people there who don't know each other, I could sit real quiet in the back, out of the way."

"I suppose you could," agreed Betsy, knowing Godwin could no more sit quietly at such an event than he could fly. He'd bawl loudly and apply a handkerchief ostentatiously, because he was Godwin, who wore all his emotions on the outside.

"Or maybe I should call Donnie and Mark and Jo-Jo and Mickey. We could throw a great party. I bet we could rent the garden at Vera's—God, we used to have some *fantastic* times there! I wonder how much it would cost?"

"I don't have any idea," said Betsy, who had never heard of Vera's.

"You know, Charlie thinks John left me something in his will. I wonder what it is."

"You're the one who knows how John's mind worked, not me."

"Huh, it's probably a gold watch. Isn't that the usual gift you give someone who's being put out to pasture?"

"Oh, Goddy, stop it. Anyhow, if it's a watch, it better be a Rolex."

Godwin giggled. "We could throw a pretty nice party on what you can get for a Rolex."

"Would you sell it? His last gift to you?"

"No, I guess not. Maybe it's not just a watch. Maybe it's money. No, no, no, it's the *house,* I bet he left me the *house!* I mean, I just *know* he'd hate to have some couple moving in with dirty-fingered children and a *dog,* a big, nasty dog that would dig up all our flowers. He knew how much I loved that house, so it's *got* to be the house, how wonderful!" He spun around with joy, hands clenched under his chin.

"Now, Goddy, don't count your chickens."

"Oh, don't be so negative! You're always the wet blanket! It *must* be the house!"

Betsy stood. "You think what you like, but meanwhile could you go get me a bottle of water?"

"Certainly!" Godwin, full of good cheer, bounced through the twin sets of box shelves. There was a little refrigerator in the back room of the shop, where a coffee maker, tea kettle, and boxes of stock were also kept.

Betsy shook her head after him. Poor fellow, his emotions

were all over the place, and of course they ruled his intellect. Goddy might grow older, but he would never entirely grow up.

She went to the checkout desk to finish making up an order for floss. Rainbow's Fuzzy-Wuzzy was selling well, and their overdyed silks, too. And Kreinik's blending filaments. And here was a note from Godwin saying they were low on Anchor 941, 137, 139, and 142—someone must be doing a big lake or sea scene to judge by the dent made in her stock of those blues.

A clear plastic bottle of water was put on the desk. She looked up and saw Godwin looking somber. "I'm such a ninny," he said. "I get carried away, like a cork on the outgoing tide. You're right about counting chickens—especially when these aren't even eggs yet. Are you mad?"

Betsy smiled. No wonder John always made up with Godwin. When he was penitent, he was irresistible. "Of course I'm not mad. It must be exciting to know you're named in a will."

"Yes, but I could've waited awhile for this. I'd rather be making up with John than wondering what he left me."

"I understand. This is a terrible time for you."

"Worse than you know." He brushed away a tear.

The phone rang and Betsy pulled herself together to answer it crisply, "Good afternoon, Crewel World, how may I help you?"

"Ms. Devonshire, this is Charlie Nye. Is Godwin there?"

"Certainly." She handed the receiver to Godwin. "Charlie Nye," she said.

"Well, hello again!" said Godwin cheerfully. He listened, the smile turning to a frown. "No, of course I didn't take it, why would I do that? Besides, the police warned us not to touch anything." He listened more briefly. "Yes, I guess you should ask them." Pause. "No, I can't imagine, either. Yes, could you let me know? Thanks, bye."

"What?" asked Betsy when he had hung up.

"John's computer is missing. Charlie was going to go through its files to see if there were some instructions for, you know . . ."

Betsy nodded.

"He told me upstairs, the police said he could go into the house, and I told him John kept all kinds of notes and things on his computer. And the computer isn't in his den. It's gone."

"Is he going to notify the police?"

"Yes. But isn't it strange? Do you suppose that whoever took our jewelry came back for the computer? He must've had a key—well, of course he did! He got in the first time without breaking a lock!"

"But who, besides you—and the Molly Maid—has a key to the house?" asked Betsy.

"No one. Well, no one I know of. Isn't that strange?" He shivered and stared at Betsy with frightened eyes.

The mystery was solved ten minutes later, when Charlie called back to say the computer had been taken by the police, who wanted to see if John had been cruising the personals, looking for a connection with someone who might have proved deadly.

"The purple robe," said Godwin, with wounded eyes. "Someone ate John's food, drank his wine, took a bath in his tub—and murdered him."

Nine

❖ ❖ ❖

BETSY and Godwin worked on Saturday. It was a busy day, lots of working women had only Saturdays to browse, so part-timer Shelly also came in. The weather was nice, sunny, and warm, which added to the number of people out and about. Jill stopped by close to noon, looking for gold Kreinik braid for a needlepoint canvas she was working on.

"Heard anything?" asked Betsy *sotto voce*.

"Mike found someone to make two copies of the hard drive out of John's computer and they sent one to the state crime lab for scrutiny," murmured Jill.

"I hope they find an e-mail from the person who was in John's house last week," said Godwin, who'd been hovering. "It gives me goosebumps to think I saw the robe he was wearing when he murdered John."

"Now, Goddy, you don't know that," said Betsy. "He might have just been a guest."

"No," said Godwin firmly, shaking his head. "I know it, *here*—" He thumped himself on the chest. "I saw the robe of a *murderer*."

Jill smiled over Godwin's head at Betsy, who smiled very faintly back—but Godwin caught it. "You don't believe me!" he accused her. He turned and repeated the accusation to Jill. "You think I'm lying!"

"Now, Goddy, I would never call you a liar. I just don't see how you can be so sure the person who murdered John Nye did it while wearing a purple bathrobe. The police don't know—yet—who wore that robe, and they don't have any evidence that he's the person who murdered John Nye. I know that preliminary testing showed no bloodstains on the robe."

Godwin took a breath, then found he had nothing more to say. Jill had that effect on emotional outbursts. It was like shouting into a duvet; she soaked up sound and fury without them leaving a trace.

"You wait," he managed to grumble and walked away.

"You're right about that. We'll find the person responsible." She said to Betsy, "I'll take these two spools, please."

As Betsy handed her her change, she asked, "Jill, what does Mike think?"

"He's trying to keep an open mind. He says it could be the visitor, it could be a lock-picking burglar, it could be someone John knew and let in. It could even be the Molly Maid." Jill smiled, took the little bag of gold braid, and left.

Sunday the shop was closed, as were almost all of Excelsior's businesses. Betsy went to church and on coming back home found Godwin cleaning the apartment. She changed clothes and started in herself, and did laundry besides. With his help, the work was soon done and Godwin cooked a

Sunday dinner of roast chicken stuffed with garlic, rosemary, and lemon quarters. That evening, after doing the books, Betsy worked on her counted needlepoint project called Independence Day.

"What do you think of counted needlepoint?" asked Betsy.

"Oh, it's okay. Easier to see the holes in canvas, of course. I like this one because each individual piece of the pattern is attractive and all, but it's not until you see them all together that you realize it's a fireworks display. I mean, look at this big one in the center: it's *square,* with a gem in the center. It could be anything."

"I've seen shaped fireworks," said Betsy.

"Yes, but not like this. And all these squiggly things— cute, but what are they? Yet, here, look at the picture of the model. Obviously, *obviously,* it's a fireworks display." He stepped back from the canvas in its stretcher bars and cocked his head at an angle, narrowing his eyes. "But it's, too early to say if your piece will work." He went back to his knitting.

Betsy, smiling, reflected that it was indeed peculiar how the human mind worked, and went back to stitching.

MONDAY they were back in the shop. At little after one in the afternoon the Monday Bunch gathered, stitchery in hand, gossip spilling from every tongue.

"Joe Mickels's sister wants to ship her triplets out for a month's stay with Joe this summer," said Martha. "I hear he's trying to find a summer camp for them up on the Iron Range." The Iron Range was in the northernmost part of the state, many hours from Excelsior. Martha had just started a large counted cross-stitch project of a lighthouse on jagged rocks with violent waves throwing foam nearly to the top of it. She turned the knobs to tighten the stretcher bars and pulled a threaded needle from the fabric.

"I heard the girls are very sweet," said Doris. She was cutting bright red DMC floss into lengths, separating the threads and putting them together again in twos.

"You heard wrong," asserted Martha, and there were smiles all around.

Then Alice dropped her bomb. "I hear Patricia Fairland is up for parole," she said, her crochet needle flashing as she worked another of her endless series of afghan squares. She was doing them in yarn that could be washed in hot water, because she was sending afghans to a missionary group caring for orphans in Afghanistan. They had asked for knitted blankets, but the notion of afghans to Afghanistan was too amusing to pass up.

Emily looked around for Betsy, who had turned to stone back behind the box shelves, out of sight.

Several years ago Patricia Fairland tried to frighten Betsy out of town with a series of near-miss attempts on her life, one of which came far nearer than she intended. That Patricia might be getting out of prison was a startling idea.

"Does Betsy know?" Emily asked.

"I don't think so, she hasn't said anything."

"Why do I think I remember that name?" asked Bershada, who was doing a counted cross-stitch pattern of a thistle on a plaid ground. "Patricia Fairland, Patricia Fairland."

"That's right, you weren't in the Monday Bunch when Betsy was nearly killed by Patricia."

"*Killed?* When was this?"

"A few years ago. Betsy was investigating a tapestry they

found in a back room of Trinity Church. We were going to restore it."

"I remember that!" said Alice. "There was a message in that tapestry that said Patricia was an adultress and the pastor was a thief."

"I don't remember hearing about any of this," said Doris, who was folding her aida fabric to find its center.

"It must be because she only *nearly* killed Betsy that Patricia is up for parole already," noted Emily, who was knitting a little yellow sweater with cable stitching up its front and down its back.

"Do you think she should get it, Betsy?" asked Martha, looking up and seeing her coming.

"Get what?" asked Betsy, stopping by the table with a chart of Maru's Aztec symbol in her hand, an innocent expression on her face. She gave it to Doris, who had brought the red and black floss from her stash, ready to begin.

"Patricia Fairland is up for parole," said Alice. "Do you want to appear out there to speak against it?"

"No, of course not."

"Why not?" demanded Martha. "If it were me, I'd go out there and have a conniption right in front of the parole board that they could even think of letting her out. She nearly *killed* you, Betsy!"

"Yes, well, she didn't, and . . ." Betsy shrugged uncomfortably. "She said she was sorry."

"Sorry wouldn't cut any ice with *me*," declared Martha. "All those felons are sorry once they're caught."

"I know. But she didn't succeed after three tries, which made me think even at the time she wasn't serious."

"She tried three times and you say she wasn't *serious*?" said Bershada, incredulous.

"You feel sorry for *her*!" declared Martha, amazed.

"No, not anymore. Now I think we're even."

After Patricia's arrest, her mother-in-law, who had never liked her, had rolled into town demanding, on pain of disinheritance, that her son divorce Patricia—and disown his son, who, Betsy's sleuthing had revealed, had been fathered by another man. Betsy had been concerned about the boy, who at eleven was old enough to understand most of what was going on.

But Peter Fairland had displayed a surprising backbone and told his mother that, so far as he was concerned, Brent *was* his son, and, further, that he was not going to abandon his wife. He told everyone his wife had "gone a little crazy there for awhile" and had done some strange things for which she was deeply ashamed, that he forgave her and was going to stand by her. Privately, he came to Betsy with a semicoherent note written by Patricia in jail, begging for forgiveness.

The details of Patricia's behavior were kept from the public by having Patricia plead guilty to three felony assault charges rather than stand trial for attempted murder. Their attorney had suggested probation, but the judge, noting Patricia had pled to three counts, said five years. Once Patricia realized her husband was not going to throw her overboard, she had been a model prisoner and so now was up for parole after less than three.

Betsy, remembering the three beautiful Fairland children and their brave father, said, "Actually, I hope she gets paroled. Not for her sake, but the sake of her husband and children."

"Honestly, Betsy, you're too good for this wicked world," said Martha.

Godwin, passing by, remarked, "And remember, the good die young."

"Hah, if that's true, I'll still be running this place at a hundred and four," said Betsy, and went back to straighten up the mess a customer had made among the Charlie Harper charts.

At two-forty the Monday Bunch was starting to wrap up. Betsy went behind the checkout desk to ring up purchases. Godwin was over by the wooden spools on the wall, helping a customer select the yarns for a Margaret Bendig painted canvas she was about to buy.

The golden bells jingled and Mike Malloy came in with two uniformed police officers, one of whom was Lars, the big uniformed cop of last Sunday's horrible discovery.

"Hi, Mike," said Betsy cheerfully, then saw the looks on their faces. "What's wrong?"

"Godwin DuLac?" called Mike.

Godwin murmured an excuse to the woman with the painted canvas and came forward. "Yes? Hi, Mike. Hi, Lars. H'lo, Phil." Betsy recognized the second uniform as the cop who'd also been at John's house that dreadful morning. All three of their faces were grim, and Betsy's heart began to pound even before Mike spoke.

"Godwin DuLac, you are under arrest for the murder of John Nye," said Mike, as the other two came to put hands on him.

"No, wait a minute!" protested Godwin. But Phil had his handcuffs out and was reaching for Godwin's right wrist.

"You have the right to remain silent," continued Mike relentlessly. "If you give up the right to silence, anything you say will be written down and may be used against you in a court of law. You have a right to consult with an attorney before any questioning. If you wish to consult with an attorney, but can't afford one, one will be provided to you at no cost. Do you understand these rights as I have explained them to you?"

But Godwin had quit listening the instant the cuffs closed around his wrists. "What do you think you're *doing*? Let me *go*!" he shouted.

"Mike, this is obviously some kind of mistake," said Betsy, coming out from behind the desk.

"Don't hand me that lie about him being in your apartment Sunday night!" barked Mike, shoving a palm toward her.

She was so astonished she could not think of a reply, and retreated behind her desk. How had Mike found out?

Alice, Martha, and Doris had scrambled back behind the baskets of knitting wool. Emily hid behind a spinner rack of overdyed silks. Only Bershada stood fast. "Be cool, Goddy, be cool!" she begged.

But he continued to yell, twist, and struggle while the two cops started for the door. His face red and streaked with tears, turned toward Betsy. "Help, *please*! Don't let them *take me*!" His knees gave out, a shoe came off. Shrieking, "No, no, no!" he was dragged to the door.

Betsy darted over and picked his shoe up, but by then he was outside, so she handed it to Mike, who didn't seem to know what to do with it.

Betsy, the customer Godwin had been helping, and the Monday Bunch members hurried to the front window to watch in awed silence as Godwin was pushed, still struggling, into the back seat of a squad car. There, his head lifted, and the cords of his neck stood out, as Mike, wincing against the racket he was making, threw the shoe into the back and slammed the door. Phil got behind the wheel, Lars climbed into the passenger seat, and the squad car, lights flashing, pulled swiftly away from the curb. Mike climbed into his own car and followed after.

"*Well!*" said Martha, turning on Betsy. "What can they be thinking?"

"I have no idea!" said Betsy, taking two steps backward.

"They think he murdered John!" said Alice, in a voice of baffled wonder.

"Well, we can't have that!" declared Martha. "What are you going to do, Betsy?"

"I don't know. I can't believe Mike did that."

"You'd better believe it," said Bershada. "And you'd better do something about it—and fast."

"What nonsense, saying Godwin murdered John," said Emily indignantly. "Of all the stupid, stupid . . . *nonsense!*"

"Of course it's nonsense!" said Betsy. She went to the window again, but the cars were out of sight. "I wonder what Mike found out that makes him believe Goddy murdered John?"

"No amount of evidence could convince me that boy murdered *anyone!*" declared Bershada. "He simply isn't capable!"

"I agree," said Emily, and everyone nodded.

Martha asked, "Where do you suppose they took him?"

"Over to the police station, of course," said Doris. Then she frowned. "Right?"

"Call over there and find out," said Martha.

"Yes, of course." Betsy picked up the phone and hit the speed dial number for Jill at work.

"Excelsior Police, this is Sergeant Cross," came the crisp reply.

"Jill, has Mike gotten over there with Goddy yet?"

"Hold on." There was the sound of a receiver being dropped onto a desk, then silence. A minute later, Jill was back. "They're not bringing him here. He's going right downtown to be booked. He's in no state to be interrogated."

"Oh, Jill! Have they hurt him?"

"You know better than that. He's acting like a crazy person."

"Yes, of course, I'm sorry. He was yelling and fighting all the way out the door. Jill, what am I supposed to do?"

"Hire an attorney."

"Shouldn't I talk to him first? Or talk to Mike? Jill, why on earth has Mike arrested Goddy?"

"I don't know. He got a call from someone this morning, and went out for awhile, then suddenly he has a warrant. Betsy, he seems awfully sure it's Godwin."

"But he's wrong, you know he's wrong."

"I can only repeat, get him a lawyer. A good one."

"Yes, all right. Thanks, Jill."

Betsy hung up. "They're taking him to Minneapolis, to the jail. Jill said . . . she said he's in no state to be interrogated."

"Well, we got a good sample of how he's handling this already," said Alice. She shivered, as if shaking off a chill. "Poor little guy."

"You've got to get him bailed out right away," said Bershada. "I mean, *right away*."

"I do?"

"Honey, think about it! We're talking Godwin. Sweet, *pretty* Godwin. They put him in a cell, and it'll be 'Fresh meat, come and get it.'"

The chill that had troubled Alice descended on them all. Sweet, pretty, *defenseless* Godwin, thrust into a cell with some enormous tattooed biker—everyone's eyes widened.

"Oh, dear God," said Betsy. She sat down again and picked up the phone. She was so frightened she had trouble finding the number on her Rolodex, and then trouble dialing it. "Mr. Pemberthy?" she said. "Oh, I'm so glad you're in! Listen, Godwin has been arrested, and we need to bail him out right away."

Attorney James Pemberthy said, "Godwin, arrested? For what?" He sounded amused.

"Murder. Mike Malloy came and got him and said he was under arrest for the murder of John Nye. Jill says they took him right down to the jail. Jim, he was scared and crying. We can't let him stay there, we have to get him out!"

There was no amusement now. "When did this happen?"

"Just now. I thought they were taking him to the police station, but Jill says he was hysterical so they just went right on down the road to Minneapolis." Betsy felt a sob rising in her chest and choked it down fiercely. "You're my attorney, can you do something?"

"Not in this case. I'm not a criminal defense attorney, and that's what you need. I can give you a couple of names, if you like."

"Yes, please. Right now, please."

"Certainly. Hold on a moment." Again, there was the sound of a receiver being dropped onto a hard surface. Penberthy was gone about a minute, too, though it seemed much longer. He picked up the receiver at last and said, "Got a pencil?"

"Yes." Betsy flipped over the order form she had been filling out and picked up her pen.

"Frank Whistler." He spelled it.

Betsy wrote that down, and the phone number.

"Thanks."

"Just in case, here's another: Marvin Lebowski."

Betsy wrote that name down and asked, "Which of the two is better?"

"Well, Frank is a weasel, while Marvin's a tank. I recommend you talk to them both and see which one you feel more comfortable with. Or better, which one Godwin will be more comfortable with. You should be warned, they'll both want their retainer up front, and neither of them is cheap. But they're both excellent."

Betsy got Marvin Lebowski's number, thanked Pemberthy, and hung up.

Ten

✤ ✤ ✤

"DOES anyone here know what kind of bail they set on someone arrested for murder?" asked Betsy of the room at large.

"Depends on the degree," said Doris, and everyone turned to stare at her.

She shrugged at them. Doris was a heavy-boned woman, nearly as tall as Alice, fond of elaborate blond wigs and bright red lipstick. A relative newcomer to stitching, she had taken to it with enthusiasm, and was never afraid to try new stitches or projects. But she retained a love for the quick, simple patterns she had begun with, and used them to decorate packages or as impulse gifts. She was a tenant of Betsy's, having taken the apartment her brother had rented before he retired to a warmer climate.

"I like to watch true crime shows on television," she explained. "And Court TV. I can tell you there's a big difference between first, second, and third-degree murder charges.

People charged with first degree usually don't get bail at all. Sergeant Malloy didn't say what degree murder he was charging Godwin with, did he?"

"No," said Betsy. "So how do I find out?"

"Well, call him and ask," suggested Emily.

"No, call the jail," said Bershada.

"Yes, call the jail," agreed Doris.

"He's probably not there, yet," said Emily. "It takes almost half an hour to get from here to downtown Minneapolis, where the jail is, and they only left a few minutes ago."

"Adult Detention Center," said Alice.

"What?" asked Betsy.

"That's the name of our new jail: Hennepin County Adult Detention Center." Alice volunteered at a homeless shelter once a week, probably the sad reason she knew this.

"Anyway," said Emily, "I don't see how he could be there yet, unless they took him by helicopter."

But Betsy couldn't just sit there, she was in a fever of impatience. She lifted the big phone book from a bottom drawer of her desk, looked up the number, and dialed it. Sure enough, no one there knew anything about a Godwin DuLac, prisoner. She dropped the receiver and put both hands over her face.

"We're all sorry about this, Betsy," said Martha. "Is there anything we can do?"

"No. Thanks."

"Come on then, it's time we started for home," said Alice, and the women slipped away, even the woman who had wanted yarn for the painted canvas she was about to buy.

Betsy put the phone book away and just sat there, her mind a frightened blank.

She still hadn't moved when Shelly came rushing,

breathless, into the shop ten minutes later. "I just heard!" she said. "What do you want me to do?"

"There isn't anything anyone can do, not yet, anyway."

"I mean here in the shop. I can work for you while you go find things out."

"What kind of hours can you work? Spring break is over and school's a long way from being finished for the summer." Shelly taught third grade in the local elementary school.

"School lets out at three, I can come straight here. I had two messages on my machine when I got home, and I came right over. I can work every day this week, from three-fifteen to five and all day on Saturday." Shelly worked part time anyway during the school year, and all summer long.

"What about—"

"Homework, schomework, I can do that after supper and on Sunday. We're talking third grade, not high school. I'll help you find another part-timer for the rest of the weekday, okay? Here, let me hang up my coat." She suited action to word and soon Betsy heard her humming in the back as she restacked and reshelved. She sighed, found Shelly's time card in a desk drawer, and noted the time she started.

The sound of all that industry brought Betsy's brain back in line; and she called the jail again. Again she was told no Godwin DuLac was there. She hung up and stuck the paper with the attorneys' phone numbers under the phone. Then she realized it was on the back of an order form. She got a new order form out and began copying the items onto it. By the time she got to the end, her brain was almost up to speed and she remembered they were out of the whitest color of Rainbow Fuzzy Wuzzy floss—what was the number? She'd better go see.

But before she could do more than stand up, Shelly came to the desk holding the Margaret Bendig canvas and a few lengths of needlepoint yarn. "I found this on the floor," she said.

And, to her surprise, Betsy sat down and burst into tears.

"What's the matter?" asked Shelly, looking at the canvas for footprints or other damage.

"What am I going to do without Goddy?" Betsy moaned. "Oh, God, I feel so helpless!"

"Here now!" Shelly came behind the desk and turned the chair so Betsy was facing her. "Pull yourself together, you hear?"

Betsy looked up, feeling indignant. Shelly continued, "Goddy can afford hysterics at present, and is welcome to them, but not you!"

"Oh, Shelly, you don't know—" Betsy started.

"Listen to me! Goddy needs you, and you're going to have to be ready to fight for him. You can't do that if you're going to break down in tears every fifteen minutes!"

"But I can't—"

"You can! You have to! And what's more, you're going to have to be both boss *and* Vice President in Charge of Operations of Crewel World, Inc.!"

"No, really—"

"Oh, for heaven's sake, you just got so used to him as your safety net you forgot to notice how rarely he's had to save your kiester lately. What the store is gonna miss is his wit and charm—plus, that boy could sell ice cubes in Antarctica. But by gosh, you're no slouch. How did we do while he was in Mexico?"

"Well, I guess we did okay. But my customers missed him. And so did I."

"Sure. And they'll miss him now. They'll probably throw a heck of a welcome-home party when he gets out." Shelly leaned forward. *"And he will get out, right?"*

"I sure hope—"

"No, no, no. We're not talking hope, we're talking *action.*" She said the word low, like a warning growl. "You are going to call on that wild card talent of yours for solving crime, and you are going to find out who really murdered John Nye, and bring our fair-haired boy home. *Right?*"

Betsy looked up into those hazel-green eyes, currently sparkling with electricity. "Yes," she said. "Yes, I'll prove him innocent and bring him home."

"Of course you will. So—" Shelly picked up a slip of paper and wrote a single, long word on it and handed it to Betsy. Kwitchyerbellyachin, it said.

Betsy read it and smiled through the last of her tears. "Thanks, Shelly."

Betsy waited an hour and tried calling the Adult Detention Center again.

"Yes, we have him here," said the man in charge of speaking to civilians.

"Do you know how much his bail is?"

"Ma'am?"

"How much will it cost to bail him out?"

The man sighed. "You can't bail him out, he hasn't been arraigned yet. That means formally charged, in court, before a judge."

"When will that happen?"

"Sometime in the next thirty-six hours."

"Can I talk to him?"

"No, ma'am. Right now the only people who can talk to him are the investigators and his attorney."

Betsy hung up and rested a hand on the receiver. "His attorney," she repeated.

"What'd you say?" asked Shelly.

"Godwin needs an attorney. Where's that piece of paper?" She began to move things around on the desk with increasing urgency until she found it. "Hah!" She looked at the two names. "Shelly, have you ever heard of Attorney Frank Whistler? Or Marvin Lebowski?"

Shelly shook her head. "Where'd you find those names?"

"Jim Pemberthy recommended them. He said Mr. Whistler is a weasel and Mr. Lebowski is a tank."

"Mike Malloy hasn't got enough of a brain for a weasel to work on. A tank running over him he'll understand."

"Yes, but a judge is different, he may resent tank treads up his back." Still, the notion of a tank appealed. "I'll call Mr. Lebowski now."

But Mr. Lebowski was in court, according to his secretary, who took Betsy's name and phone number. Betsy made sure she had Godwin's name spelled right and understood that he was in the Hennepin County Adult Detention Center, charged with murder. Then she hung up and dialed Mr. Whistler's number.

Mr. Whistler's secretary put Betsy right through. "Mr. Whistler, my name is Betsy Devonshire, and I got your name from Attorney James Pemberthy of Excelsior."

"Yes? How is Jim?"

"Very well. But he doesn't practice in criminal defense, and that's the kind of help we need right now."

"Who is 'we,' Ms. Devonshire?" Mr. Whistler had a rich, confident, good-humored baritone, and a way of very slightly over-pronouncing his words, as if he thought her slightly deaf. Or dull-witted.

"Actually, it's my store manager, Godwin DuLac. He's also a close friend. He was arrested about an hour ago for murdering his lover, John Nye."

"Nye: Are you speaking of the senior associate at Wellborn, Hanson, and Smith?"

"You know him?"

"I've heard of him, he has—had a very good reputation." There was a pause. Betsy wondered if what Mr. Whistler had heard was nothing about John Nye the person, but that an attorney with an important law firm had been killed. "Is Mr. DuLac able to handle an attorney's fee?" First things first, of course, thought Betsy.

"Probably not. But I can. That is, I think I can. How much do you charge?"

Mr. Whistler named a rate per hour—or fraction thereof—that was surprising, even with Mr. Pemberthy's warning.

"All right," said Betsy, wincing, writing that number down and underlining it. "I think we can manage that."

"And, of course, I will need a retainer." When he said how much that would be, it left her unable to speak for several seconds.

"Are you there?" asked Mr. Whistler, concerned.

"Uh, yes, I'm still here. Gosh, that's a lot of money."

"And it's payable in advance."

Nothing weaselly about the way he asked for money, thought Betsy, rudely. "I . . . see. Well, Mr. Pemberthy did give me the name of another lawyer—"

"I understand."

"Good. I'll call you back."

"Hold on a minute. If you do hire me, I'll have to start fast. So, with the understanding that you may not hire me, may I nevertheless ask you some questions?"

"What kind of questions?"

"For example, where is Mr. DuLac now, do you know?"

"Well, he went a little crazy when they came for him, so they didn't interrogate him, but just took him right down to the jail."

" 'Crazy'?"

"Hysterical is a better word, I suppose. He was here, at work, and they just walked in and handcuffed him while the detective read him his rights. Goddy is an emotional sort of person, and he started screaming 'no, no,' and they had to more or less drag him out. It was awful, just awful." Betsy closed her eyes and swallowed hard.

"That must have been tough to watch."

"It was. Tougher on him, of course."

"What kind of business do you own, Ms. Devonshire?"

"It's a needlework shop, called Crewel World."

There was a brief pause, then rich laughter. "Very clever, Crewel World!" he said.

"Thank you."

"In your opinion, is there enough evidence in the hands of the police to convict Mr. DuLac of this crime?"

"No. In fact, I can't understand what Mike was thinking when he arrested Goddy."

"Who is Mike?"

"Sergeant Mike Malloy, Excelsior Police."

"You know him?"

"Yes, I've had several run-ins with him."

"I . . . beg your pardon?"

"I sometimes do some investigating on behalf of people wrongly accused of a crime. Sergeant Malloy does not always appreciate what he calls my interference."

"No, I can imagine that he wouldn't. Well, thank you, I hope I have the beginning of an understanding of the situation here. I want you to let me know as soon as possible if you wish me to represent Mr. DuLac, so I may advise the police that they are not to question him without my presence."

"All right, I'll do that."

"Let me give you a phone number where you can reach me at any time." She wrote that down, too, and they hung up.

Eleven

✤ ✤ ✤

BETSY was upstairs in her apartment trying to think what to have for supper. She finally found a small pepperoni pizza at the back of the freezer, which made her happy until she thought how Godwin would sneer at frozen pizza and make something far more interesting. That made her think about the cold balogna sandwich he was probably eating in his cell—and that made her burst into angry, frightened tears.

But the storm soon passed. She pulled herself together, turned on the oven, and had just put the pizza in when the doorbell buzzed. At the same time, the phone rang. She grabbed the phone and said, "Hold on a second, someone's at the door," and went to ask into the intercom system, "Who's there?"

"Charlie Nye. I really need to talk to you."

"Come up, I'm the door on the left," she replied and pushed the buzzer to unlock the downstairs door. She left her own door slightly open and went back to the phone.

"Thanks for waiting," she said.

"Is this Ms. Devonshire?" said a man's voice with just a hint of sand in it, and a faint accent she couldn't place. Maryland? Nebraska?

"Yes?"

"I'm Marvin Lebowski. You wanted to talk to me about a case?"

"Yes. My employee and good friend Godwin DuLac has been arrested for the murder of John Nye, and I'm seeking a lawyer to represent him."

"John Nye the attorney, right?"

Was there the merest hint of avarice in his voice? Honestly, lawyers! "Yes," she said.

"When was Mr. DuLac arrested?"

"This afternoon. The police took him right out of the shop."

"And am I right that Mr. DuLac is the young man who found the body?"

"Yes. Actually we both found the body. Godwin was scared to go over to the house by himself and persuaded me to come along."

"Ah, yes, that's right, the newspaper said two people were found in the house by police. And now they've arrested one of them. But you are not considered a suspect?"

"No. Godwin, you see, lived with John until shortly before the murder. They had a quarrel, and Godwin moved out. He was staying with me."

"Do you think the police have enough evidence to bring a conviction?"

Interesting, that was the same question Mr. Whistler had asked. Must be a lawyerly way of trying to find out how tough the case was going to be. "No, of course not."

"You said you're Godwin's employer."

"Yes, I own Crewel World, a needlework shop in Excelsior. Godwin was my store manager."

Betsy heard the snick of a doorknob turning and looked around to see Charlie Nye sticking his head through the open door. She gestured at him to come in and go forward into the living room, and returned her attention to her caller.

"Were Mr. Nye and Mr. DuLac engaged in a homosexual relationship?"

"Yes."

"A long-term one?"

"Yes, I believe something close to eight years."

"Was Mr. DuLac taken to the Excelsior police station?"

"No, he's in the Hennepin County Adult Detention Center. He became hysterical when they arrested him, and so he was taken directly to jail. I can imagine what it's like down there, and I'm—well, I'm afraid for his safety. He's very obviously gay."

"Now don't worry about that, he's perfectly safe there. They have experience with gay prisoners and are careful not to place them in jeopardy."

"Oh, thank you for telling me that!" said Betsy.

"No charge. However, if you think Mr. DuLac would like me to represent him, I'll need a retainer before I can act on his behalf."

Betsy braced herself and asked, "How much of a retainer?"

He named a sum even larger than Mr. Whistler's.

Betsy sighed. "Rats. Okay, I'm talking to another attorney as well. I don't know which of you to choose, but I think it should be someone Goddy is comfortable with. Would it be possible—is it even ethical, to ask both of you to visit him, and let him decide?"

"I don't see why not. How about I call the Detention Center right now to ensure that Mr. DuLac knows he has potential representation, and that he should not consent to talk with a police investigator without the presence of an attorney."

"I'd be grateful if you could do that. Thank you."

Mr. Lebowski took Betsy's cell, home, and office phone numbers, and they hung up.

Betsy shut off the oven before she went into the living room, where she found Charlie Nye looking at the glass case holding her late sister's collection of Lladro statues.

"What can I do for you, Mr. Nye?" she asked.

He straightened and turned. "I heard Godwin has been arrested for the murder of my brother."

"Has it been on the news already?"

"I don't know. I heard it at that little restaurant over by the movie theater."

Betsy smiled. She couldn't help it. "Yes, of course, the Waterfront Café is the very root of the grapevine that covers this town."

He grinned. "We have one of those back home, too." He sobered. "So it's true."

"Yes, I'm afraid so."

"I'm sorry to hear that. He sure had me fooled; I never thought a fellow like him would be capable of a violent crime like that."

"He didn't do it, Mr. Nye."

"No? How can you be so sure?"

"Goddy and I have worked closely together for several years, and I'm convinced he would never murder John. I'm hiring an attorney to defend him, but I also intend to do my own sleuthing, of course."

"Of course?"

"I have a certain talent for it."

Now he was really confused. "Are you a private investigator?"

"No, I'm a shop owner and landlord. But this won't be the first time I've been asked to prove that someone accused of a crime is innocent."

He looked her up and down and shook his head. "You are a remarkable woman, Ms. Devonshire."

"Thank you. May I ask you some questions about your brother?"

"If you like."

"Have a seat. May I offer you a cup of coffee, or tea? I think there are some soft drinks, too."

"You Scandihoovians really do drink coffee at all hours of the day, don't you?"

"I guess some do. I, personally, am going to have a diet soft drink without caffeine."

"Do you have bottled water?"

"I have filtered water. Almost the same thing. With ice?"

"Please. And thank you."

Charlie was sitting on her couch when she came back with a tall glass of water for him and a diet orange drink for herself—Godwin had drunk up all her Diet Squirt. She took a seat in the overstuffed chair that had her knitting bag beside it and said, "Just start anywhere telling me about your brother."

He'd been thinking about it, she knew, because his reply was prompt. "Johnny was a deeply troubled man." He took a drink of water, held the glass up at eye level, and nodded at it.

"What makes you say that?"

He made a surprised face at her, though he didn't actually say, "Duh." He held up one finger. "First, he was committed to the gay lifestyle." He changed that to two fingers. "Second, he liked young men, *very* young men, practically boys. Third, and you probably didn't know this—or even if you did, you might not—Well, let me back up a bit. The brother I used to know was a responsible person. One of the things he did when he got his first job out of law school was set up an investment account. He put every spare nickel into that account. When he finally decided to buy a house, he bought it outright, cash on the barrelhead. Then he decided he wanted to be gay. It was—"

"Pardon me, but it doesn't work that way."

He nodded, taking her rebuke courteously. "So some people say. But that's not the point. The point is, apparently of late he was *spending* every nickel he was taking in—and he was making damn good money."

"How do you know that?" asked Betsy, feeling her investigative antenna swivel around to point at him. The word *blackmail* crossed her mind, all caps, twenty point, elephant font.

"I've been looking at his records. The police let me into the house and I pulled some files from a cabinet in his den. Pay stubs, credit card bills, checkbook. It looks like he was living right up to the limit of his income."

"Do you know where the money was going?"

He shrugged. "Mostly he was buying art and jewelry, a new car, expensive suits and shoes." He grimaced. "Some of it for his little friend."

Betsy thought about that for a few moments, while her antenna circled, confused. "That's interesting," she said at last. "I didn't know that. You mean he had nothing left in savings? No IRA or investments of any kind?"

"I didn't find any evidence that he had cashed in anything, but I've only begun looking. As another complication, Johnny seems to have kept quite a bit of information on his computer, which the police have taken away. I was hoping to talk to Godwin, to see if he could shed any light on this, but now, of course, that won't be possible."

"Not right now, no. How long will you be in town?"

"I've taken a week's vacation, but I can get another if I need it. I was hoping to collect the information I needed to work on the estate at home—I'm Johnny's executor. What do you suppose the police want with the computer, anyway?"

"I imagine they're trying to see if John met someone on the Internet. There's evidence he had . . . company the day he was killed."

Charlie grimaced. "See? *Deeply* troubled."

Betsy chose to change the subject. "Are you the older brother?"

"Yes. We have two sisters, too. The oldest of us is Melanie. Then me, then Johnny, then Mandy."

"Goddy told me John had told him that his family refused to accept his sexual orientation. Yet Goddy said you seemed to get along pretty well with him."

"Me, I don't care what an individual does in his private life, so long as he doesn't insist I come to the party. On the other hand, my family is old-fashioned about some things." Charlie drank deeply, put the glass down. "And, of course, it's different when it's your brother. When Johnny made it clear a long time ago that he was not going to give me a sister-in-law or nieces or nephews, it took awhile before I could come to terms with that, but I did. That made it possible for us to reconnect. You see, he and I were pretty close growing up, and I couldn't just toss him overboard like the rest of the family wanted to do when they found out. I worked out a deal: I told him he had to stiffen his wrist if he came home, and talked the rest of the family into letting him come home for Christmas and weddings and all. They didn't ask, and he didn't swish."

Betsy smiled. "He didn't swish here, either. Not all gay men do, you know."

"Unlike his boyfriend."

Her smile broadened. "Oh, yes, Godwin swishes. He prances, even."

He burst out, "God, how can you stand someone like that working for you?"

"Mr. Nye, you would not believe what an asset Godwin is to my shop. Or how valuable he has proven himself to me, over and over."

"Oh. Then I beg your pardon. Obviously, I have stepped wrong here."

"Yes, you have. But never mind. Have you stayed in touch with your brother between his visits home?"

"Yes, mostly by e-mail, but phone calls once a month or so as well."

"Has he seemed different lately? Worried about something?"

"No."

"When did you see him last?"

"At Christmas. He spent an hour at my house, with just the two of us talking. My wife, God bless her, took the kids to Grandma's to give us time alone. And for the first time I said something about his lifestyle. I'd heard some of them make a kind of match and settle down, so I asked him if he was going to play the field all his life. He said no, that he was amazed that he'd found someone he never grew tired of."

Betsy marked that comment for easy retrieval. What a comfort it would be to Godwin!

Charlie continued, "But he did, in the end, didn't he? They quarreled and separated."

"Yes, but there's been a pattern of that for about as long as I've known them. They'd have a big fight, and John would throw Goddy out, and then a few days or a week later, John would call, and they'd get back together again. I am quite sure this was just another round in that fight. Goddy was too, and that's why he's so devastated by this. They didn't get that chance to make up before this happened."

"What would they fight about?" Charlie put that delicately, not sure he wanted to know.

"Different things. John was jealous and Goddy loved to flirt, for example. I don't know what it was about this time— Goddy insists he doesn't know, either. I suspect something happened while they were down in Mexico. Goddy won a trip to Mexico City and so he got to play host for a change. That may have felt threatening to John." She looked inquiringly at Charlie.

He frowned and shook his head. "I haven't a clue. He didn't talk about that side of his life except in generalities; he knew it made me uncomfortable. I got an e-mail a couple of weeks ago, he said he was going to Mexico City for a week. He sent gifts from down there to each of my kids. He said that museum, what's it called, the Museum of Anthropology? He said it was a wonderful thing to see. My oldest, Annie, wants to be an archaeologist, and he sent her a book on the exhibits *in Spanish,* telling her to let him know when she could read it, and he'd pay her way down there to take some classes at the museum. She went right out and signed up for a summer immersion course." He made a sad face. "I never told him that."

"How old is Annie?"

"She'll be sixteen in November. I've got a boy, fourteen, and another girl who'll be eleven in two weeks."

"Nice family."

"They're good kids. And Marti is great with them." He shook his head. "Such a waste."

"What is?"

"Johnny. He could have had all that, too, if he really tried."

Twelve

❖ ❖ ❖

THE next morning, after a water aerobics session during which even Renee's hearty instruction could not make her move briskly, and a breakfast left half-eaten, Betsy started down to the shop with a heavy heart. Of course she wanted to keep the place open; this was her one point of sanity in a world gone crazy. But she couldn't ask Messrs. Whistler and Lebowski to drop by so she could interview them. One would probably be better than the other for Goddy, but how was she to choose without talking to them? Would they both want a retainer before they went to see Goddy, so he could choose? Say, wouldn't it be great if sending them both set off a bidding war?

If she did set off a bidding war, it had better be a short one. Goddy couldn't stay hysterical forever. Once he calmed down, Mike could begin the interrogation. Goddy surely had the intelligence to invoke his right to an attorney—didn't he? Of course he would. It would be prudent for him to have a good one, not some underpaid, overworked fellow still blowing on the ink on his law degree to dry it.

For Goddy's sake, it would be the best Betsy could buy.

Thirty-six hours was the most they could hold him incommunicado, the man at the jail had said. That had been confirmed through Google.com, which seemed to open doors to all information, including the Minnesota criminal law code. Godwin had to be arraigned in court within thirty-six hours or let go.

Which was interesting and helpful, except it didn't answer the most basic question: What had Mike Malloy found out that made him arrest Goddy in the first place? That was what she couldn't figure out. What clue, what form of evidence had he uncovered?

Or thought he'd uncovered. Goddy was innocent. Wasn't there some kind of "discovery" attorneys for the defense got to do, where they had access to the evidence? When did that happen, at the arraignment? Maybe the attorney she hired would share that information with her.

That thought turned the urgency to go talk to them into a screaming gargoyle that rode her head down the stairs.

At the bottom, she turned toward the obscure door to the hallway that led to the back door into her shop. Other worrying thoughts whispered into her ear.

How had Mike broken Goddy's alibi? Goddy had told Betsy he hadn't talked to anyone or seen anyone he knew on his late-night drive around Lake Minnetonka. So how had Mike found out he wasn't at her house in bed?

Mike was angry at Betsy for lying about that to Lars, which was totally unfair. She hadn't lied, or not exactly. Godwin *was* staying with her, just as she'd said. And he *had* slept in the apartment that night. She'd just let those two statements imply that he'd been there around the time John was being murdered.

Even though he hadn't.

So, okay, maybe she'd taken a few steps down the road to perdition by planting that idea in poor Lars's head. But who on earth could seriously think Godwin could murder *anyone,* much less the man he loved?

Besides Mike Malloy.

And Charlie Nye.

Hmmmmmmm.

Sophie trotted ahead of Betsy to the back door of Crewel World. Betsy unlocked and opened that, and Sophie bustled in, eyes and ears on the alert for a customer who might have something edible.

You'd think, Betsy thought, Sophie would know that customers couldn't get in until she unlocked the front door, too. But hope springs eternal in the greedy heart, and Sophie peered around every corner until, satisfied no treats were in the offing, she jumped up onto "her" chair, the wooden one with the powder-blue cushion, to wait.

Betsy went to the checkout desk, picked up the phone and dialed the police department's number. She asked, when the phone was answered, "May I speak with Mike Malloy, please?"

"He's not here right now. Do you want his voicemail?"

Betsy hesitated. "No, never mind, I'll try again later."

Betsy went through her opening-up routine, putting cash into the register, turning on lights and the little radio tuned to a classical music station, starting the coffee urn perking and plugging in the tea kettle, then walking to the front door at two minutes to ten, head swiveling from side to side to assure herself all was neat and ready.

She was surprised to find four customers waiting at the door. Not just customers, four members of the Monday Bunch. Bershada Reynolds, Alice Skoglund, Martha Winters, and Doris Valentine stood in a little cluster, smiling at her surprise.

"Well, good morning, good morning!" said Betsy on unlocking and opening the door. "What brings you all out so early?"

"We're here to take over the store til Shelly arrives, so you can go off and do your thing," announced Bershada.

"What? What thing?"

"Your sleuthing thing, of course. So go on, get out of here!"

"Oh, I can't let you do that!" said Betsy.

"And why not?" demanded Alice. "I'm sure that the four of us together know where every item in Crewel World is."

"And could answer any question about stitches, fabrics, flosses, or designers," said Doris.

"And I know how to operate a cash register," added Martha, who until recently operated a dry cleaning establishment.

"Plus, we work for free," concluded Doris, producing an empty goldfish bowl.

"What's that for?" asked Betsy.

"We're starting a defense fund for Goddy, of course," said Doris, surprised that Betsy had to ask. She walked to the checkout desk, put the bowl on it, and pulled a ten dollar bill from her skirt pocket. "There, let me be the first."

The other three hurried over to put money into the bowl. "You'd better open a special bank account while you're out today," said Alice. "We're going to fill this up at least twice before the day is over."

"Oh, ladies . . . this is . . . too, too wonderful," said Betsy, her eyes filling. "But really, I should be here, you don't have to do this."

"Oh, p'shaw!" said Doris. "We can't just sit around wringing our hands; we want to *do* something! We can't sleuth, but we can run the shop while you do. Have you found a lawyer yet?"

"I've talked to two of them, actually, just on the phone, and I can't decide which one to use."

"So go see them both in person," said Alice. "Then you'll know."

"We promise to make correct change and not set the place on fire," said Doris. "You just be back in time to close up at six."

Betsy blinked away her tears and yielded. "Well, thank you, I do want to go out. But all of you need to work only this morning," Betsy said. "I've got a part-timer coming in at noon, so maybe two of you can leave then." Betsy didn't mind working by herself in the shop, but preferred two part-time clerks there when she was gone. Two volunteers should equal one trained clerk.

"Okay," said Martha. "Who's coming in?"

"Rennie Jones."

The women nodded; they knew her.

"Now, if all of you have had enough by noon, I've got my list of part-timers in the desk. You can start calling and find someone else to help Rennie."

"Don't worry about a thing, we're fine, we'll be fine," said Martha briskly. "Now go along."

"All right."

Betsy went back upstairs to call the two attorneys and found Mr. Lebowski was in court this morning, but could see her right after lunch. Mr. Whistler could see her right now, briefly, if she could come at once to his office in Wayzata.

Wayzata is a town on the north side of Lake Minnetonka, almost directly across from Excelsior, half an hour by slow boat. It takes a little longer to drive to it, because Lake Minnetonka is a big lake with a complex shoreline.

Betsy drove through a long string of little towns, big towns, hamlets, and collections of beautiful houses that lined the shore. Forty minutes later, she came into Wayzata.

The city was built on a series of terraces rising from the lake. The lowest level was very beautiful, with upscale shops and restaurants that rather reminded Betsy of the nicer sub-urbs of San Diego. Wayzata didn't go in for the shaggy, country-town look Excelsior had, with its main street per-pendicular to the lake. Wayzata went for the luxury-vacation look of white buildings facing the water.

Mr. Whistler's office was on the second tier, top floor, in a nice old three-story office building. He and his two partners were served by a receptionist of striking good looks. Two other secretaries were making their computer keyboards rat-tle nearby.

The receptionist took Betsy into a good-sized office where a large mahogany desk sat on the far edge of a beauti-ful Persian rug. Bookcases full of law books lined one wall. On the opposite there was a large Victorian oil painting of a great stag held at bay by a pack of angry dogs—symbolic of a sympathetic understanding of how clients felt, no doubt. A big picture window beside the painting looked over the roofs of the buildings on the first tier into the blue lake. Already a pretty scene, it must be a wonderful, soothing picture in the summer, when the trees filled in and sailboats dotted the lake.

Behind the desk a slender black man was writing something in a notebook. He looked up at Betsy, closed the notebook, and a very charming smile appeared. He stood. He was wearing an expensive pinstripe suit of somewhat extravagant design and a yellow tie with diagonal black stripes the same width as those on the suit.

"Ms. Devonshire?" he said, offering his hand.

"Yes." She shook it briefly.

"Won't you sit down?"

There were two grass-green wing chairs in front of the desk. Betsy took one. "Thank you," she said.

"I have taken the liberty of informing the arresting officer that counsel is pending in the case of Mr. DuLac, and that Mr. DuLac is to be so informed."

"Thank you," said Betsy, wondering what the jailers thought about getting two calls with that message. "I'm afraid I don't know what questions to ask. I assume you are competent, or Mr. Pemberthy would not have recommended you. But what can you do outside of the courtroom? I mean, I want to be sure that Godwin is treated fairly, with respect. He is a . . . vulnerable person."

"Do you mean that he is retarded?"

"Oh, no! He's just . . . gay. Not big and strong, or macho. I saw him not long ago trying to act straight, and it wouldn't have fooled anyone for more than a minute. I've heard they are more careful with people like that than they used to be, but I'm still concerned."

"Hennepin County would never put your friend into a cell or quad where he'd be in any danger."

"Good, I'm glad to hear you say that. I guess when two lawyers say it, it must be true." Betsy blushed; she could feel the heat climb up her cheeks. "I'm sorry, I didn't mean that the way it sounded. I just meant that perhaps the first person to tell me that was just trying to comfort me."

"Whereas you don't think two lawyers in a row would do that," said Mr. Whistler, his grin showing again.

Betsy laughed. "I guess I was thinking something like that. You are kind not to take offense."

"My dear, you would not believe what you'd have to say to make me take offense. I deal with difficult people having a difficult time."

"I want to help you."

"How's that?"

"I have a talent for investigating. Seriously, I have helped other people wrongly charged with a crime." She quickly described a case in which she found a contractor popularly suspected of murder to be innocent. He listened, his eyebrows going higher and higher.

"How remarkable," he said, sounding impressed. "I may indeed need someone with a talent like that." He glanced at his watch.

Betsy stood. "I understand you have somewhere to go. I want to thank you for talking with me on such short notice."

"You are very welcome. You'll let me know soon about Mr. DuLac, right?"

"Yes, probably this afternoon."

As she climbed into her car for the drive downtown, she thought, *The other one is going to have to go some distance to beat Mr. Whistler.*

Betsy had a quick lunch at Peter's downtown, a very old-fashioned restaurant with its original forties décor intact.

Before she left, she dialed Excelsior PD again, to find Mike Malloy was still out. She sighed, over-tipped the waitress, and walked the four blocks to the Wells Fargo Center Building, a new skyscraper built in the Art Deco style.

Mr. Lebowski worked on the tenth floor with a much larger law firm, Franklin, Morris, and LeBarge. His name was on the door, fourth in a list of nine partners. The receptionist was Asian, with quiet manners and too-correct English, which made Betsy think she might be Japanese-born. She directed Betsy to an office at the end of a high, narrow corridor. Mr. Lebowski had his own secretary, a black woman who reminded Betsy of Claire Huxtable on the old Bill Cosby show. She had the same pleasant voice and air of intelligent competence. She checked Betsy's name against a list or calendar on her computer and asked her to be seated for a moment.

The outer office was as beautiful as Mr. Whistler's inner sanctum, though the painting on the wall looked to be an original Erté, and the carpet was also Art Deco. The walls were paneled in a wood stained mahogany. Or maybe it was real mahogany. Certainly the desk looked like real mahogany.

Betsy couldn't decide if this was conspicuous consumption or a way of reassuring clients they were buying the services of a top-flight attorney.

The secretary returned and said, "Mr. Lebowski will see you now." She gestured at the open door.

Mr. Lebowski stood right inside the door, his hand extended to greet her. He was very tall, with a barrel chest that went all the way down to the top of his legs. Where Mr. Whistler was the color of dark chocolate, this man was milk-chocolate. His hair was white, cropped short, his eyes light brown and very penetrating. His hand was enormous;

it engulfed Betsy's entirely. His suit was two shades darker than his skin, his shirt snow white, like his hair. His necktie was many colored flowers on green.

He led Betsy to a very comfortable chair and went behind a desk. A big desk, which he nevertheless dominated.

Betsy finally realized that she was staring, blinked, and looked into her lap. When she raised her eyes, he was smiling at her. "I—" she began, and stopped there.

"My mother was the great-granddaughter of a slave, my father was the son of a Polish immigrant," he said. His smile broadened, as if he'd pulled off a clever practical joke, and Betsy laughed.

"I bet you enjoy watching people meet you for the first time," she said.

"Yes, I do; I really, truly do. Now, what can I do for you?"

"I have spoken with Attorney Frank Whistler, and am here to speak with you, to decide which of you will represent Godwin DuLac, who has been arrested for murder."

"You are assuming the cost of an attorney, is that right?"

"Yes, Godwin couldn't afford someone like you or Mr. Whistler. I rely on Godwin, he is my most valuable employee, so I'm hoping also to bail him out. Do you know when he will be arraigned?"

"No. They haven't started to interrogate him yet, because they're waiting for counsel. I hate to pressure you, but we really need to get that question settled quickly. What questions do you have for me?"

"Both you and Mr. Whistler asked me if I thought the police had enough evidence to convict Goddy. Were you trying to find out if I thought he was guilty?"

Mr. Lebowski laughed softly. "Yes, that's right. It's a question I will ask Mr. DuLac, too. It is never a good idea to ask a client directly if he is or is not guilty. But the reply to that question often tells me what I want to know."

"I see. Do you think bail will be high?"

"Depends on what he's charged with. I think the first thing we ought to do is get me down there to talk to him, and allow him to be interrogated with me present. Get this show on the road, so to speak, so we'll know where we're headed."

"There's a process called 'discovery,' right? Where you get to see the evidence against him."

"Yes, but that's not something that will happen very soon, either."

"You see, I have a talent for investigating crimes. And I want to know what they know, so I can understand what they're thinking happened. That will help me find out what really happened."

His look was very keen. "A 'talent'?"

"Yes." Betsy quickly relayed some of her experiences with sleuthing. His eyes never left her face.

"That's very good," he said when she had finished. "It's not uncommon for an attorney for the defense to hire a private investigator to look into the circumstances of a case. I might want to do that here—but if I can rely on you to do that, it will save expenses. And—" his eyes twinkled—"I suspect it will relieve some of the anxiety you are feeling to be doing valuable things for me and for Mr. DuLac."

"Yes, you understand that, don't you? All right, you may act as Goddy's attorney. Your retainer—" She opened her purse. "Do you take Visa?"

He did.

Thirteen

✤ ✤ ✤

THE courtroom was small and low-ceilinged. The judge's desk was of honey-colored wood, very plain—it looked made of sheets of varnished plywood. The jury box was empty, of course, this being an arraignment. The judge looked bored, the bailiff looked bored, the attorneys looked bored as they came forward to announce they were representing this client or that. They often had several clients, and had to read their client's name off a file folder.

It was all routine, and terrifying.

Betsy sat in the front row—there were only six rows of seats, mostly empty—with Jill beside her in civilian clothes, and Lebowski on her other side in a dark blue suit and bright yellow tie.

"How is Godwin doing?" Betsy asked Lebowski in a low voice.

"As well as can be expected," he replied quietly.

"When do you think—"

He touched her arm. Godwin was being led in. He looked small and frightened in his too-big orange jumpsuit, and didn't seem to see Betsy, Jill, or his attorney. Without an "ah, ah," of warning, Jill sneezed. It was a big, loud sneeze. Betsy jumped, the two people sitting behind them giggled, the judge looked up repressively—and Godwin looked over his shoulder. He saw Betsy, and his face lit up. Betsy smiled and gave a thumbs–up. The judge smacked his gavel once, and Godwin returned his attention to the podium. But his shoulders were straighter; even, somehow, his hair was brighter. Jill, following through, wiped her nose with a wrinkled Kleenex she'd pulled from her purse, and sniffed three times. Betsy bumped her with a "that's enough" elbow. Jill had her coolest Gibson Girl look going, but her eyes were shining.

The charge was second-degree murder, and Godwin said, "Yes, your honor," in a low voice when asked if he under-stood. And he said it again when asked if he understood his rights when read aloud by the judge.

When the judge asked if Godwin was represented by counsel, he turned to look at the big black man sitting be-side Betsy. Lebowski rose and said in a firm voice, "Counsel is present, your honor." He made his way to the low wall and then through the swinging door in the center of it.

He stood beside Godwin and the judge asked, "Do you wish to confer with your client before you enter a plea?"

"I want to say right now that I am innocent, your honor," said Godwin.

Lebowski said, "My client pleads not guilty, your honor."

"A plea of Not Guilty will be entered in the record," said the judge.

The next item of business was bail. The prosecution rose

first to make a statement. The prosecuting attorney was a lanky young man with thick brown hair at the top and cowboy boots at the bottom, the two connected by a cheap blue-gray suit. He talked earnestly about the heinousness of the crime, the defendant's lack of family in the area, and the fact of his recent trip to Mexico City. Further, he noted, a grand jury would be considering first-degree murder charges against Mr. DuLac. All this, he was sure, added up to a certainty that Mr. DuLac should be held without bail.

Lebowski countered that his client had no criminal record of any kind, that he had lived in Minnesota for fifteen years, at one address for eight, and had held the same job for nearly six. He said that he was confident that a modest bail would ensure the appearance of his client. The judge studied Godwin, who was looking as un-dangerous as he could, and said he was setting bail at one million dollars. Smack went the gavel, and Godwin was led away, Lebowski following behind.

Betsy turned to Jill and said, "Where do I find a bail bondsman?"

T HE answer to Betsy's question was, "Around the corner." It was like learning a new word: Suddenly you see it everywhere. Driving around the several blocks that held City Hall, the County Courthouse, and the Adult Detention Center, Betsy was surprised to see that there was a bail bondsman's office at or near every intersection.

She picked one that had a parking space across the street from it. A neon sign in the window said it was Bookman's Bail Bonds, and printing on the window offered 24-hour service and a phone number.

The office was a little shabby, with acoustic-tile ceiling and a worn, no-nap carpet on the floor. There were harsh lights set into the ceiling and a faint smell of despair. A stocky man with hair dyed black sat behind a low counter that separated his much bigger side of the room from Betsy. He was talking on the phone.

"Thirty thousand for weapons," he was saying. "The house is valued at seventy-four thousand, but she has a mortgage for one twenty, so nothing there."

There were a great many file cabinets making a maze of his side, and on a back wall T-shirts were advertised for sale: *Dad, I'm in Jail,* read one. Who could possibly think a stint in jail deserved a souvenir?

A black woman with a sad, worn face sat on a bench on Betsy's side of the counter, and from the back came the in-and-out sound of a vacuum cleaner.

"Yeah, a long history of DUIs and weapons. Yeah? Okay, in about an hour." He hung up, made a notation on his computer, and looked up at Betsy.

"May I help you?" he asked.

"A friend of mine has been arrested, and the bail was set at a million dollars. I want to know what I have to do for you to bail him out."

"We'll need ten percent of that amount, in advance," said the man promptly.

"That's one hundred thousand," said Betsy, who had already heard that bail bondsmen wanted ten percent.

"Correct, in cash or securities," he said.

"Hmmm, I think I can manage that," said Betsy, whose net worth was a little over three million. It would be a strain, but it was temporary, after all. "What is your fee for arranging bail?"

"A hundred thousand."

"Yes, for a hundred thousand."

"The fee for a million dollars bail is one hundred thousand dollars."

"No, that's the amount I have to give to the court to get Goddy out."

"No, ma'am," said the man patiently. "The amount you have to give to the court to release your friend on bail is one million dollars. We will do that for you, at a cost of one hundred thousand dollars."

Betsy stared at him. "But . . . but, you . . . I understand you get the money back when the person charged turns up for his trial."

The man nodded. "That's correct. We get the million back, less certain fees. You pay ten percent of the bail to us for giving the court the bail money. That's our fee."

"I see." Without meaning to, she blurted, "But I don't think . . . I mean, I could raise that much, if I knew I'd get it back, but I don't think I could take a loss of a hundred thousand dollars right now!"

"Ma'am, if I might be so bold as to offer you some advice?"

Betsy nodded faintly, still looking at one hundred thousand dollars flying away, like birds heading south in autumn. Only these could not be back in the spring.

"Let your friend sit. He'll be fine. Use the money to hire a good lawyer."

"Thank you, I'll think about that."

Betsy stumbled back out to her car and sat behind the wheel for a couple of minutes. A hundred thousand dollars! It would take weeks, maybe months to free up that much money! That goldfish bowl, filled even eleven times a day, wasn't going to amount to a hundred thousand dollars.

Besides, that money should go to pay attorney fees, not to allow Godwin to come back to work.

His sad face rose before her. Standing humbly in the courtroom, while all the might of law and law enforcement ganged up to put him in prison forever. . . .

She put her head down on the steering wheel, but before the first tear escaped, she remembered Shelly's advice: kwitcherbellyachin. Don't whine, go find the evidence that would set him free.

All right, but first, she had to tell Goddy he wasn't getting out on bail.

The Adult Detention Center in downtown Minneapolis was a modern brick building whose entrance was slanted across the corner of Fourth Avenue and Fourth Street. The entrance lobby was large and also diagonal. A nice young deputy behind a long counter took Betsy's name. She knew Godwin's full name—Robert Godwin DuLac—but had to think for a moment before she could recall his date of birth.

Poor Goddy, he had sworn her to secrecy before telling her how old he was, and now his age had become a password!

She followed the directions that led to an elevator to the fourth floor, down a highly polished corridor, to a small room in a row of them. Inside, the room was divided in half by a wall that was plaster on the bottom and glass on the top. There was a phone on the wall near a chair, and another phone on the other side.

She sat down and a couple of minutes later a door on the other side opened, and there was Godwin, still in the official orange jumpsuit of Hennepin County prisoners. It hung loosely on him; not a big man to start with, Godwin seemed to have dropped twenty pounds. There were dark shadows under his eyes.

But he smiled broadly and waved at Betsy, then picked up the phone on his side and gestured at her to pick up hers.

"I'm *so* glad to see you!" he said. "Have you come to tell me I'm bailed out?"

"No." The smile vanished. He looked stunned, then sadder even than he had in court. He sat down like an old man. "Goddy, I can't afford to bail you out! You know what your bail is: a million dollars!"

"You don't have to come up with a million, just ten percent."

"Yes, but that's still a hundred thousand."

"Are you saying you can't raise it? It's just temporary, you get it back when I'm found not guilty."

"No, hon, the hundred thousand is the *fee*. The bail bondsman has to put up the million, and he charges a hundred thousand to do that. The bail is given back to them when you turn up in court, guilty or innocent. But it doesn't matter, we're still out the hundred thousand."

Now Godwin, as store manager, had become aware of Betsy's financial status. He knew she was rich, but he also knew she kept her money working, not sitting in a big money bin like Uncle Scrooge's, ready to tap. She would have to cash in profitable investments to raise the money.

Betsy knew he realized that when his next question was a jest. "And what if I run to Costa Rica?"

"They send bounty hunters after you. Big, mean men, with guns, who don't care about extradition laws, and who have no code of conduct to make them play nice."

"Well, nuts. I guess I'm stuck in here."

"Is it really awful, Goddy?"

"Well, more depressing-awful than scary-awful. I'm in Quad Eleven, where they put the not-dangerous-but-odd ones. Sigmund Freud would love meeting those people. The most depressing part is to think I belong with that bunch."

"Yes, well, another Bunch is going to be so relieved to hear about Quad Eleven. They were all picturing you sharing a cell with Lice Cutthroat, an enforcer in the Hell's Angels."

Godwin smiled sideways and shook his head. "Believe it or not, I think I could handle Mr. Cutthroat more easily than these people. There's a man in my quad who insists we call him Dorothy and complains to the nurse that he's got PMS. And then there's George, who is worried sick about his wife, who is a collie dog. And Frank, who quarrels with invisible people. You don't think I'm one of the crazy people, do you?"

"Of course not. So why did they put you in with them?"

"Oh, not all of them are weird. Some are just sweet and pretty, like me. My choice appears to be staying there or sitting in solitary. And I got a taste of that when they first brought me here." His face puckered, close to tears. "Betsy, they took *all* my clothes away and gave me this smelly yellow blanket and put me in this tiny, *tiny* room, all alone, with a cement bench and a steel toilet—oh, *ugh!* I *couldn't* go back to that!"

"No, of course you couldn't. Oh, Goddy, I feel so guilty, asking you to stay in jail!"

"Don't, *please* don't, it's all right, *really* it is. I didn't understand what bailing me out meant. I don't mind, not *too* much. It's going to be hard enough to pay for that lawyer. By the way, I *like* Marvin, he's like a big, strong daddy—and you would not *believe* how much respect he gets around here." He looked from side to side as if for eavesdroppers, and said, *sotto voce,* "The *best* part is that Mike has a hard time with him. You can almost hear his teeth grind when

Marvin says, 'Wait just one second, Sergeant Malloy, I don't think my client should answer that question.' *Such* a hoot!"

Betsy smiled at this grand display of courage. "Well, then, we'll keep him on retainer, won't we?"

Godwin nodded. "Are you going to sleuth?"

Betsy nodded, then remembered a warning John had given her long ago: There are things about Godwin you don't want to know. "Are you all right with me doing that? You know how deep I dig."

"If it means getting me out of this mess, you may dig away. Carte blanche—that means do what you will, right?"

"Yes. All right, I'll start by talking to Jill this evening. Maybe she knows why Mike arrested you."

"Shoot, I can tell you that. It's John's new will. He was killed before he could sign it."

"What's in it?"

"Nothing for me. And that's the problem. In his old will, he set up a . . . a testamentary trust for me. Or a spendthrift trust, they use both words, so I don't know which is the correct one. A big hunk of money goes into a special account and I get the interest from it for the rest of my life." His face went blank, then sad. "He really *was* mad at me this time, I guess. But he died before he could sign the new will—and Mike thinks I murdered him so I'd get the money."

"But if you didn't know about it—"

"Yeah, well, Mike thinks I did know about it. It's a sweet motive, you have to admit. It might even have tempted me, if I had known about it."

"I trust you don't say things like that where Mike can hear you."

"Never fear." But he looked sad at having to guard his mischievious tongue.

"Actually, I don't care how big it is. I just hope I get to spend it on something besides the prison commissary."

"It doesn't work like that, Goddy. If you're found guilty, you won't get it at all. You aren't allowed to profit from a crime." She added hastily, "But never mind about that. You know perfectly well you won't be found guilty. In fact, it won't come to trial. I'm going to find out who really murdered John, and they'll have to drop the charges."

"Do it fast, okay? If I stay here too long, I may start missing the missus, too."

Fourteen

❖ ❖ ❖

BETSY got caught up in rush-hour traffic all the way out to Excelsior, but managed to get to the exit to Excelsior before five. The long, slow drive out had given her a chance to think a bit about this case. Where to begin? Well, that was obvious. What she needed was the name of that person who had used John Nye's whirlpool bath and purple bathrobe.

And she knew where that information was.

She walked into Crewel World at four minutes to five, to the cheers of Bershada, Shelly, Rennie Jones, and Phil Galvin. Phil was a member of the Monday Bunch. A retired railroad engineer, his beautiful counted cross-stitch patterns of railroad engines sometimes graced the walls of Crewel World as models to encourage others to buy the charts. He waved at Betsy from behind the checkout desk, where he was ringing up a sale under Rennie's watchful eye.

"Hiya, Betsy!" he called cheerfully. "How's Godwin?"

"Not happy," said Betsy briefly. "Hello, Mrs. Cunningham," she greeted the customer.

"Hi, Betsy" Mrs. Cunningham nodded.

"Whom did you hire?" asked Shelly.

"Marvin Lebowski." Betsy turned and fixed Bershada with a gimlet eye. "Did you know?"

"Know what?"

"He's black. I wish you had warned me, I stared at him like a tourist, which, fortunately, amused him."

Bershada stared at her. "Marvin *Lebowski* is *black*?" A broad smile appeared. "Are you serious?"

"Well, his mother was African-American; his father was a second-generation Pole from Chicago."

Phil said, "Why do white folks think black folks all know one another?" He shook his head at Betsy for harboring such a notion.

"I don't think any such thing—do I?" Betsy did a brief examination of her conscience. "No, of course not, it's just curious. Mr. Whistler is black, too."

"Now him I know," said Bershada. "Was he wearing one of his fancy-schmancy suits?"

Betsy smiled. "He sure was."

"Fancy suit?" asked Rennie. "What are you two talking about?"

"Attorney Frank Whistler wears suits that are on the very leading edge of fashion," explained Betsy. "You should have seen the lapels!"

"You mean like the beautiful things Goddy sometimes wears?" asked Mrs. Cunningham.

Betsy shook her head. "Godwin would sooner wear that

orange jail coverall than the suit I saw Frank Whistler in today; Frank wouldn't be caught dead in one of Goddy's unconstructed sport coats." She put a hand to her forehead and continued in a faint voice, "Dear lord, I am becoming far, far too knowledgeable about men's clothing. Is there hot water in back? I need a cup of tea."

"I was about to unplug the kettle, but hadn't yet," said Shelly, and Betsy went to the back room of the shop.

There, she started to smile, remembering Goddy's over-fastidious fashion sense as she looked through the little box of tea packets for the raspberry-flavored one, but her smile quickly turned upside down. Godwin took great pride in dressing well, and to see—and be seen—in that ugly, ill-fitting jumpsuit was genuinely painful to him. Another reason, an odd, but real, reason to see that he was set free quickly.

She brought the cup back out front, inhaling the fragrance of the tea. Mrs. Cunningham had departed. Phil was at the front door, turning the needlepointed sign from Open to Closed.

"You want me to run the register?" asked Rennie.

"Yes, go ahead. What kind of day did we have?"

"Really good," said Shelly. "Lots of people coming in to say how sorry they are about Goddy."

That reminded Bershada. "Did you open that Godwin Defense Account?"

"No, I didn't get to the bank. Why, how much did you take in?"

"Seven hundred and forty dollars. We emptied the bowl about five times."

Betsy gaped at her. "Wow. That's amazing."

Phil snorted. "Yeah, it'll pay for less than one working day for that fancy-suit lawyer you hired."

"Every dollar counts," countered Bershada. "Right, Betsy?"

"Right. And since you all are putting your money where your mouth is, I want to ask your opinion about something."

"Shoot," said Shelly, sitting down at the library table.

"Godwin's bail has been set at a million dollars." There were gasps at that. "I can't possibly raise that amount, and a bail bondsman will charge me a hundred thousand to post it for him. I don't think I can raise that amount, either, not in a hurry."

"I bet the bank would loan you that amount. I mean, after all, you get it back, right?" said Rennie.

"No, and that's the problem." She explained how bail bondsmen worked.

"Well, that doesn't seem fair," said Shelly. "A hundred thousand is a lot of money for a short-term loan of a million."

"Sometimes it takes years for a case to work its way through court," said Phil, still standing at the door, hand on the knob. "So it's not always a short-term loan. And if the accused runs away, bounty hunters aren't cheap. Think about that."

"My question is," said Betsy, "is it wrong of me to ask Godwin to sit in jail when I could, just possibly, get him out on bail?"

"But if you have to run around trying to raise the money," said Shelly, "then you couldn't also be trying to find out who really murdered John."

"If you did raise it," noted Phil, "Godwin would feel obliged to pay you back. That would make him your slave for years to come."

Betsy shuddered. "Yes, that's true."

"So I think—" Bershada looked around the room

and collected nods—"*we* think you should concentrate on sleuthing."

"From your description," added Phil, "Godwin is unhappy but not in danger where he is."

"That's right," nodded Rennie.

Betsy sighed, partly from relief, partly from concession. "All right, then, Goddy has to sit where he is."

"I've got to go," Phil said. "See you tomorrow." He waved to the room to large and went out the door.

A minute later Rennie handed Betsy the record of sales from the cash register. Betsy ran her eyes down the tape and smiled. "Very nice!" she said. "Now the rest of you run along, too. I'll close and make a night deposit. Rennie, can you work all day tomorrow?"

"Yes, ma'am."

"And I'll come in, too," Shelly said.

"Emily and Martha want to work tomorrow morning," said Bershada. "And Doris will come in the afternoon."

Betsy put her cup of tea down. Gratitude was making her hand tremble. "You people . . ." she began, then had to swallow before she could continue. "I have the best friends in the world," she said. "I don't know how I can ever repay you."

"Sure you do," said Bershada. "Bring him home safe, okay?"

"I'll do my best."

Up in her apartment that evening, Betsy opened a can of tuna and made a little salad for supper. In her one exception to Sophie's strict regimen of Science Diet, she put the emptied can down for the cat to lick dry.

She chopped some leaves off the bunch of cilantro into the salad as she built it and the scent made her smile. Some day she'd have to pay her own visit to Mexico City, stay at the

Del Prado, and eat their version of that chicken rice soup.
Though she doubted it would be any better than Goddy's.

After supper she picked up the phone and dialed Jill at
home.

They talked a bit about Betsy's day—Jill approved of
Marvin Lebowski, having heard stories about him—and
then Betsy said, "Jill, I need a special favor."

"Sure, if I can."

"I want to borrow one of the copies Mike made of John's
hard drive. How do I go about doing that? Should I have
Goddy's attorney ask for it? Subpoena it?"

"What are you hoping to find?"

"For one thing, the name of the young man John brought
home the night he was killed."

"Why not just ask Mike?"

"Could I do that? You know what he thinks about me,
the interfering civilian. On the other hand, he's not using
the hard drive, is he? He's sure he's got the guilty party, so
what would he care? But he must know I'm wild to find another suspect in John's murder. Mr. Lebowski said he often
hires private investigators to help him in a case, and he's all
right with me filling that role, at least for now. If I tell Mike
that, would that make it worse or better?"

Jill snorted softly. "Worse, probably, as far as your personal
relationship with Mike goes. There's cops in the area still trying to heal the scars Lebowski leaves on cross–examination in
a courtroom, including Mike. On the other hand, having an
official role in the defense gives you some authority. You're not
just a snoopy female this time. You're working for one of the
big guns. Not that Goddy deserves any less than the best, in
my opinion."

"So you agree with me, Goddy couldn't be guilty!"

"Oh, you bet. But it looks bad. He's got a heck of a motive."

"You know about the will?"

"Yes, Mike was talking about it to the county prosecutor and I overheard some of the conversation."

"Goddy didn't know about the first will, much less the second."

"That's not what Mike understands. He found an e-mail to Goddy, suggesting he write his own will, since John had written his."

Betsy groaned softly. "Oh, gosh, Goddy even mentioned that to me. He said John told him to make a will, but Goddy said he planned to die broke and so didn't need one. But wait, did the e-mail Mike found say anything about what was in John's will?"

"I don't know."

"I bet it didn't—but now I have another reason to want to see that hard drive. Do you know where Mike is? I've been trying to call him all day with no luck."

"I imagine he's at home."

"Would he mind if I called him there?"

"He'd mind if you called him at work."

"True. And this is urgent. All right, thanks, Jill. Bye."

Betsy looked up Mike Malloy's home phone number in the Excelsior phone book—virtually no one had an un-listed number in Excelsior—and dialed it. A child an-swered.

"Hello, this is Betsy Devonshire. I'd like to speak to Sergeant Malloy, please."

"Are you going to try to sell him something?"

"No."

"Okay, just a minute."

Less than a minute later, Mike said, "Ms. Devonshire?" He did not sound pleased.

"I'm so sorry to bother you at home, but I wasn't able to connect with you at work, and this is urgent."

"What do you want?"

"I want to look at the hard drive—the copy of the hard drive—from John Nye's computer."

"Why?"

"Now, Mike, you must know I'm trying to help Godwin. I want to talk to the person who was John's guest the day he was killed."

"That young man didn't murder John."

"He was among the last to see him alive, right? Maybe he can tell me something."

"Did Marvin Lebowski put you up to this?"

"Not this specifically. But he's allowing me to act as his private investigator. Do you need a letter from him stating that? I could get it to you—would an e-mail be all right? I'm in kind of a hurry."

"Why don't you just bail him out?"

"You know what the bail is."

"You're a rich woman. Don't tell me you couldn't raise a million dollars if you had to." Was there envy in his voice?

"If it meant Godwin's life, certainly. If it only means setting him free a couple of weeks early, no. I'll get him out, Mike. But it will be as a free man, not someone under some Mickey-Mouse indictment, all right?" Betsy stopped and took a breath. She was getting angry and that was stupid and dangerous. "Please, Mike. If he's guilty, it can't do any harm—and I may even find something to prove that."

"Yeah, and you'd be quick to tell me about it, wouldn't you?"

"Of course I would, why not? Look, I'll make you a deal. If I find proof that Godwin knew about the old will, I'll hand it over to you. I promise. In fact, I'll even tell you something now that you probably don't know. Godwin's computer is here. I'll swap with you: a copy of John's hard drive, for a copy of Godwin's."

Mike's voice was suddenly eager, even warm. "Deal! Come to the police station tomorrow with your copy, and I'll let you have the one off John's."

"Thanks, Mike."

Betsy hung up. How on earth did you make a copy of a hard drive?

She went in to her guest bedroom, where her own computer was, and booted up. It took some research, but she found that she needed a USB external drive. They cost around a hundred dollars, and they came in different sizes. Once you had that item, it was as easy as downloading a single program.

Funny how intimidating computers seemed. Betsy had resisted learning anything about them other than what she absolutely needed to know—all that talk about gigabytes, for example. What was a gigabyte? She wasn't sure, except it seemed like some kind of large number.

But when you stopped trying to understand how they worked, suddenly it was easy. She didn't need to know how the internal combustion system worked to figure out how many gallons of gas it would take to drive to Fargo and back. Same here, all she needed to know was that a gigabyte was a unit of storage, and Godwin's computer had—how many of them?

She signed off and booted up Godwin's computer. She went to "My Computer" and selected "Properties" for

Godwin's hard drive. That told her, among other things, that he had a forty gigabyte hard drive—so she needed another hard drive at least that large. Probably a little larger. She remembered an early computer that, when its memory was full, didn't have the smarts left to operate the printer. So maybe a sixty gigabyte hard drive.

Hard drives were for sale in any store that sold computers. Tomorrow she'd go to CompuWorld in Minnetonka and buy one.

Fifteen

✤ ✤ ✤

THE next day was Saturday. Betsy made three phone calls right after breakfast. One was to Hower House, the bed and breakfast on Water Street where Charlie Nye was staying. She was told Mr. Nye had eaten early and was already gone. She called John Nye's house next, thinking he'd probably gone there, but the phone had been disconnected.

Then she called Gary Woodward's house, and got his father, a retired army officer. "Hi, Frank, this is Betsy Devonshire. I need to borrow Gary, if that's all right."

"Got a computer problem or a knitting question?" he asked jovially. Some while back, Betsy had helped Gary prove to his father the marijuana found in his bedroom wasn't his. Subsequently, the father became closer to his son, and, in gratitude, the teen had volunteered to help Betsy solve any computer problems she had. Betsy knew Gary before the marijuana incident; he had learned to knit in grade school and haunted the sales bin in Betsy's shop for yarn. Betsy enjoyed knowing Gary, he had the same deep under-standing of knitting patterns he had of computers.

Now Betsy said, "A computer problem. I need him to show me how to copy a hard drive onto another hard drive. I'm on my way out to buy the new hard drive. Could you have him call me?"

Just before ten, she went down to open up and found Rennie just coming up to the door. Betsy let her in and told her that Nikki Marquez and Shelly would be in in an hour to help out.

"Where are you going today, Betsy?" asked Rennie, as she watched Betsy put the start-up cash into the register.

"First, to CompuWorld. After that, well, it depends on if I can buy a computer part that I can make work."

"Ah, spyware," nodded Rennie wisely.

Betsy smiled. "I wish I could use some spyware, but it's too early in this business to even know whom to spy on. I'm hoping to hear from Charlie Nye today, because I want to see him. If he calls looking for me, give him my cell phone number and tell him I'll be back in about an hour. And if Gary Woodward calls, ask him where he'll be today, so I can get hold of him. Tell him it's urgent."

Betsy wrote her cell phone number down on a card and put it beside the phone on the desk. "You can also call me if you run into any problems. I'll stop back in here when I get back from Minnetonka."

Minnetonka was a lake, but also a town adjoining Wayzata that ran east along the I-394 corridor. Near its eastern end was a nice mall called Ridgedale. In the manner of such things, Ridgedale had inspired a couple of strip malls and a gathering of big box stores: Best Buy, PetSmart, Office Max—and, next to a Porsche dealer, CompuWorld.

Betsy was deeply intimidated by computer stores. Big signs advertising features she sometimes didn't know the use of made her feel defensive. She was sure the clerks could tell just looking at her, a blond, middle-aged woman— "Look, Harold, a three-fer!"—that she was ripe to be sold some defective product at an outrageous price.

And it was true, she was woefully ignorant. She wished Gary had been at home when she called, she could have brought him along.

She would have walked out of the place, except a fragment of common sense made itself heard. All she needed was a hard drive somewhat bigger than forty gigabytes; she *knew* that. And knowledge is power. Beside, look, right over there, on that bin, a sign saying *SALE: Hard Drives, Priced as Marked*. The bin was nearly full of silver boxes, about the size of a hardcover novel, except longer. They looked metal but were plastic, and were not in boxes or other wrapping. Betsy quickly found labels on their undersides that announced the number of bytes. The Internet site she'd found said hard drives generally sold for around one hundred dollars; none of these cost more than seventy. She found a sixty-gigabyte one for fifty-eight dollars. The case had no damage she could see, and it didn't look at all shopworn. It should do nicely for the temporary use to which it would be put.

She carried it proudly to the checkout and was careful to store the receipt in a zippered pocket of her purse. Maybe she could get at least some crumbs of her retainer money back from Attorney Lebowski when she turned in her receipts.

Back at the shop, Rennie had been joined by Shelly, Emily,

Martha, and Phil. With the addition of four customers, the place looked jammed. Sophie, reclining regally on her chair, was trying to conceal a fragment of a chocolate chip cookie with one fat paw.

Rennie said Charlie hadn't called but Gary had, and the teen was at home waiting for her to call him.

"Thanks," said Betsy, and, after subtly removing the portion of cookie from her cat's custody, hurried upstairs.

Gary didn't live far away, he was ringing her doorbell within minutes of her phoning him.

He was a slender boy of sixteen, a little undersized, with a thick shock of dark hair shading gray eyes. He wore an unbuttoned plaid flannel shirt, too-big jeans, and unlaced sport shoes. Betsy bit back the smart-aleck remark about people who went out before they finished dressing, and showed him the way to the computer.

"Is this the right kind of hard drive?" she asked anxiously, showing him the silver box. "I can't see how to open it, so I just left it alone."

"You don't open it," he said, turning it over. "How many gigs on the drive that's in it?" He gestured at Godwin's laptop, a Toshiba Satellite.

"Forty," she said.

"You bought a sixty, that's good," he noted, and sat down, shifting his backpack onto the floor beside him. "Where's your USB cord?"

"Um, I don't think I have one," she confessed.

He nodded and opened his backpack and pulled out a cord with a metal rectangle near one end and a square sort of plug-in at either end. "Well, let's see if we can do this."

He booted up Godwin's computer, went searching in

various places, attached the cord to the computer and then the hard drive, clicked on an icon, and clicked on various choices on the various boxes that came down with each click, and sat back.

"Now what?" asked Betsy.

"We wait. It'll take maybe an hour."

"Well, then, how about lunch?"

He brightened. "What've you got?"

"Not much in the place, how about we go down to Sol's?" Sol's was the deli next door to Crewel World. "You can have any sandwich in the place, soup, too, if you like."

"All right."

"We could go to Licks for dessert." Licks, over on Water Street, had many flavors of ice cream.

"All right!"

When they got back, the download was still going on, so Gary washed his hands and produced a knitting project from his backpack. He liked working with beads, and had once shown Betsy a pattern he had worked out on his own, suitable for any kind of cuff, whether a baby's sock or the bottom of an extra-large sweater. He was currently working a series of red and blue beads onto the cuff of a white sock, a gift for his little sister.

Seeing the white sock, Betsy was reminded of Godwin's knitting of an endless series of white cotton socks. Perhaps they would allow Godwin to knit while he was in jail, a happy thought. Then, looking at the needles Gary was using with the eyes of a jailer—sharp, slender, easily-hidden objects—coupled with yards of strong yarn, she thought perhaps not. Still, she could ask.

Meanwhile, she got her own project out. Bershada's inquiry into an entrelac pattern had inspired Betsy to start that sweater. The pattern was from Spincraft, and knit from side to side. Betsy was using overdyed silk yarn in rich shades of wine, purple, blue, and gray. Like the purse Bershada was making, it was knit on circular needles. Betsy couldn't wait to see how the pattern worked from the sleeves into the body—she wasn't like Gary, she couldn't look at a pattern and see how it would look for real.

After about half an hour, Gary went to check on the download, and pronounced it finished. "What are you going to do with it?" he asked.

"I'm going to trade it with someone for another hard drive. After I do that, will you show me how to access the new hard drive?"

"Sure. Just let me know. Say, is this for a case you're working on?"

Betsy nodded. "Yes, it is. That's why I can't give you any details yet. When it's all over, I'll tell you how valuable you were to the solution."

His gray eyes shone. "Am I really important?"

"Yes, very important. But I can't tell you any more about it right now."

"Wow, thanks! Wait'll I—no, I shouldn't tell anyone, should I?"

"Just tell them exactly what you did, you copied a hard drive for me because I'm too lazy to take a class and learn how to do it myself. And that you don't know why I wanted it copied."

He smiled, pleased at sharing a grown-up secret. "All right. You'll call me again if you need me?"

"*When* I need you. And when this is all over, I'll tell you what I did."

After Gary went tripping down the stairs, she called

Mike Malloy and found him in. "I've got that hard drive, if you still want to trade."

"All right, come on over."

The brick and stone one-story building wasn't far away, but Betsy drove over, first because she was in a hurry and second because she was afraid she might drop the hard drive and have the copying to do all over again. She carried it in two hands up to the door of the police station.

Mike was waiting in the airlock between the two sets of doors that made the entrance. "Here," he said, handing her a clipboard after taking the hard drive.

"What's this?"

"A receipt, of course."

"Oh. Of course." Betsy signed it and was given a copy along with a silver plastic box identical to the one she'd handed over. Except for the strip of white adhesive tape that marked it as Copy Two of John Nye's hard drive.

"Did you find anything useful on this?" she asked.

"Nah, most of it is password protected and the rest is encrypted." He showed her an evil smile, turned, and went back inside.

Yeah, thought Betsy, *getting back into her car, but I've got a secret weapon that can, I just betcha, break this thing wide open.*

On her way home, her cell phone rang. "Yes?" she said, after pulling over and fumbling it open. She could talk and drive, but she couldn't get the doggone thing open while driving.

"Hello?" she said, hoping it was Charlie Nye.

"Betsy, it's Shelly. Can you come right away?"

"What's the matter?"

"I'll tell you when you get here."

At the shop Betsy found Rennie and Shelly behind the desk, looking flustered. Nikki was standing by the entrance to the back, and there was an air about her as of being on guard. Betsy glanced through the double set of box shelves and saw Phil sitting at the little round table with a customer Betsy recognized, though she couldn't remember her name. They were not conversing. Phil was looking very firm, the woman was looking half-defiant, half-ashamed. Betsy sighed.

"Is she our shoplifter?" she murmured, walking up to the desk.

"Yeah." Shelly sighed. "I walked into the back and caught her putting a kit into her slacks. I told her to put it back and asked her to sit down while I called you, but she couldn't sit down, she had two more kits down her trouser legs and another one down the back of her slacks. And her coat pockets are full of floss." Shelly smiled. "She said she had no idea how that stuff got into her clothing."

Rennie spoke up. "Yeah, but she's either got two pairs of slacks on or some kind of lining like a giant pocket down both trouser legs, because they look loose but those kits didn't fall out the bottoms."

A pro, then. Betsy went for a look. The woman was middle-aged, with thin lips, tired eyes, short hair dyed dark brown. She wore baggy trousers, sneakers, a loose-fitting coat over a baggy sweater.

Betsy came back to the desk to ask, "Did she admit she's been having a problem with charts and kits hopping into her clothing before?" Crewel World had been suffering from theft all year.

"She said no, of course not, but I don't believe her."

"I hope she's the one who's been doing all of it, all by herself," said Betsy. She considered her options. If it had been just a pocketful of floss, or even a kit, they might have had her pay for the stuff, told her she was banned from the shop, and let her go. But if this was the chronic thief . . . Like most small businesses, the profit margin at Crewel World was thin and a determined thief could put a shop into the red in a hurry.

"What did she take?"

Shelly brought out the biggest Crewel World bag, heavy with merchandise. The Rowandean crewel kit alone retailed at more than a hundred dollars, the Nan Heldenbrand Morrissette kimono kit was sixty-five, and the two Marilyn Leavitt Inblum kits were seventy and eighty dollars—plus the shoplifter had filled one pocket with Caron's Waterlilies floss at six-eighty a skein, and the other with Betsy's new stock of beautiful, hand-dyed Olde Willow Stitchery Threads' Quaker flosses. "What we took off her totals over three hundred dollars," said Shelly. "That's felony-level theft."

Betsy turned and asked Nikki, "Did Mr. Nye call?"

"No, ma'am."

Betsy started to weigh the various possibilities against the various consequences. She wanted to have this woman arrested as a lesson to her and any others who might be thinking of stealing. She wanted to hurry upstairs to start looking at the hard drive and find the clue that would free Godwin. It would take time to get this woman arrested; they'd gotten everything back and none of it was damaged. And if they called the police, that was just more time Godwin would have to spend with those odd people in Quad Eleven. She turned and looked at the sad woman at the table, then at the heap of expensive goods on the desk. Anger won. "Call the police," she said.

"Betsy!" exclaimed Rennie.

"I don't care, I'm sick and tired of this. If she's the one who's been stealing all along, we've lost nearly a thousand dollars thanks to her, and I am not going to stand for that kind of thing. *So call the police!*" Betsy said that last bit nice and loud and was rewarded with a burst of weeping from the sad woman.

Phil looked at Betsy and nodded once, firmly.

"Did you also see her take anything?" Betsy asked Nikki.

"No, ma'am." Nikki's eyes were wide; she'd never seen Betsy on the warpath before.

It took a few minutes for Lars to arrive. Betsy was fairly jittering with impatience before his squad car drove up. "Now what?" he said, coming in large and aggressive. *Still mad about me lying to him about Godwin's whereabouts the night John was killed,* she thought.

"Shoplifter," she said briefly. "I wasn't here. You can talk to Shelly, she caught her in the act. I'll be upstairs if you want me to sign the complaint." She started to walk away, but then turned and went back to intercept him on his way to the desk and Shelly. She put a hand on his forearm and, looking up into his frosty blue eyes, said, "I'm sorry I misled you last Friday."

"You ought to be," he said, but already the frost was melting.

"Well, I just knew he didn't do it, so I thought I'd save Mike the trouble of thinking he did."

"And now you know you were wrong."

"No, I wasn't. You'll see. Goddy's no murderer."

"Aw, you and Jill and all you women, you always think the sweet little ones can't do any wrong."

"We're right about you, aren't we?"

Lars blinked, grinned, and said, "Got you fooled, don't I?"

Betsy turned and this time went all the way through to the back door and out.

She imagined it was a full thirty seconds before a massive frown formed on Lars's broad, low forehead. Work? Upstairs? But she worked here.

Only most of the time, my friend.

When she got upstairs, she realized she still didn't have a USB cord and so couldn't even begin to access John's hard drive. She called Gary.

"I hate to bother you again so soon, are you busy?" she asked.

"Playing computer games is all," he said. "What's up?"

"I have a new hard drive, or rather a different one, another copy of someone else's hard drive. I've been told it's protected by a password and that some of it is encrypted. Any ideas?"

"Is this more of that special deal you're working on?"

"Yes, it is."

"Great! Can I come over right now?" He sounded eager.

She was pleased to be able to say with equal eagerness, "I'd love it if you could come over right now."

He rang the doorbell a few minutes later, and within minutes of that was happily hooking up her computer to the hard drive. She stood behind him, hoping to learn something esoteric about computers—then her phone rang and she hurried away to answer it.

"Hello, Ms. Devonshire, this is Charlie Nye. I understand you've been wanting to talk to me."

"Yes, I have. I've got good news for you. I have a copy of your brother's hard drive, and we are at this minute trying find a way past his passwords."

"Would you be willing to let me look, too?"

"Certainly. Can you come over right now?"

Sixteen

❈ ❈ ❈

B ETSY went back into the guest bedroom. Her computer
monitor was showing the Microsoft Word screen under
the smaller screen on which files were listed, and, partly
covering that, another screen asking for a password. There
was a faint grinding sound, as of a disk turning, coming
from her computer, and suddenly the password icon went
away. Gary gave a grunt of satisfaction as a file opened.

He clicked and typed a command and clicked again. "I
took off the password protection," he said. "You'll be able to
open any of these by just clicking on them."

He opened a few to show her, then one he opened filled
the screen with gibberish: rows of dots, random numbers
and letters, swatches of white space. "Encrypted," Gary explained. He took out his password-finder disk and put it in.
Seconds later, the screen changed, but only to more gibberish, which immediately faded to another screen of gibberish.

This continued for a couple of minutes, and then the fade was to English.

She touched Gary on the top of his dark hair. "You are so brilliant!" she said, and he grinned. She bent forward to look at the now-decipherable screen. "What have we here?" she said.

It appeared to be a financial statement of some kind, but one belonging to Christopher Bright, who banked at First Wisconsin of Menomonee, a town down I-94 from the Twin Cities. He was further identified with what was probably his Social Security number, and a birthdate that made him about twenty-seven. He had a substantial balance of close to two hundred and fifty thousand dollars, split among a savings account, a money market, and an investment fund called QuikGro.

"Who's Christopher Bright?" Betsy asked herself, but out loud.

"I never heard of him," replied Gary. "But he's rich, isn't he? And wasn't Mr. Nye a lawyer? Maybe he was doing some legal stuff for Mr. Bright."

"How do you know this is about Mr. Nye?"

"Goddy's in jail for killing Mr. Nye, it was on the news. So of course this is about that. You're helping Goddy."

"Yes," admitted Betsy. "But the details are secret, okay?"

"Sure. Is Mr. Bright a suspect?"

"I don't know." Betsy looked closer. It wasn't a real spreadsheet, it looked like something typed up from notes. But why did John have this information on his home computer, rather than on one at his office? "Maybe he was moonlighting."

"That's a word I've heard before . . . what does it mean?" asked Gary.

"Working a second job, usually at night. Otherwise this file would be on his office computer."

Gary went through the other two encrypted files. One used the same encryption, and contained biographical information about Mr. Bright, who had been born in St. Paul of parents named Angela and Edward Bright. The other had a different code that took his magic disk another five minutes to change into plain English. This one seemed to be entries in a journal—or maybe, judging by the florid language, parts of a romance-adventure novel.

"That's enough, just close it," said Betsy, catching a phrase she thought Gary's mother would have a hemorrhage over if she thought her son had read it.

Gary, smiling, complied. "It's okay, I've seen stuff like that before," he said.

"Never let it be said that *I* was a party to showing you literature like that," said Betsy.

He shrugged. "Whatever eases your mind." He clicked it closed and turned in the chair to look up at her. "Will this help you solve your case?" he asked.

"I don't know. It's what you might call 'raw data' right now. Maybe I can find facts among them that will be useful."

She offered to pay Gary for his services, which he, as usual, refused. She stood in her apartment door a minute after saying goodbye, listening to him bound down the stairs, and heard him exchange a quick "Hi" with a man coming into the building.

The man started up the stairs. "Who is it?" called Betsy, ready to close her door.

"Me, Charlie," the man said, so she waited to let him in.

He was looking tired, and his jeans and sweatshirt were

grungy. "Be they never so clean, houses have dusty garages," he remarked.

"Did you find anything useful?" she asked.

"Not really. Old law books, old tax returns, a flat basket-ball, a croquet set, two kites—the usual. Nothing valuable."

"Was his car in the garage?"

"Yes. A Mercedes, of course. SLK Roadster, a convertible. Deep gold, only two years old, beautiful condition. He took good care of it, he kept records of oil changes and tune-ups, and he never missed a mileage mark."

Betsy imagined Charlie, mourning a dead brother, faced with the complex task of sorting out the detritus of his life, nevertheless sitting down and going page-by-page through the little book given all car owners about upkeep. "You're being very thorough."

" 'Thorough' is a good CPA's middle name."

"Back home, do you work for a big company?"

"I'm a partner in a small one. Guthmann, Nye, and Do-herty." He sat on her couch with an audible sigh, then im-mediately leaped up again, brushing at the seat of his jeans and looking at the couch for signs of his passage.

"Here, just a minute." Betsy went into the guest bed-room closet and pulled down an afghan crocheted in some of Alice's washable squares. She floated it over the couch, and he sat down on it, putting one ankle on his other knee.

"You look tired," she said. "Are you taking care of your-self? May I offer you something to eat or drink?"

He looked at his watch, raised his eyebrows. "Later than I thought," he said. "Maybe a sandwich of some kind, if you don't mind?"

"Tuna all right?"

"Sure."

"Then I want you to take a look at John's computer."

"You have it?" He was definitely surprised.

"I have a copy of his hard drive, and the passwords and encryptions have been removed, so all the files are readable."

"I almost never do this, but would you mind bringing my sandwich to the computer?"

She smiled. "Fine. Do you like onions?"

"Only if there are no cucumbers instead."

There weren't. Not that he would have noticed if the sandwich had been made of jalepeno peppers and sardines. Betsy put the sandwich, wrapped in a napkin, into his hand, the glass of water on the table beside him, and crept away.

He emerged two hours later to hand her the empty glass. He had a small notebook in his other hand, which he had raised to shoulder level and was shaking gently. "Something's screwy in there," he said.

"Christopher Bright?" she asked.

"That's one thing. But I think the explanation for that is obvious."

"You do?"

"Certainly. John was Christopher Bright."

Betsy stared at him. "How do you know—wait, I saw that the bank in Menomonee uses Social Security numbers as ID numbers. They're the same, aren't they? John's and Christopher Bright's?"

"No." Charlie shook his head. "John set up a false ID to open that account."

"How do you know that?"

"What started me thinking that had happened was that, in the biography file, Bright gives his address as a post office box number in Rusk, a little town near Menomonee. John has used a post office box number from time to time, and he always tries to get a box number that corresponds to a number important to him, the month he was born in, the month and day combined, whatever. The post office box number for Mr. Bright is the year John was born."

Betsy wanted to say, "Coincidence!" But she didn't, because Charlie was smiling and obviously going to make another, better point.

Charlie said, "What's interesting is that he didn't just use a false name, but came up with a whole new identity, a different Social Security number and all. However, I went to the St. Paul Municipal Records site and discovered that Christopher Bright, son of Angela and Edward Bright, died of kidney failure at the age of four." He came and sat down on the afghan again.

Betsy sat down in her upholstered chair. "Do you mean he did that old graveyard thing?"

He laughed out loud. "You *are* a sleuth at that!" he said.

"Thank you," said Betsy. She had learned the technique from a thriller, actually. People seeking to create a new identity sometimes went to graveyards to find the tombstone of a child born the same year, or close to it, that they were born. They would write to the municipality nearby, seeking a copy of a birth certificate, and once they had that, they could get a Social Security card and a driver's license, the three solid proofs of a person's legal existence.

"Wait a second," said Betsy. "If John was spending every nickel he was making, where did he get two hundred and fifty thousand dollars to put into the Menomonee bank?"

"That, my dear Ms. Devonshire, is a very good question."

"A lawyer learns a lot of unsavory things about his clients, doesn't he? Maybe John was blackmailing someone."

"I don't think so. Blackmailers tend to say, 'That is going to cost you five hundred dollars a month' or some such regular amount, and the deposits into the Bright account were much bigger, varied in amount from five thousand to twenty-six thousand, and were made at irregular intervals."

"Maybe he was selling something," said Betsy.

"Could be," nodded Charlie.

"But he wasn't dealing in antiques or something else honest, because why go to all that trouble setting up a false identity? Drugs, maybe?"

"I don't think drug dealers put money into bank accounts. Banks are required to report transactions larger than ten thousand dollars. I suspect Johnny, as Christopher Bright, was a tax-paying citizen."

"So what do you think he was doing?"

"I don't know. But it's possible that, whatever it was, it got him killed."

"So you've changed your mind about Godwin being the murderer?"

"No, not entirely. It's possible that Godwin was also involved in whatever shenanigans Johnny was into, and that there was a danger from somewhere that the scheme was about to be revealed, and Godwin murdered Johnny to keep from being indicted."

Betsy refused to be drawn into an argument about Godwin. She asked instead, "Did you ever do your brother's tax returns?"

He sat back with a satisfied smile. "Every year from his first job until about two years ago. Even when we were barely speaking because of this homosexual thing. I did his returns."

"What excuse did he give for stopping?"

He had to think about that a few moments. "He said an important client offered him a referral and he thought he should take it."

"Maybe it's true."

He shrugged. "Maybe it is. I know I believed him at the time."

After Charlie left, Betsy went in to look at the files on John's computer.

The homemade financial statement showed only deposits, no withdrawals. Betsy noted the date the account was opened, and some of the deposit dates.

Then she went to the biography of Christopher Bright. He was born, said the bio, at St. Luke's Hospital in St. Paul going on twenty-eight years ago. John was a great deal older than twenty-eight. Evidently he had planned to take some lessons from Godwin on knocking a decade off his appearance. His parents were missionaries and set off with their little boy to Cancun, Mexico, where they stayed until he was twelve. He came back home to live with a relative (not further identified) until he was sixteen, then he went back to Mexico until he was twenty. There followed a gap in the chronology, until he appeared in Menomonee, Wisconsin, two years ago, in need of a driver's license.

There was no mention of his education, nor a resumé of his employment record, or even his career choice—which must have been pretty remunerative, for him to have saved so much in that short a time.

Betsy closed that work of fiction and went to the torrid-language one.

This seemed to be a collection of anecdotes, descriptions of romantic encounters, or what was desired by way of romantic encounters—of course. This was boilerplate: sentences, phrases, brief scenarios that could be lifted and dropped into advertisements. "A casual walk by the lake, a romantic dinner, an evening, by the fire . . ." read one. There seemed to be a great deal of that sort of thing. "A clean, discreet young man, inexperienced in love . . ." And here were love letters, not one of which was addressed to Dear Goddy. Heavens, there were pages of the stuff! Betsy slapped the computer closed, her lips thinning in anger. How long had this been going on? Certainly longer than the brief time since John and Godwin had broken up!

She had to get up and walk through the apartment, letting her anger cool. And when it did, there followed a chill. What if Godwin had seen this? Why, he'd be brokenhearted—and then he'd be angry. Or so Mike and that slender lady from the BCA might convincingly conclude.

Seventeen

SUNDAY morning Betsy went to church to pray for help. Sitting in the familiar surroundings, hearing the familiar words was a comfort, but not an inspiration. She had more hopes of the sermon. Father Rettger's sermons were generally good. As he did on occasion, he began with a joke, the one about the man who prayed for years to win the lottery, with no success. Finally, an old man, he grew angry and demanded of God why he, a good and devout man, had never won. There came a crash of thunder and a mighty voice called down to him, "Because you never bought a ticket!"

When the mild laughter at this rather elderly joke ended, the priest continued, "So I bought a ticket—" more laughter—"and as you can see, here I am as usual, standing in the pulpit, not at home negotiating a purchase of ocean-front property in Miami. Why didn't I win? If I should ask God why, I'm pretty sure His answer would be: 'There's a million people who bought tickets ahead of you. Be patient.'"

Betsy shifted uncomfortably. She didn't feel patient, she felt impatient, with herself, this case, the sullen facts that refused to come forth and make sense. She wanted the crash of thunder and the deep, loud voice.

"Patience occurs in the Gospels frequently. The debtor in one of Jesus's parables cries, 'Be patient and I will pay you all.' Paul writes in Corithinians, 'Love is patient, love bears all things, endures all things.' In Galatians, he says patience is one of the fruits of the Holy Spirit, and in Hebrews it was the important trait of our forebears in faith. And, it is not only a virtue for humans, it is a characteristic of God, spoken of in first Peter.

"Now it is true, there are times when God acts quickly, in the twinkling of an eye. It can be frightening as well as rewarding when justice is swift. It is recommended that children be corrected at once, and criminals be prosecuted quickly—'justice delayed is justice denied' after all, and tyrants need to be brought down as fast as possible to prevent their doing more harm. In fact, when it doesn't happen like that, in the twinkling of our eye, we grow impatient, and wonder, Where is God?

"Where indeed? He will come to us, but in His own time. Do your part—buy a ticket. Then be patient."

"Amen," she repeated after him, and rose with the rest to recite the Creed. Be patient. Buy a ticket and be patient. Well, she was trying to buy that ticket, but it seemed very elusive. Or had she bought it, and just couldn't tell? She began going over the case in her head, looking at the few clues she'd collected—useless, most of them—and got so tangled up in her thoughts that a few minutes later, going to the communion rail, she looked blankly at the goblet of wine when it was offered to her, unable to remember for a moment whether she was a sipper or a dipper.

She didn't even notice that Jill had been sitting only a pew over until, making her way out, Jill touched her on the arm. She turned, an apology forming for getting in someone's way, when she saw who it was. "Oh, hi, Jill."

"You seem a little distracted," Jill noted. "Though it's not hard to guess why."

"Yes, I guess I am."

"Don't be afraid for Goddy, he'll do fine."

Tears formed on Betsy's lashes, but she blinked them away. "I know."

"Meanwhile, I think you need a break. Come over to our house for brunch. Lars is home cooking up a storm. He makes a very good omelet."

Something in Jill's voice brought Betsy out of her focus on herself. The woman's normal cool was slightly overridden by something else, pleasure or excitement; and Betsy, knowing how rare that was, said, "All right. Thanks, in fact. What time?"

"Eleven all right?"

"Yes. See you then."

She went home to change out of her Sunday best into comfortable slacks and shirt, then decided to tackle the contents of John's computer until it was time to leave for the brunch.

John had liked the computer games Spider Solitaire and Doom. He had kept a calendar of appointments on his computer, though it was far out of date—Betsy made a mental note to check if John had one of those pocket computers so many business people carried now.

His word processing program contained mostly correspondence. There was a letter written to an attorney John seemed to know well, greeting him by his first name and asking about his family before going into crisp legal language about the new will John wanted drawn up. He was going to leave slightly larger bequests to his nieces and nephews and a slightly smaller bequest to the William Mitchell College of Law in St. Paul. He also wanted to eliminate a provision in the old will, which set up a spendthrift trust for Goodwin DuLac. "Our situation has altered of late," he wrote, "and so with regret I am ordering this change."

She braced herself when opening John's e-mail files, but most of them were newsy little chats between friends. There was a thank you e-mail from Charlie for the Spanish-language book on the Museum of Anthropology sent to his daughter. But some were flirtatious, and there was a small set of increasingly torrid exchanges between John and a young man named Beni Greenleaf. Beni's spelling was as atrocious as his sentiments were naïve. Betsy noted that Beni was local, that he was eighteen, "not very tall," with a slender build and "curly auburn hair," and worked as a waiter in an uptown restaurant.

Then she closed her notebook, shut down her computer and left for her brunch engagement.

Lars and Jill lived a modest house out St. Alban's Bay Road. Betsy drove slowly down the road, noting the late spring flowers and breathing the clean, damp air—it was overcast today, with a promise of rain before nightfall. Weekend Street was a short lane between St. Alban's and the lake. The Larson house was at the foot of the street, though mature trees blocked all but glimpses of the water. The lot was large and oddly shaped, bordered with flowering shrubs. It contained a good-size barn-shaped shed in which, Betsy knew, Lars kept his beloved 1908 Stanley Steamer. Jill's big old Oldsmobile and

Lars' regular-use car, a new red Volvo, had to sit outside until Lars got around to building a regular garage for them.

Betsy pulled up behind the Oldsmobile and got out. The air was full of the scent of lilacs just opening, and Betsy walked by a ten-foot-high bush of them on her way to the house. She climbed onto the screened porch and pressed the doorbell.

It was opened immediately by Jill. That look of suppressed joy was still on her face, and Betsy smiled up at her. "Please, I can't bear this; tell me what's got you so happy," she said.

"Ask Lars," replied Jill, and led the way to the breakfast bar that marked the border between the kitchen and dining room. There was a delicious smell of eggs, onions, and sausages frying, and coffee brewing.

Lars was bustling around the little kitchen, whistling something loud and off-key, looking fit to burst with good news.

Betsy was pretty sure now she knew what it was, but didn't say anything: first, not to spoil their joy in telling her, and second, what if she was wrong?

Lars took a plate out of the oven. It was piled high with toast. He opened the refrigerator and brought out a Mason jar full of raspberry preserves. He stuck a knife into the jam, and placed it with a flourish in front of her.

"We're having a baby!" he said.

As soon as she got home, Betsy phoned the jail and found out there was no one to fetch a prisoner on weekends unless the caller was an attorney. She sighed deeply and said she'd call back Monday.

She went into the guest room and sat down at Godwin's laptop with even greater reluctance than she'd had opening John's e-mail messages. But very likely at this minute Mike Malloy was rummaging through Godwin's private life.

She started Godwin's computer and found it wanted a password. She tried a few of the more obvious ones and none worked. Annoyed—and relieved—she shut it down.

Then she recollected that she had some urgent, if more mundane, tasks to complete, and spent the next several hours doing books. She also made a record of who had volunteered to help out in the shop and how many hours each had worked. She didn't know what use she would make of that record, but it was something she felt she needed to know.

That done, she cleaned her apartment and did laundry, then had an early supper and sat down with her entrelac pattern. It took a little while to get used to knitting sideways, but at least she wasn't changing colors of yarn all the time. She'd changed from knitting in the round to knitting straight on the body, and was now at the neck. "Work 7 step5 Rectangles, then out 2 step6 TTri and finish row with 7 step5 Recs." she read. She struggled awhile, then, rather abruptly, something in her brain flipped over, and she understood. She continued knitting for another forty minutes, then put it aside.

It was nearly bedtime by then. She spread a sheet saved for the purpose on the little table in the dining nook and put Sophie up on it and combed her thick fur, taking the collected hair off as it clogged the brush and putting it into a Ziploc bag already half-full. Sophie shed year-round, but most heavily in the spring. If she was not brushed every few days, the fur matted so horribly that it could not be picked apart and combed out. The year that happened, Betsy had

had to resort to scissors. When the mats were cut out, the cat lost her ovoid silhouette and looked as if some small predator had taken bites out of her.

Fortunately, Sophie loved being groomed and started pacing and mewing impatiently as soon as she saw the sheet being spread on the table. She purred through the entire process, and kept turning and pushing her face against the comb, eyes half-closed in pleasure.

It also gave pleasure to Betsy, happy she could at least bring comfort and joy to one member of her household.

That finished, they retired for the night.

B Y nine the next morning, Betsy was at the jail, asking to see Godwin. She had dressed carefully in a good, navy-blue, linen-blend suit, snow-white blouse, and spectator shoes. She ostentatiously carried a notebook in one hand. All this—or the fact that she'd been there before—shortened her wait, and soon she was sitting in the depressing little room, waiting for Godwin.

He came in looking a whole lot less like a dog being given a bath than last time. Amazingly, his jumpsuit fit him. It was an old one, washed so many times it was more a peach color than the by-God orange he'd worn before. He looked almost chipper, and brightened further when he saw her. He threw up his hands and made an admiring face at her before sitting down and picking up the phone.

"You look *smashing!*" he said into the receiver.

"Thank you, and you look rather fine yourself."

"Oh, *this* old thing?" he said, and rocked to one side with laughter.

"All right, young man, explain yourself," she ordered.

"Well, you know that old saying, 'In the valley of the blind, the one-eyed man is king'?"

She nodded.

"In Quad Eleven, the one most nearly sane is in charge."

"I thought the guards were in charge."

"They can't be everywhere all the time. So they rely on sensible people to help keep the peace. In Quad Eleven, *c'est moi*." He pointed to himself, grandly smirking. "I helped Felix write a letter to his dog-wife; found out that Dorothy really is transgendered and was on estrogen before she got arrested and so she's really suffering, though they won't give her estrogen while she's here; and I arranged for some of us to sit for half an hour twice a day while Mark repeats wonderful stories one of his voices tells him. He should write them down, some of them are wonderfully sad and some are *so* romantic." He heaved a dramatic sigh.

"Godwin, you are the most amazing person I have ever known," said Betsy sincerely.

"I am?" he said. "Thank you, but how so?"

"I swear, only you could find the beauty part of being in jail."

"Well, it isn't all roses. I don't suppose you have any good news for me?"

"How's this: Jill and Lars are pregnant!"

His mouth fell open. "Hey, good for them! When is it due?"

"Around Christmas or New Year's."

"How jolly! Boy or girl?"

"They don't know yet, and may not want to know. They're back and forth about that."

"Buying presents for them this year will be easy, anyhow."

His good mood suddenly vanished, as if someone had let all the air out of it. "If I'm able to go shopping for presents."

"Oh, of course you'll be shopping!"

"But you haven't made any progress yet, have you?"

"Well . . . some. I went through John's computer and found some interesting things. Did you know he had set up a different identity?"

"What does that mean?"

"He was salting money away in an account in Menomonee, Wisconsin, under the name Christopher Bright. Do you have any idea why he might want to do that?"

Godwin stared at her through the Plexiglas window. "Not a clue. How strange."

"Does the name Christopher Bright mean anything to you?"

"No." He thought about it a few moments, then shook his head and repeated, "No."

"Did John go out of town a lot?"

"No, not very often. Well, once in awhile, and then just for a day or overnight. Interviewing people about cases he was working on. Witnesses, or clients."

"Did he fly or drive?"

"Either, or. Sometimes one, sometimes the other."

"Can you remember the last time he drove out and back in a single day?"

Godwin thought, casting his eyes upward, wrapping a forefinger around his chin. "About a week before we went to Mexico. I can't remember the exact date, though maybe I could if I had a calendar. I remember it was on a weekday; he left early to get out ahead of the rush hour, and he took me out to dinner that night."

Betsy wrote that down. "Very good," she said, nodding. "Now, I have another question for you."

"Shoot."

"I've got the name of someone John was seeing." Betsy went back a page, where she had written it down. "Beni—spelled Bee, ee, en, eye—Greenleaf. Do you know him?"

"Beni, Beni . . . No, I don't think so—wait, yes, I do! Skinny little twerp with a home perm and hardly any manners?"

"I don't know, I've never seen him. All I have is his name. He and John exchanged e-mails and John invited him out for coffee one night and . . . to the house the day he was killed."

"Him? John brought *him* into our house? My God, what was he *thinking*?"

"Is Beni dangerous?"

"*Dangerous?*" Godwin snorted. "God, no! Oh, wait a second, that's not the answer you're looking for, is it?"

"No, but don't change it to make me happy. Tell me about him."

"Yeah, well, what can I say? Beni might be dangerous to an ant with a broken leg, but only by accidentally squashing it trying to put a splint on."

Betsy grimaced. That was not at all what she wanted to hear. "Still, I want to talk to him. He was among the last to see John alive. Where can I find him?"

"I have no idea where he lives. Try Vera's. He hangs out there most evenings, hoping to be picked up."

"Is Vera's a bar?"

"No, a coffee house. Don't go alone—and don't go with a man, if you want Beni to talk to you."

Eighteen

* * *

FROM the Adult Detention Center, Betsy walked a few blocks north and west, to the IDS Center, a tall, green-glass building on Hennepin Avenue in downtown Minneapolis. It was Minneapolis's first modern skyscraper, shaped like four very wide, shallow steps up, a broad landing, and four steps down—set on end. Inside it still had the tall escalators Mary Tyler Moore rode under the opening credits of her old television sitcom.

Betsy went to the bank of elevators on the west side and rode up to the thirtieth floor. She walked into a very nice reception area, all marble and hand-loomed art carpets—were there any poor lawyers? she wondered—where an attractive black woman with a professional air spoke into her phone: "Ms. Kravchenko, there is a Ms. Devonshire here to see you."

Soon a petite woman with a Slavic face and short straight hair a peculiar light brown color came into the lobby area. She was wearing a black skirt and a white blouse with ruffles that stood up on her shoulders and made dizzy circles around her wrists. "I don't think I've ever met you, have I? And yet you look familiar." She had a very faint Russian accent that only added to her allure.

"I came to see Mr. Nye summer before last."

"Oh, yes." A speculative glint flickered in Tasha Kravchenko's slanted eyes. "Now I remember, you have the needlework store that Mr. DuLac worked in. Will you come with me?" She turned and walked back the way she had come in, Betsy following.

They came to a double row of cubicles which fronted a double row of private offices. Tasha turned into one and said, "Perhaps we should use Mr. Nye's office, we can be more private in there," and led her into a nice office with paneled walls, furnished with a soft carpet and two green wing chairs facing a mahogany desk Betsy remembered from her first visit here. It was profoundly quiet in the office. Betsy wondered if special instructions were given to the architects or decorators when putting up attorneys' offices to use extra insulation in the walls. She was sure someone could have a huge tantrum in here without disturbing anyone in the offices on either side.

Tasha gestured at the chairs, and Betsy turned the left one towards the other—it was surprisingly lightweight—and Tasha did the same, so they could sit facing one another.

"Now, how may I help you?" asked Tasha.

"I am looking into the circumstances surrounding the death of John Nye."

A tiny smile flickered across that exotic face. "I can understand why you don't think Godwin did it. He is a friend as well as a good employee, am I right? You came to defend him that first time you visited this office."

"I came primarily to ask Mr. Nye to confirm some work he had done for an artist. But yes, I defended Godwin. He is my most valuable employee as well as a good friend."

"All right, I understand. I also understand that you do some investigating of crimes. But you are an amateur, right? So don't you think you should leave this to the police?"

"No, I don't. I have hired Marvin Lebowski to represent Godwin, and he has said I may act on his behalf in conducting an investigation."

She was surprised, and was not able to hide it. "You are officially working for Mr. Lebowski?"

"Yes. He would normally hire a private investigator—and he might still do so—but he has decided to allow me to see what I can find first." Betsy shrugged. "If I am successful, it will save me the money for a PI's fee."

"That is . . . interesting." *Which,* wondered Betsy, *my doing private investigations or that I'm able to afford Marvin Lebowski?*

She tried, "I have conducted successful investigations before."

"Are you also putting up the bail so Godwin can get out?"

Oh. "No, I can't afford both Mr. Lebowski and a hundred thousand dollars for a bail bondsman."

Tasha smiled, showing small, white teeth. She seemed to have felt she'd won a point, or perhaps learned something about Betsy, without Betsy knowing it. In any case, she relaxed in the chair as much as its stiff design would allow. "I understand. Very well, what do you want to ask me about?"

Betsy opened her notebook. "Tell me something about Hanson, Wellborn, and Smith. How big a company is it?"

"There are thirty partners and a little over or under one hundred attorneys—people come and go all the time."

"When was it founded?"

"Let me think. Around 1939, I believe."

"Could you tell me who some of the clients are?"

Tasha frowned prettily. "I suppose our most important client is Sweetwater. We handle all their product-failure litigation. We also handle St. Luke's and Children's Hospital's malpractice litigation."

Betsy nodded. "Impressive. What did Mr. Nye specialize in?"

"He was good at taking raw information, analyzing it, and making it into plans of action," said Tasha. "He was also what they call a good rainmaker."

" 'Rainmaker'?"

"He could find new business for the firm."

"The partners must have found that equally valuable," said Betsy. "How long did you work for Mr. Nye?"

"Four years. Well, nearly four years—three years and ten months, actually."

"What was he like to work for?"

Was there the merest hesitation? "He worked very hard. He was a good lawyer, he knew what he was doing all the time. That is, he knew the law—no, he *understood* the law. Do you know what I mean?"

"I think so. Do you mean that he hadn't just memorized a bunch of rules, he understood how the law could be used to advantage?"

Tasha smiled. "Yes, exactly. That is exactly what I mean. When you combine that with his ability to analyze, you can see he was a very valuable person." She gestured at Betsy to write that down.

Betsy did, then asked, "Did you like him?"

Again that brief hesitation. "It was more that I admired

him. He was very . . . focused on his work. He liked everything to be done exactly right." She raised her chin. "I was the secretary who lasted the longest with him because I could be as . . . correct, I think that is the word, in my work as he was in his."

"Perhaps 'accurate' is the word you want."

Tasha thought about that. "Yes, I believe you are right."

"Did you like working for him?"

"Yes." A firm nod. "He was pleasant and did not lose his temper, or not very often. He was going to be a partner in this law firm, and he said I could still be his secretary when that happened. I was looking forward to that." She added, confidentially, "Secretary to a partner in a law firm, that is a good position." She nodded. "More money, too, that would be nice. He said I would have a raise."

"Was he an easy boss?"

"No, not at all." But Tasha didn't think that a negative. "He was proud of me, he would brag about me, he would say, 'Here is a woman who knows how to work!'" This time her eyes lit up and her chin was very high. Then she looked out of the corner of her eyes at Betsy and laughed softly. "You don't think that is so wonderful."

"Oh, but I do! To find someone to work with who appreciates your efforts, who admires your hard work, that's always a blessing." Betsy made and note and said, "Now, I didn't know him well, but I have gathered that he could be difficult, because he had strong feelings about how things should be done, and preferred things to be done his way. He would get . . . unhappy when he couldn't get others to agree to go along with him."

"Well, yes, but that was because he was so very intelligent, and so was pretty generally right." Tasha frowned and shifted position slightly. "He was a good man, very talented," she said, taking the edge off his being difficult. "But perhaps not patient."

"I understand why you would think well of him. You must have been a good match for him."

She nodded proudly. "Yes, I was." Then her face went sad. "I will miss him."

"I'm sure of that, too. Will you be able to stay on here at the law firm?"

"I don't know yet. I don't even know if I want to."

Taking the opening, Betsy asked, "Did John Nye have any enemies here at Hanson, Wellborn, and Smith?"

Tasha looked scandalized. "That is not a nice question!"

"Murder is not nice."

She frowned. "You are right there, certainly." She shifted uncomfortably, then said with firmness, "But I am sure no one at this place would have ever, *ever* thought to murder Mr. Nye. Such an idea is ridiculous."

"I understand that John's superior here was Mr. David Shaker. Did you know him?"

"Of course I know him. I see him—I saw him every day, or nearly every day."

"Did he and John get along?"

"Of course they did. Mostly."

"Were they friends?"

She hesitated. "I don't think I should say that. They had a . . . professional relationship. Very correct. Mr. Shaker is a partner, after all, and John was a senior associate, but still . . . only an associate."

"How long had John worked here?"

"I don't know. I was hired five years ago, and I worked for

a year for two new attorneys, then for Mr. Nye and Preston
Marson. Mr. Marson quit a year ago and I have worked just
for John ever since. I have heard that Mr. Nye's work was always very good. I remember it was only a few weeks ago
that Mr. Kedge, who is a *managing partner*—" she said that
title with awe—"said to Mr. Nye, right in front of me, that
he never knew anyone who understood the law on executive
compensation as well as he did." Tasha inhaled, basking in
the reflected glory of that moment.

"Was Mr. Kedge a friend of Mr. Nye's?"

"Not really. Mr. Kedge is—" Tasha lifted her hand over
her head, palm down, and again spoke with awe—"a *managing partner*. He is also the nephew of Mr. Wellborn, who is
retired. I could see his compliment made Mr. Nye sure he
would be made a partner very soon."

"How about Mr. Shaker—he's a partner—did he get
along with Mr. Kedge?"

Tasha shrugged. "That is far outside my area."

"I understand," said Betsy. "I'm not asking you to make
an official report. Nor am I a police investigator or even a li-
censed private eye who will make an official report. I'm asking as a private citizen, as a friend of Mr. Nye's very dear
friend, who is innocent of murder yet sits in jail, his future
in the balance. Please, won't you help me find out who really
murdered your boss?"

She wavered, but then stiffened her spine and said, "I
don't want to repeat gossip. I don't know, myself, if those
two might have been friends or not." She unbent enough to
add, "Of course I want to know who murdered Mr. Nye.
I want the murderer caught and sent to prison. But I still
think it is the responsibility of the police to discover that."

"Well, I want to help the police, if I can," said Betsy, closing her notebook. "Thank you for taking the time to talk with me."

"You are quite welcome."

Tasha led Betsy out into the hall and started for the lobby.

"Betsy!" called a voice. They both turned. Susan Lavery, tall and slim in something pale green, her improbably-red hair a flame on top, waved at her.

"Why, Susan!" said Betsy. "I didn't know you worked here!"

"Ms. Lavery," said Tasha in greeting.

"Tasha," replied Susan. Which meant Susan was not a fellow secretary.

"Are you an attorney?" asked Betsy.

"Yes, ma'am," said Susan. "I don't suppose I mentioned that when I came into your place for stitching materials."

"Probably not," said Betsy.

"Are you here seeking legal advice?"

"No, I'm investigating the murder of John Nye, helping Godwin's defense, I hope."

"She's doing private investigator work for Marvin Lebowski," noted Tasha.

"Hiring the big gun, I see," said Susan in her dry drawl.

"I want the best for Godwin," said Betsy.

"Yes, I was startled to hear he'd been charged with the murder. I know you think the world of him. Are you on your way in, or out?"

"She was just leaving," said Tasha.

"Would you like a cup of coffee before you go?"

"Thank you, I would love a cup of coffee."

Susan made a detour to a break room for two mugs of coffee. Betsy picked the decaf variety and doctored it with almond-flavored creamer and Splenda sweetener. Out of Tasha's hearing, Susan said, "What's up?"

"I'm trying to learn more about John. Tasha was his secretary, but she isn't much of a gossip."

Susan looked at Betsy out of large eyes the exact green color of her suit. "I am. Follow me."

They stopped in Susan's cluttered office, where they found her officemate tapping at his computer. "Just passing through," said Susan. She sat at her own computer and clicked through several screens. "Here we go. I'll be in Conference J, Chris."

"Uh huh," he said absently.

When they were comfortably seated in a very small conference room furnished entirely in shades of garnet except for the table, Betsy said, "What do you know about Tasha?"

"Not a whole lot. She's polite, correct in her dealings— she's kind of class-conscious, did you notice that?"

"Yes. I suppose that's a question to be asked: How rigid is the caste system in this place?"

"If I tell you that Tasha is completely in her element here, does that answer your question?"

Betsy laughed and opened her notebook. Susan had fetched their coffee herself; she evidently was not a supporter of the caste system. Betsy said, "Tasha used words like 'polite' and 'correct' and 'professional' to describe the relationship between John and David Shaker—was he John's boss?"

"Boss is not the right term. Superior, supervisor, those are closer. And only until John made partner."

"Anyway, she didn't say 'friendly' once. Is that significant?"

"Oh, yes. There was bad blood between John and David. What did Tasha tell you about David?"

"Nothing, really. Except that he's a partner."

"She didn't mention the big fight they had in John's office the day before he was found dead?"

Betsy hauled her sagging jaw back into place. "No, she didn't." Then she recalled the silence of John's office and asked, "How did you come to overhear it?"

"Overhear? I didn't overhear anything!" Susan laughed. "I just saw things I've seen before. David Shaker is the company pit bull. He can be obsequious, sweet, or enraged, depending on the situation, and what you see of him depends on where you stand in the upper echelon's opinion. They send David out to do their dirty work. He is really good at lighting fires under attorneys, and he doesn't mind if people don't like him. He's not the best attorney in the world, and there are people who think he's a partner because he has the goods on several other partners." She paused to take a drink of her coffee and look out the window. "Is it as warm out as it looks?"

"Yes, a beautiful day out there."

"I'll have to take Liam for a walk when I get home. They grow up so fast—he's going to be eight in just another month." She blinked and returned her attention to Betsy. "Where was I?"

"Telling me how you know Mr. Shaker and Mr. Nye had a fight."

"Oh, yes. Well, for one thing, when David's been reaming someone out, he walks like . . . like Popeye the Sailor." Susan lifted her arms straight out from her shoulders, then bent her elbows so her hands hung straight down. She moved her upper torso back and forth and smiled with only one side of her mouth.

Betsy laughed. "Come on, he does not!"

Susan laughed, too, and brought her arms down. "All

right, not as obvious as that. But he does have this cocky walk he does after he's laid into someone. Sometimes he even whistles. And last Thursday morning, he came out of John's office just like that. Whistling 'Mexican Hat Dance,' I think—did you know John went on vacation to Mexico a couple of weeks ago?"

"Yes. Goddy took him. They had a great time."

Susan twinkled at her. "That's what you think."

Betsy frowned. "What do you mean? Godwin told me in so many words, they had a great time. And John's brother, Charlie, told me John raved about the Museum of Anthropology they toured down there."

"John whined to Dick Kennison—those two went to college together and came to Hanson Wellborn at the same time and they're good friends. But Dick is a gossip, and he said John whined to him that he didn't like Mexico City. It's too big, it's too dirty, the air is thin and smells funny, there's no ocean . . ." Susan was counting on her fingers. She paused to think, bending one long, white finger back until Betsy feared it would come out of its socket. "Oh, the hotel was third-rate, and full of school children who ran wild while their teachers danced in the lobby."

Betsy, writing frantically, said, "Teachers dancing in the lobby? Godwin never mentioned any of this."

"No? Maybe he was having too much fun trying to learn the steps. Bill said John said something to that effect. Oh, and also that Godwin took to flirting with the native guide he hired."

"Native guide? Oh, that must be the taxi driver. Godwin said he was a hoot, and really knew the city well, took them everywhere."

Susan closed her eyes and shook her head, evidently

imitating Bill imitating John. "Tacky, the man was *tacky*.
He was short and pudgy, he wore double-knit fabrics, and
his cab smelled of cigarette smoke."

Betsy was surprised into laughter. "That does sound like
John, even third-hand!" Then she sobered. "Sorry. After all,
he's dead."

But Susan was smiling, too. "That's one reason I repeated
it to you; it sounds *exactly* like John."

"How well did you know him?"

"Not all that well, but well enough. He treated me like a
paralegal, giving me scut work to do. Not that he wasn't a
very busy man." Susan frowned, trying to decide whether to
continue. She nodded abruptly and said, "It's my never-
humble opinion that he was being seriously overworked.
David was trying to spoil his chances of getting that partnership. Wanted to push him out of the firm entirely, if he
could."

"Are you sure?"

"Well . . . pretty sure."

"Why? Was it David's idea? Or someone else's? After all,
you said he was the company pit bull. Who sicced him on
John?"

Susan sat back in her chair and tapped the side of her
nose while she considered that.

"I think getting rid of John was David's own idea. I
heard this story a month ago about a conference John was
called into with a client of Mr. Kedge. David was there.
Some kind of problem had come up before the conference,
and Mr. Kedge had asked David to work on it. I don't know
what the problem was, exactly, but it involved setting up a
contingency compensation plan for a CEO. David did what
he's done before, palmed it off onto John. John came up

with a very complicated solution that, I believe, involved foreign investments. And when David tried to present the solution as his own, Mr. Kedge seemed to think something about it didn't make sense. So David said something on the order of, 'I don't understand it, either; it's something John Nye dreamed up.' Mr. Kedge said, 'Get Mr. Nye in here.' John came in and explained his idea, and Mr. Kedge said, 'Oh, is that what you meant?' and the two of them explained it to the client, who was very happy to implement it. Mr. Kedge sent John off laden with trophies, medals, and rose garlands. David tried to say John explained it to him poorly, but then said something that showed he still didn't understand it. He would have it that John deliberately didn't make it clear, but Mr. Kedge knew better. The thing was over David's head."

Betsy had been taking notes. Now she asked, "How sure are you that what you're telling me is really what happened?"

"Well, it's a funny thing, but some of the research done into that little problem of Mr. Kedge's—" she raised an eyebrow—"I did myself. Now I am willing to admit I don't understand what John was getting at myself. And neither does his little Russian secretary, who typed up the thirty-page memo on it. But John did—and so did Mr. Kedge."

"And David Shaker didn't."

"That's right—or that's what I understand. David won't lose his position over this. He's a partner, after all. And he's damn useful to Hanson Wellborn. But he hates John's guts for showing him up like that, especially in front of a client. Well, that is, he hated John's guts. And he had some kind of confrontation with him the day before John died."

Nineteen

❖ ❖ ❖

Bᴇᴛsʏ looked back at all the information she'd gotten from Susan and said, "I would like to know if you'd do me a really big favor."

"You want me to poke around and see what else I can learn," said Susan promptly.

The offer took Betsy's breath away. She hadn't dared ask so great a favor. On the other hand, she grabbed it quickly now that it was offered. "But if it will get you in trouble—" she began.

"Oh, I'm in pretty deep already. In fact, I updated my resumé a few weeks ago and put it into circulation. I'm not cut out for corporate law. I'm going to try for the county prosecutor's office. Failing that, public defender. Or maybe I'll get out of law entirely. It's a heartbreaker of a profession."

"With your attitude and nose for information, you'd be great in any kind of investigative business, newspaper reporting, maybe, or private investigations," said Betsy. "Or anything you'd care to turn your hand to."

"Why, thank you, ma'am," said Susan—Betsy understood by now that "ma'am" was just a kind of nickname Susan used. Like men used to say "pal". "Meanwhile, I'll be your mole."

"Keep track of your hours," said Betsy. "I can pay you for this."

"I ought to say, no, thank you, I'll do it for the love of it—but thank you. Because if they catch me, I'll be out on my ear with no references, and I've got a child to support." They negotiated a bit, and finally agreed on an hourly fee that both could live with.

"Now," said Betsy, "I'll ask another favor that, I hope, is less difficult."

"Name it."

"Can I meet David Shaker? Even just for a minute?"

"I think I can arrange that." She stood. "Come on, follow me."

She led Betsy up one corridor and down another, finally stopping at a door like many, of red-brown wood, with a name printed in black on an ivory board that slid into a holder—a reminder, perhaps, that while the door was to last, the occupant of the office might not.

They went in, to find a lovely little outer office furnished in deep green leather and richly grained oak. The secretary behind her desk was a well-groomed fiftyish woman of slender build and a cool, competent gaze.

"Hi, Stormy," said Susan. Betsy blinked in surprise. Stormy? People who name their babies ought to realize that one day they'll be middle-aged. This sedate, middle-aged Stormy seemed more like clear and mild.

"H'lo, Ms. Lavery," said Stormy. "Have you brought a client to see Mr. Shaker?"

"Not exactly. This is Ms. Devonshire, who is working for Mr. Marvin Lebowski. She has a couple of questions for Mr. Shaker, if he has a minute."

Stormy did not so much as raise a speculative eyebrow as she rose from her chair. "I'll just see, all right?" She opened the door to an inner office, and came back less than a minute later to say, "Will you step this way?"

Betsy could not have said beforehand what she expected to see in David Shaker—but she was surprised to see the tall, slim young man with dark hair, blue eyes, and sensitive features. He put out a large, thin hand to greet her, and she took it, noting how warm and firm it was. "Ms. Devonshire?" he said, peering deep into her eyes. "Do I know you?"

"No, sir. I'm Godwin DuLac's employer, and I'm working with Marvin Lebowski on his defense."

His hand abruptly released hers. "I see. And you think I might be of help in your quest?" His tone indicated grave doubt.

"I'm interested in the character of John Nye. You probably saw a great deal of him at work, and I'd like your opinion."

He smiled. "Certainly. He was an excellent attorney, his knowledge of the law was comprehensive, and he had a subtle intelligence that left many of us in the dust." He gestured, elbows in, hands wide with palms up, helpless against such an intellect. "His death leaves Hanson Wellborn much the poorer."

"Did you consider him a friend?"

He took a breath to reply, then his eye was caught by something behind Betsy—Susan Lavery. For the merest instant his nostrils were pinched white and his brows lowered, then he was all sweetness again. "I suppose not," he said, speaking slowly. "He kept to himself a great deal—I suppose now because he was gay, and didn't want anyone to get too near for fear they might ask about his family or something."

"You didn't know?"

"No." He shrugged. "It just never occurred to me. It should have, I suppose, no picture of the wife and kiddies on his desk, his never coming to the annual picnic given for families. But you know how it is, hindsight is always twenty-twenty."

"Was there anyone here at the company who'd quarreled with him recently?"

"You mean a really serious quarrel? No. I had words with him a day or two before he was killed, but ask around, you'll find I have words with just about everyone, sooner or later." He smiled, a very boyish and charming smile.

"Well, that's all I can think of for now. Thank you."

"You're welcome." He extended his hand again. Betsy took it and was surprised to find it chilly and damp.

Outside in the hall again, Betsy said, "Now there's an interesting personality."

"Did you catch his glance of death at me?"

"Yes, I did. Is he going to come around to shout at you?"

"Not today. Maybe not tomorrow. But before the week is out, yes." She frowned. "Or maybe not. He doesn't want to become a suspect in a murder case."

"Too late," said Betsy, and Susan laughed.

"Anything else I can do before you head out?"

"Could I meet Mr. Kedge?"

"You plunge right in and fly high," said Susan, mixing metaphors in her surprise. "But all right, let's see if we can get a minute of the old man's time."

They went into a fancier district of the company, where doors were farther apart and of a better grade of wood, and the carpet in the hallway more plush. Mr. Kedge's private secretary was frankly beautiful, her black suit costly, the solitaire diamond on her hand at least a carat and a half in size.

"Hello, Karen," said Susan. "This is Ms. Betsy Devonshire, who is looking into the death of John Nye for Marvin Lebowski. She would like just to meet Mr. Kedge, if that would be possible."

"Oh, I don't think so. He's with Mr. D'Agnosto. Though, if she could wait for just a few minutes, I think they're almost finished."

"I can wait," said Betsy. She turned to Susan. "But I've kept you from your work long enough. Thank you so much, you've been a great help to me."

"You're most entirely welcome. I'll call you this evening, all right?"

"Yes, thanks."

With a wave of her long-fingered hand, Susan left. Betsy looked around and chose a settee with what looked like antique brocade upholstery. She opened her notebook and went back over what she'd written in haste, making the writing less scribbly, occasionally putting the next of a consecutive series of numbers beside a sentence or phrase, then going to a blank page and expanding on the note.

She finished quickly, then looked up to see Karen looking at her speculatively. "Who is Mr. D'Agnosto, one of the partners here?"

"Yes, he's our signatory officer, among other things."

"What's a signatory officer?"

"He handles certain accounts. Money coming in that will be going out again, for example."

Betsy thought a moment. "You mean, when someone sues, the money isn't paid directly to the client, but goes through here."

"Yes, that's approximately correct."

"Does Mr. D'Agnosto also function as an attorney?"

"Yes, of course."

"That's interesting, that you have attorneys doing corporate functions as well as, er, lawyerly things."

"Is it? These are people who specialize in corporate law. They are very likely to understand better what they are doing, and how to do it legally, than someone with no legal training."

"Yes, of course. What does Mr. D'Agnosto specialize in as an attorney?"

"He handles the malpractice suits."

"You mean the Children's Hospital and St. Luke's?"

Karen raised an eyebrow, a little surprised at the depth of Betsy's knowledge about the firm. "Yes, that's right."

The door opened then, and two men appeared. One stayed just inside the office; he was a short man with thick, curly white hair and a three-piece suit that fit him so well it must have been custom-made. The other was about medium height, his hair almost as white, but with a hint of tan in it—he'd been a redhead when young, thought Betsy. He had the heavily-freckled and weather-beaten complexion of a fair-skinned sailor, and the deep creases around his light eyes indicated many hours of squinting against sun reflecting on water.

Karen had risen when the door opened. The sailor looked at her and she looked at Betsy and then at the short man.

The two men looked at Betsy. "This is Ms. Devonshire," said Karen. "She would like just a moment of your time, Mr. Kedge. She's working for Mr. Lebowski, investigating the circumstances of John Nye's murder."

"Really," said the short man, frowning at her.

"Well, isn't that interesting," said the sailor. "Are you Mr. Lebowski's partner in his office?"

"No, sir, I'm actually acting on behalf of Godwin DuLac, who has been charged with Mr. Nye's murder. Mr. Lebowski has been kind enough to give me official status at present, as an investigator."

"Have you a license as a private investigator?" demanded the sailor.

"No, sir. But I have helped the police in other cases. I would do this in any case, because Godwin is a dear friend and I absolutely know he did not murder Mr. Nye."

The sailor made a faint snorting sound, turned, and shook the short man's hand. "Well, I'm off to a meeting with Doctor Knopf. I think we can settle this before it goes to trial."

"Good luck," said the other. They all waited until Mr. D'Agnosto left, and then the short man came toward Betsy.

"What did you want to see me about?"

"I'm looking to talk to anyone who can tell me something about Mr. Nye," she said. "I'd met him through Godwin, but didn't really know him."

"Here, come into my office," he said quickly, then looked at his watch. "I can give you perhaps five minutes."

"Thank you."

His office was not palatial, but it was on a corner, and had two windows. He sat her in a comfortable club chair then hurried behind his desk as if anxious to put something substantial between himself and her.

Betsy said, "Did you know before this happened that John was gay?"

"Well . . . yes. It didn't interfere with his work, and he was not obvious about it, but it wasn't something generally known, and I preferred it be kept that way. So this happening was rather a blow. We have a number of very conservative clients and it's been an interesting process soothing them down."

"Why should they—" Betsy started, then shut up. It was impossible to direct peoples' feelings and prejudices, and arguing with them about it never helped.

Mr. Kedge smiled and nodded at her, reading her mind. "John was a very valuable member of Hanson, Wellborn, and Smith," he said. "He'll be sorely missed."

"I understand he came up with a solution recently to a golden parachute problem you were having. A particularly clever solution."

His brow lifted in surprise. "You've done your homework, Ms. Devonshire."

"Don't ask me any questions about the solution, and you'll not be disappointed in my homework."

He laughed, a very pleasant sound.

"On the other hand," continued Betsy, "I also understand there is a partner who was not pleased that Mr. Nye showed him up with the cleverness of the solution."

That killed the laugh dead on the spot. "What?"

"I understand that Mr. Shaker was very angry at Mr. Nye."

"Oh, that! Well, David is a valuable member, too. It's just that his talents lie in another plane than John's."

"So you didn't think he was right to be embarrassed about his failure to grasp the implications of John's work?"

"Oh, he could be embarrassed all he liked. David has a very high opinion of himself, and it's good for him to be taken down a peg or two now and then. John was going to become a partner within six months or so, and then they'd have the same status, and David could stop being uncomfortable about being pecked by someone he didn't think was his equal." Mr. Kedge's tone was dismissive of the whole matter.

"I've heard that one of Mr. Shaker's responsibilities was to 'light a fire' under employees when that was felt necessary, and that he wasn't one of the more popular partners because of that."

Mr. Kedge bit his upper lip and stared at Betsy—a very intimidating stare, which she returned as calmly as she could. He nodded once, and said, "Yes, that's true. He has a heck of a mouth on him, and he enjoys applying the lash when it's needed. Since this is a pleasure not everyone appreciates, we sometimes use him as a surrogate. But—" he pointed a stubby forefinger at her—"David could also be a sweet man. There's many a time he'd lay into someone one day and take the same person to lunch the next."

"Yes? A pity he didn't get a chance to make up with John."

"Yes. Yes, indeed, a great pity."

"What did you think of John as a person?"

Mr. Kedge leaned back in his high-backed leather chair and thought about that for a few moments. "He was personable, intelligent, clever, and charming. He worked at least as hard as any attorney here. He could be tough when it was called for, and he had drive, but there was also a human side to him I liked. I think he could have gone much further than he had, if his life hadn't been cut short."

Betsy wrote most of that down. "This is kind of a hard question to frame. There's the law, I mean like the 'letter of the law' and then there's fairness and balance and values like that. Which side was John on?"

"Well, my dear, he was a lawyer. It was his job to follow the law. Outside of his office, he might have been all for fairness, as you call it, or balance. Within this place, we're all for following the law."

"I see. I think that's all. You were kind to give me this much of your valuable time. Thank you." She stood. "Who was the sailor you were talking with before you talked to me?"

"Sailor? Oh, you mean D'Agnosto! You *are* perceptive! He is, in fact a sailor when he can find the time. His goal was to sail all seven seas, and he finished that last year."

"Does he work here, or is he a client?"

"Oh, a partner, has been for many years—almost as many as me. He handles the money as it flows in and out, and tries to dam up as much as possible on our side. He also has the unhappy job of trying to keep litigants from testifying against our clients at trial by arranging settlements. Another of those little 'letter of the law' problems we lawyers deal with." He gave her a condescending smile.

"Well, thank you again," said Betsy.

"Can you find your way out to the lobby, or shall I call for someone to guide you?"

"I can find my way. Good-bye."

Twenty

❈ ❈ ❈

Betsy went back up and across Fourth Street to the Wells Fargo Center Building where Mr. Lebowski had his office. She couldn't believe it was only 11:47, she was actually going to be a couple of minutes early for her luncheon engagement.

Yet he was waiting for her in the anteroom to his office. He seemed nervous about something. "Let's roll," he said on seeing her, but he paused to glance both ways out the door to the hallway before he hurried her out, and into the stainless steel and marble elevator going down. Once the door closed, he relaxed.

Betsy didn't. What if they ran into the person he was clearly trying to avoid down in the lobby? He hadn't seemed frightened, only a little anxious, and maybe even that was on her behalf—he was probably used to angry clients. Criminal defense attorneys had a lot of clients with a history of not handling anger issues well. Who was this one? What did he look like? What if he was waiting at the bottom? She finally dared to ask, "Who are we running from?"

"My brother. He's in town and he's a leech. He's on his way over and I don't want to take him to lunch, too."

"Oh."

Out front he hailed a cab. "The Polonaise Room, across the river on Hennepin," he said to the driver. And to Betsy, "It's a nice little Polish restaurant—have you eaten there?"

"No."

"I haven't been there in a long while, which is too bad. The food there takes me right back to my grandmother's house."

The cab turned onto Hennepin Avenue, and a couple of blocks later crossed the Mississippi on what was probably the shortest suspension bridge in the world: the two towers were a stone's throw apart. The Polonaise Room was a block further along; the cab pulled over and they got out.

It wasn't a fancy place. It had vertical white siding and a sharply angled roof that shouted, "It was remodeled in the fifties!"

The interior was from the fifties, too. The entrance led into a long bar, with booths in golden shimmery plastic along one side, and black globular lights suspended from the ceiling with knobs of colored glass in them.

"Gosh," said Betsy, suddenly feeling very young—or was it old?

The maitre d' was a stocky older man with an Eastern-European face. *"Dzien dobry!"* said Marvin, adding to Betsy, "That's Polish for hello."

The maitre d' overheard his explanation and smiled. "I am Lebanese, not Polish," he said, showing you can't judge a book by its cover. "My sons own this place. But the food is still the best Polish in town."

Marvin looked disappointed and doubtful as they were led to the dining room and seated. "Well, it looks the same," he said, looking around. The room was paneled in dark wood, with big, rectangular picture frames around black-and-red wallpaper. More of the chunky black globes hung from the ceiling. The tables and chairs were of an early version of imitation wood, with thin, black, v-shaped rods for legs. If there had been a calendar on the wall, it would have featured a wasp-waisted woman in a long, full skirt looking admiringly at a green Pontiac with tail fins. Very, very fifties.

A nice blond waitress, not at all a fifties relic, brought the menus.

"Here we are, all *right*!" said Marvin on opening it, doubts wiped away. "Look at this! Pieroges! Bigos! Golabki!"

Betsy wasn't Polish, but she grew up in Milwaukee, which has a large Polish-descent population. But the only Polish item on the menu that she recognized was kielbasa—Polish sausage, a thinner, spicier bratwurst. She'd had a good friend from junior high through high school, Marlene Sobolewski, and had dined at her friend's house about as often as Marlene had dined at hers. Kielbasa with kraut was a favorite in Marlene's house, like sloppy joes were in Betsy's.

Right there on the menu was hunter's stew—the "bigos" Marvin happily noted—a combination of kielbasa, beef, and sauerkraut. That sounded a whole lot like a meal Betsy had shared at the Sobolewski table many a time. "The Polish National Dish," said the menu, which was interesting; Betsy had thought adding kielbasa to beef was Marlene's mother's way of stretching Sunday's leftover roast beef into Monday's dinner.

Smiling in nostalgia, Betsy decided that's what she would have. Marvin ordered it, too, and a beer to drink.

While they waited, Betsy opened her notebook.

"What have you found out?" asked Marvin.

"Well, not much, I'm afraid. John may have had an enemy at his law firm: a partner named David Shaker, who was John's supervisor. Mr. Shaker is known as the company pit bull, because he's willing to confront other attorneys about their shortcomings. It seems the upper echelon at the firm are all cowards. They send him to do their dirty work, and he appears to enjoy it. He came to say some hard things to John the day before he was killed."

"So far, that's nothing to get excited about," said Marvin.

Betsy raised her right arm and waggled her hand. "I also heard that Mr. Shaker was made to appear a fool in front of a managing partner and an important client by John. John had to be called in to explain a complex legal plan he had drawn up and that Mr. Shaker was willing to claim as his own idea until he had to admit he didn't understand how it worked. Mr. Shaker was very angry and embarrassed about this. It's entirely possible he came down to talk to John about that and words were exchanged. David was supposed to work up that plan on his own, but he had been loading John with work he couldn't do himself and/or was trying to so overburden John that John would quit."

"What kind of legal plan?" asked Marvin.

"It had something to do with executive compensation, and involved foreign currencies. It was probably a way of giving someone a golden parachute. The person who told me about it did some of the research on the plan for John and said she didn't understand how the parts she looked up fit together, either. The memo on it was thirty pages long."

"Only thirty?" said Marvin, smiling. "Must have been a summary. Did this person you talked to write the memo?"

"No, it was dictated by John and typed by his secretary, Tasha Kravchenko."

"But it wasn't Tasha who told you about this?"

"No, Tasha was reluctant to say anything bad about anyone at the firm, and she was a big fan of John's. She did say John was a hard taskmaster, but that he praised her to everyone as the one secretary who could keep up with him. She was very proud of that."

"So scratch the abused secretary as a suspect."

"Oh, I'd say so, yes."

"On the other hand, there's David."

"Yes," said Betsy. "Of course, maybe he cleared his anger just shouting at John. Certainly if I became angry enough at someone to kill him, it would be because I sit in silence, nursing grudges. Especially I wouldn't go shouting at him at the office, where people might find out. On the other hand, maybe there was some further provocation." Even as she said it, Betsy was thinking that over.

Suppose that was what happened? Suppose that later John had said something to David? Like what? Well, suppose that incident Tasha had talked about, where Mr. Kedge had come in and said how wonderful John was, had happened because of this incident? And suppose John had taunted David with it?

Tasha might know. She had said something about John never shouting, or "at least not very often." Maybe Betsy needed to talk to Tasha again.

"Penny for that thought?" said Marvin, bringing Betsy back to The Polonaise Room.

"Oh, sorry, just thinking."

"About what?"

Betsy didn't want to offer a theory with that many supposes in it, so she said, "The person who told me about David and John said she's willing to act as a spy for me, see if there's anything else about John she can dig up for me."

Marvin nodded. "Very valuable, informants are."

When the food arrived, Betsy found just the smell of it sent her winging back to old times in Milwaukee. She dug in, and when, after a couple of minutes, she looked across at Marvin she saw the same look of happy nostalgia on his face.

He saw her smiling at him and said, lifting a forkload in salute, "Just like mother used to make."

Betsy said, "Where did your mother learn to cook Polish dishes?"

"From Babushka Lebowski, of course." Babushka, Betsy knew, was the Polish word for headscarf. Since older Polish women universally wore headscarves, it also meant Grandmother.

Lebowski continued, "We ate over at her house two, three times a month. Mama refused to make some of it, of course. Blood soup, I remember she wouldn't even taste it at Babushka's house. On the other hand, Daddy wouldn't touch chitterlings." He made a face. "I didn't like them, either. But greens and pot likker, black-eyed peas, corn bread and pork chops—now that was a feast!" His accent had broadened just a bit, and he smiled at her. "I got the best of both worlds, and a cholesterol number that scares my doctor."

"I believe you." Ethnic diets like these were designed to sustain men who performed grindingly hard labor in the fields, coal mines, and factories. People who sat at desks but still ate like that found their arteries clogged up.

From The Polonaise Room Betsy went back to Excelsior,

to the shop. A big shipment of books had come in and the volunteers had unpacked them and stacked them on the library table—and looked through most of them. They had been kind enough, however, to only open one of multiple copies, aware that there were customers who insisted on virgin spines. She had ordered three of Carol Phillipson's *Cross-Stitch Designs from China,* and five of Herrschner's *200+ Holiday Quickies* cross-stitch charts and projects—one of the latter was already sitting on the checkout desk for Doris to take home. Betsy herself paused to page through a copy of Barbara Baatz-Hillman's beautiful collection of cross-stitched flowers, birds, and cats. For the sword and sorcery set, there was *Cross-Stitch Myth and Magic*. There were three copies of Teresa Wentzler's lush, beautiful—and difficult—cross-stitch charts called *Christmas Collection*. The cover featured a delectable procession of six angels, so wonderful Betsy was sure she'd have to reorder that title soon.

She was relieved to see that four copies of *Stitch 'n Bitch* had arrived. This was the second time already this year she'd had to reorder this "book with attitude," and last time it had gone on back order.

She helped Nikki shelve the books, then went to call Jill at work.

"I wonder if you can do me a favor as soon as you get off."

"Probably. What's up?"

"I need to go to Vera's Coffee House in Uptown, on Lyndale. I'm looking for the young man who was at John Nye's house the day he was killed. I have his name and a description, and Goddy says he hangs out at Vera's—but he also said I should go there with a female companion."

"All right. I'll have to go home and change out of these clothes. I'll pick you up at six, okay?"

"Thanks, Jill." She hung up and ignored the inquiring glances of her employees the rest of the day.

Jill turned up at six wearing chinos, walking boots, and a flannel shirt open over a T–shirt that advertised Buzzard Billy's Armadillo Bar-N-Grillo. She had also pulled her hair back into a tight braid down her back and wiped her face clean of makeup.

Betsy looked at her own more dressy outfit of new gray sandals, light wool slacks, and a sweater, also gray. Her purse was gray, her jewelry gold.

"Should I change?" she asked.

"No, you look great."

"But you . . . uh."

"Didn't you know I'd play the butch?" Jill held up her left hand to show that she'd replaced her wedding band with a ring shaped like a horseshoe.

Betsy began to giggle, and she giggled off and on all the way into town. Jill called on all her reserves of ice to maintain her cool expression, but her eyes twinkled and one corner of her mouth twitched. Neither trusted herself to say a word, and Betsy had her giggles under control by the time Jill turned off Lake onto Lyndale.

Vera's was a modest place, one story of red brick with two big plate-glass windows. Right inside was a dilapidated couch marking the entryway. The room had a collection of tan Formica tables and brown wooden chairs. A young man sat in a corner with his laptop open and operating. A counter at the back featured a chill box with a selection of salads and sandwiches. A big menu was written on a collection of wood-framed blackboards on the wall behind it. Betsy selected a chicken salad and sparkling water; Jill ordered a sandwich on a hard roll and a double latte. They saw an open door on the side and went to look out.

Beside the building was a wooden ground-level deck open to the air. About a dozen mostly young men sat at long wooden tables down the middle and at smaller tables around the edges. An iron fence with ivy growing over it guarded the deck from the stares of passers by on the sidewalk. Two trees growing up against the rough brick wall of the neighboring store would offer shade from the summer sun, and strings of lights criss-crossed overhead, to make evening out here attractive. It looked inviting, and ordinary enough until one noticed that the men were talking only to other men, and the few women exclusively to other women.

"I see what Goddy meant," said Betsy. Jill went through the door and held it with an elbow for Betsy.

They received only perfunctory glances as they took a table in the far corner. Jill deliberately slouched in her chair, Betsy deliberately didn't. There were four other females sitting at a single table kitty-corner from them, dressed alike in jeans and long-sleeved T–shirts.

"Maybe we shouldn't have dressed so differently," said Betsy in an undertone.

"We can dress any way we please," said Jill curtly. Betsy stared at her. "Sorry, just getting into character." She took a slug of her latte.

Betsy smiled and shook her head. She looked around at the other tables. "Goddy said the guy we're looking for is a little twerp—"

"Twink," interrupted Jill.

" 'Twink'?"

"That's the current slang for a very young gay man. Not to be confused with 'tweaker,' one who uses drugs to, um, enhance performance."

"Do I want to know where you learned these things?" asked Betsy, amused.

"Probably disappoint if not bore you."

"The problem is, there are at least three twinks here. Ours is named Beni Greenleaf, and he has a home perm."

Jill looked around the space, looked at Betsy, and murmured with a grin, "That cuts it down to two, I think."

Betsy took a bite of her salad—it was delicious, with chunks of apple, and flavored with dill—and said, "Only one really bad home perm, though." A young man—a boy, really; he looked barely fifteen—was sitting with a group of five men at the long table. After a minute's observation, it was clear the other four were two couples and the boy was a hanger-on. The other four were eating, and he wasn't. Also, he was looking lonesome and unhappy. He wore very tight-fitting white jeans and a red tank top, and now that the sun was setting he looked cold, too. The boy's dirty-blond hair was mostly frizzy, except here and there a strand was straight.

"What do you think?" asked Betsy.

"I think I'll go see." Jill rose and stalked—there was no other word for it—across the deck to bend suddenly and say something to the boy. He looked startled, then smiled and shook his head. He nodded toward a table up against the iron fence where two young men were sitting.

Jill straightened to look for several moments at the pair, then said thanks—Betsy could read her lips—and went to the table.

If it had been Beni and an older man, Jill wouldn't have been able to pry them apart. But they were a duo, not a couple, and when Jill handed the one with the tight curls a bill, he nodded and went back into the coffee house.

Jill came back to Betsy and sat down. "That doesn't look like a home perm," said Betsy.

"Evidently he had it fixed professionally. He says he's Beni Greenleaf."

"Is he coming back?" Betsy asked.

"I hope so, or I'm out a twenty. If you want him to stay after he finds out who you are, put another twenty on the table."

"Did you promise him that?" asked Betsy, opening her purse.

"No."

"What did you tell him?"

"Just that you wanted to talk to him and would buy him supper if he'd agree. He said sure, so now we wait and see."

The young man came back a few minutes later carrying a paper plate and a paper bowl, with napkins hanging out of a jeans pocket. His tank top had a very rude boast printed on it. He put his food on the table and sat down.

"Are you Beni Greenleaf?" asked Betsy.

"Yeah, that's me," he said, and took a huge bite of his sandwich. After chewing awhile, he washed it down with a gulp of soup. "Who are you?"

"My name is Betsy Devonshire, and I'm a friend of Godwin DuLac."

He nodded several times, then froze. "Uh oh." Betsy was afraid he was going to get up and leave, but he only took another big bite. His eyes flickered from Betsy to Jill to the twenty on the table and back again.

Jill shook her head. "No," she said quietly. "No hag fags, no badges."

"Oh. Okay. How did you know to look here for me?"

"Godwin told me," said Betsy.

"How's Goddy doin'?" asked the boy.

"He's just fine," said Betsy.

"So they let him go, huh?"

"No, not yet. I suppose the police talked to you already?"

"Oh, yeah. But I told 'em it wasn't me. Good thing they believed me, huh? Or I'd be the one in the orange jump-suit." He seemed pretty snotty about it.

"Goddy didn't do it," said Betsy. "So to help him, I'm looking for the one who did."

His eyes widened in alarm. "Now just one freakin' minute!"

Jill said, "Tell us all about it, so we can think you didn't do it, either."

He studied her face, then nodded. "Sure," he said, but grudgingly, and picked up a fat pinch of potato chips that took a few seconds to work into his mouth.

Betsy said, "First, I want to talk to you about your relationship with John Nye."

He swallowed and said, "What relationship? We met in person twice, once here and once at his house. I thought we were getting along fine, but it's bing, bang, boom, here's cab fare, go home."

"What do you think made him change his mind?"

"How should I know? Maybe he didn't like—" He suddenly realized he didn't know how to finish that sentence without offense. "Me," he concluded lamely.

"How did you meet?" asked Betsy.

"On the Internet. I'm surfing at a cyber café and he's putting out a line and I bit. We e-mail back and forth for awhile, he seems hot but nice, so we set up a meet here. He still seems nice, old but not a geezer, got some bucks, not a muscle Mary, not a gym bunny. He's clean, I'm clean." Beni shrugged. "So he goes, 'Why not come out to my place,' and I'm like, 'Great.'"

"How long were you out there?"

He frowned at her, then a sly smile appeared.

"Looking for the gory details, huh?"

"Not for all the tea in China," Betsy assured him. "I want to know how long you were out there, what you talked about other than the obvious, and why you didn't stay the night."

"I was out there from sometime around six til probably eight-thirty, nine. Then I go to the toilet and when I come out, he's holding my clothes in his hands and he says, 'That's it, I'm sending you home.' I'm like, 'Why?' and he goes, 'None of your business, get dressed. I already called a cab.'"

"Did he get a phone call?" asked Betsy.

"I didn't hear it if he did, but—" He shrugged and tugged an earlobe. "Can't hear the ring when the water's running."

"How much did he pay you?"

He feigned a look of shock very badly. *"What?"*

"He gave you money before you left. How much was it?"

He put on a sulky face. "Two hundred."

"Was that agreed on ahead of time?"

His look of shock was genuine now. "No, of course not! I'm not one of *those*!"

"Did you murder him?"

"No!" He couldn't look any more shocked than he did already, but now it was overlaid with fear.

"Where did you go after you left John's house?"

"I went to a friend's house."

"The friend have a name?"

He nodded. "Miguel Alvarado." He gave a phone number.

"That's his cell, he's moved out since I stayed there, I don't know where he's staying now."

"Did you spend the night?"

"Sure. I brought a bottle so we had a little party." He grinned. "I think that's what got him tossed out, it kind of turned into a big party."

"Any arrests?" asked Jill.

He cocked a suspicious eye at her, but she did her trick of absorbing his look while giving nothing back and after a moment he shrugged. "No, though the cops did come by. My friend told them I was a co-host, so they took my name."

"All right, thank you for talking with me," said Betsy. "You've been very helpful."

"Yeah, yeah, well, thanks for the soup and sandwich." He reached for the twenty and tucked it, not without effort, into a jeans pocket, picked up his plate and bowl and walked away, trying for some kind of attitude.

Jill smiled at Betsy and shook her head. "You did all right, kid. Can we go home now?"

Twenty-one

❖ ❖ ❖

BETSY worked in her shop all the next day, finding pleasure and relief in just doing the everyday shopowner things. She dealt happily with difficult customers, put disarranged stock back in place without complaint, checked sales slips for errors, and talked with her employees and the Monday Bunch volunteers.

Late in the afternoon, Mrs. Phelps came in with a knitting problem. She was a middle-aged woman, tall and commanding, who had come to knitting late in life. She was doing her first sweater with a Norwegian pattern, in six colors.

"I'm tired of all those bobbins in the back," she complained. "They clatter around, they twist around one another, and they make an uncomfortable pile in my lap. Any other suggestions?"

Betsy took the almost-finished sweater—Mrs. Phelps had started at the bottom and the many-colored part was the yoke at the top—and said, "You're always going to have a problem when you're doing multicolored patterns. If you don't use bobbins, then the yarn will tangle. What I don't like is a pattern like this, that uses three stitches of one color here, and again over here, then doesn't use it again until up around the neckline. This one does it with several colors, so you'll wind up with these long lines of yarn across the underside, that will snag the fingers of the person putting them on."

"I always look my patterns over so I don't wind up with lots of colors of yarn," said Nikki, unhelpfully. "Because what can you do?"

"Well," said Betsy, "here's something Carolyn Potts taught me at CATS when it was here a few years ago. When you're knitting, catch up the yarn behind." She put a strand of yarn down the back of Mrs. Phelps's sweater. "Like this." She showed how to knit the yarn into the back of the piece so that it didn't show on the front. "Just tack it down like that as you go along."

"Well, I'll be," said Mrs. Phelps. "You learn something new every day."

Betsy pulled the loose piece of yarn out. Mrs. Phelps was so pleased, she bought another multicolored pattern, this time of a sleeveless argyle sweater, and the yarn needed to knit it.

An hour later, the shop closed. They went through the closing-up routine, washing out the coffee urn, unplugging the tea kettle, turning out lights, taking eighty dollars in start-up money out of the register for tomorrow. Betsy sent Nikki with the day's earnings to the bank, and went upstairs to give Sophie her evening scoop of diet cat food, then sink onto her couch and not think about anything for awhile.

That lasted until her stomach growled hungrily. She went into the kitchen—and saw the message light on her phone blinking. She picked it up, dialed star and two numbers, then punched in her code number. "First message," said the recorded voice, and then Goddy's: "Hi, Betsy, hope you're not there to answer this because you're out running down a hot clue! How are things? Call me tomorrow during working hours, okay? Or better, come to see me. Oh, and could you bring me some money? Twenty will do. I need commissary things. Thanks."

She turned to her refrigerator and wrote herself a note, then punched seven to erase the message. "Next message, sent . . . today," said the hesitating recording, searching among options, "at . . . four . . twenty . . . pee-emm."

"Hello, Betsy," said Charlie's cheerful voice. "I want to know if I can have another go at Johnny's hard drive. I hope he kept his bank records on there, and also information on his stock portfolio. What I'm finding at his house doesn't correspond with what his bank is telling me. By the way, I found something in his safe deposit box that you'll be interested in. If I'm not at Hower House, you can leave a message there for me."

Betsy erased that one, too, then found the number for the bed and breakfast and dialed it. The manager cheerfully took a message for Charles Nye. He was even cheerful about not knowing when Charlie would be back.

Betsy opened her last can of soup and sliced a tomato onto a plate for her supper.

Then she called Susan Lavery at home. "How's it going?" she asked.

"These people are the most careless people in the world!" Susan crowed. "You would not believe how much stuff they leave on their computers with no protection at all from prying eyes like mine. It's the senior partners who are the worst; when forced to use a password, about three-quarters of the time it's 'password,' and the other quarter it's their first or last name. They seem to have the notion that when information is in electronic form instead of on paper, it's invisible." She snickered.

"Susan, for heaven's sake, be careful! If you go wading through other peoples' computers, someone is going to notice!"

"Not these people. And what will they do if they find out?" she asked in her signature dry drawl. "Fire me? I gave my two weeks' notice this morning."

"Quitting can still net you references; being fired won't," warned Betsy.

"Are you kidding? I now know where so many bodies are buried, they'll give me sparkling references—or else."

That turned Betsy's fear into curiosity instantly. "What bodies? Have you got something I can use?"

"Well . . . not exactly. Not yet, anyway. But something's rotten in the financial department, I think. Mr. D'Agnosto has been careless about his record keeping—or crooked, and I think it's the latter. He's also copied a *lot* of information from the accounting department's files."

"D'Agnosto, why does that sound familiar?"

"I don't know, I didn't take you to his office, only David Shaker's and Walter Kedge's."

"Oh, right, he was talking to Mr. Kedge, remember? Mr. Kedge's secretary said so."

"Yes, that's right."

"I saw him come out while I was waiting. Tall man, used to be a redhead, he's freckled all over."

"That's our boy. He ought to have a pegleg and a parrot on his shoulder, I think he's some kind of pirate."

"What do you mean?"

"I mean he's keeping two sets of books, maybe. Or he's found some way to cook the originals."

"Pirates don't go in for bookkeeping, they just swarm onto your ship with knives and take things."

"So cancel the pirate image. I still think he's double dealing."

"How? I mean both how do you know, and how is he doing it?"

"I don't know how he's doing it, but I'm sure he is. There's no reason for him to have that much information, even as the official check signer. And it's the only part of his computer material that's hidden behind a password. I'm going to find out more."

"Is he being shady, or is he really doing something illegal?"

"Illegal, definitely."

"Then shouldn't you tell the police?"

"I don't have any real evidence yet. But I will, I will." She was crooning with happiness.

"Now hold on a second. What connection does all this have with John Nye?"

"Oh. None at all that I know of. I don't think John and D'Agnosto ever so much as had lunch together."

"Then stop turning over rocks that don't concern you! I need you to find out who at Hanson Wellborn had a motive to murder John."

"But this does concern me. At least for the next two weeks it concerns me. I work here, remember?"

"Susan, for the love of justice, please. I hired you to help me find someone with a motive to murder John."

"Yes, but—oh, all right. I was going to say this is more fun, because it is, but I get your point. Very well, Mr. D'Agnosto can go on skimming the company profits for a little while longer. I'll go back to looking for people who thought of John Nye as a deadly enemy."

"Thank you."

Betsy had no more than hung up when the phone rang. "Hello?" she said.

"Hello, Ms. Devonshire, it's Charlie Nye."

"Hi, I got your message. You can come over anytime."

"Is it too late to come over right now?"

"No, of course not."

"Good, I'll be there in about ten minutes."

He was as good as his word. He came up the stairs flushed with excitement, a big brown envelope in one hand, attaché case in the other. Inside her apartment, he went to the dining nook and spilled the envelope's contents on the table. "Look at this!" he said. "It was in John's safe deposit box."

There was a man's brown leather wallet, separated from its contents: a Social Security card, driver's license, ATM card with a logo identifying it as from a First Wisconsin bank, and sixty-three dollars in cash. The photograph on the driver's license was recognizable as John's.

"Notice there are no credit cards," said Charlie.

"Is that significant?"

"It probably means he couldn't get a credit card—no credit rating. No work history, no job. He didn't own any property, not even a car. Never bought anything on time. He did rent a small apartment in Rush—and look at this." He picked up a small rectangle of paper Betsy hadn't noticed. It was a scrap of newspaper, a want ad that began: *Two Blocks from Lake Winnebago!* and offering a vacant lot for sale.

"I don't get it, was he going to move away?"

"Eventually. I think he was going to work some more on this new identity. Buy some land, pay cash, then put a manufactured home on it. Then mortgage the property, make regular payments, construct a credit rating. Pay property taxes, buy a car."

"But . . . why? I mean, why did he have this need to become someone else?"

"I have no idea."

"He couldn't practice as a lawyer; Christopher Bright doesn't have a law degree."

"I know. I don't know what he meant to do. Maybe buy one of those degrees from a mill. Not a law degree, but a bachelor's degree in something." He tossed the scrap of paper down, and shook his head. "He had a great job, he was doing really well—wasn't he? You've been poking around, have you talked to people at his law firm?"

"Yes." Betsy nodded. "He and his supervisor weren't getting along, but no one gets along with David Shaker. John had a good reputation, he was definitely close to making partner. One of the reasons Mr. Shaker didn't like him was because John was a lot smarter and more clever than he was."

Charlie smiled. "Johnny never was one to hide his light under a bushel." He wiped the top of his head with one hand. "But if he was about to make partner, then Shaker was not a threat. So why quit? Why quit the law?"

"It's possible he knew something about financial illegalities at the firm. My spy there says at least one partner was cooking the books—or at least she suspects he was, she's still digging for proof. Why don't you go look on his hard drive and see if anything turns up there to show he knew about it?"

"Or was involved in? I can't believe he'd take part in something like that. But if he knew, and was afraid of the consequences of knowing . . ."

"Yes, that would explain this Christopher Bright business, wouldn't it?" said Betsy. A troubling thought—especially with Susan Lavery poking her long white fingers into the secret places of that same firm.

Charlie had also brought his own laptop. It nested in his attaché case, atop a stack of papers. "With your permission, I'll attach that hard drive to my own computer."

"Fine. Will you need to go on-line?"

"No, or at least not for awhile."

"Good, I need to make a phone call."

But when Betsy dialed Susan's number the line was busy—and it stayed busy. That most likely meant Susan was on the Internet. Betsy wondered what line she was investigating and prayed it wasn't something that might endanger her life, as it had ended John Nye's.

Twenty-two

�֍ ✤ ✤

CHARLIE said he was sorry he'd taken so long, but he didn't seem particularly sorry, perhaps because he had gotten some more account numbers and some figures that were more in line with what John's two banks had told him. He left with a cheery "So long, I'll call you tomorrow, if that's okay."

"Certainly," she replied, and shut the door after him.

She felt restless, and made a cup of tea which she had with a cookie. She was so distracted, she actually gave Sophie a fragment.

She tried calling Susan again, but her line was still busy. At last she sat down with the one thing she had found always soothed her: knitting. The entrelac pattern took all her concentration and after an hour of it she felt calm enough to go to bed.

The next morning she rose very early and drove into

Golden Valley for water aerobics. The streets were wet, though it wasn't raining, and there was a small buildup of traffic as she neared the Highway 100/394 interchange. As she pulled into the sunken parking lot on the west side of the building, her headlights swept over a red fox. The creature was looking back over its shoulder at her, unafraid. She found a slot (most of the slots in the lot were restricted to handicapped drivers), got out and peered around in the faint light, but the fox was gone. Had it been an illusion?

In the locker room she greeted her fellow early birds, and mentioned the fox.

"Oh, did you see him this morning?" asked Jackie.

"You mean there really was a fox there this morning?"

"I didn't see him this morning, but I've seen him other mornings. He doesn't run, he just kind of fades into the bushes."

"I know, that's what made me think my eyes were deceiving me. If he'd taken off up the hill, I would've known he was real."

"Sly as a fox, I guess," said someone behind Betsy.

She turned to see Barbara, a tall woman with a serene face and a lot of allergies.

"Yes, very appropriate," agreed Betsy. "Have you seen him?"

"Strangely enough, no."

Betsy tried to work off some of her frustration by pushing herself through the routines, and was thinking pretty well of herself until she caught a glimpse of Trisha, a young marathoner who did every movement faster and harder even than the instructor—and without breathing hard.

When they all grabbed a "noodle," a Styrofoam stick

about three inches in diameter and four feet long, and headed out to the deep end, riding them like horses, Betsy again tried to lose herself in the repetitions, but the only part that worked for her was the thirty seconds right at the end when the music changed to a thoughtful Indian pipe and they all shifted the noodle to under their arms and hung still in the water.

Betsy hated for that part to end, when they had to go back to the shallow end and do stretches before heading for the showers. She would have liked to just hang there all morning.

Instead, she slipped into the heavy morning traffic heading downtown, found a space in a parking ramp, and went into the extensive "skyway" system that went between buildings. She managed to get lost twice before she found a box of printed maps, took one, and sat down in a little café to have a cup of coffee and a bagel while she read the morning *Star Tribune.* Called the "Strib" by locals, it served even more than the coffee to stir Betsy's blood. She snorted at an editorial and turned to the funnies.

They lasted until it was time to go over to the jail. She left forty dollars in cash at the front desk for Godwin, for which she prudently took a receipt, then went up to the depressing little room to wait for him.

His appearance didn't help. "What's the matter?" she demanded, once he was seated and had picked up the telephone receiver on his side.

"Nothing," he said mournfully.

"Goddy . . ."

He rolled sad eyes at her. "I'm sorry, but I miss my stitching. They won't let me knit or do needlepoint and my fingers are getting all soft and lazy. It's going to take me weeks to get them back." He held up one hand and twiddled the fingers. "See?"

"Poor fellow," she said, and meant it, though his fingers looked as slim and flexible as ever. Needlework was pleasure and relaxation and meditation and even a form of exercise for Godwin. It kept his fingers nimble, his vision sharp, and his brain alert.

"That book you suggested we order, on rediscovering crewel? You were right, we should have ordered four copies. We're sold out already." Talking shop helped, and after ten minutes of business and gossip he was in a better frame of mind.

"I've been talking to someone over at Hanson, Wellborn, and Smith," she said. "And I'm afraid she says John didn't have a good time in Mexico City."

"Did John tell her that?" Godwin seemed sincerely surprised.

"John told a friend name Dick Kennison—do you know him?"

"I've met him a couple of times. He and John went to law school together."

"That's right. Anyway, Dick is a gossip, and he told Susan—she's my source at Hanson Wellborn—that John whined to her about the trip." Betsy found the page in her notebook. "He said Mexico City was too big, too dirty, smells funny, and has thin air."

Godwin looked stricken. "He did say things like that, but not like he was angry about it."

"Did he also complain about children running around the hotel while their teachers danced in the lobby?"

"Now just a minute, that was a nice thing! The kids were part of that children's government thing, you know, like we have here, where kids take over the city government for a day. Down there it's called, let me think, *Parlimento de Los Ninos y Las Ninas de Mexico.* A real big deal for the children, and the teachers had this reception for the child elected governor or president or whatever it was. They had these paper shakers, like pom poms, and they sang and danced in the lobby. It was like a line dance, only in a circle." Godwin took the receiver away from his ear to move his hands back and forth, then in a circle, tilting his torso from side to side. Then he resumed. "The kids got to stay overnight, and they were pretty well behaved, considering. All I remember John complaining about were the balloons. There were thousands of them, stuck to walls and making big twisted chains all over the place. Balloons in that quantity smell, did you know that? But it was only in the lobby, and John never spent more than three minutes in the lobby. I did, I was trying to learn that dance the teachers were doing." He moved his hands again, looking over his left then right shoulder.

Then he stopped and said, "What else didn't he like? If you say the museum or the pyramids at Teotihuacan I will scream, I promise you. Because he said he loved them."

"No, the last thing he complained about was your native guide." When Godwin looked puzzled, she said, "The taxi driver."

"Mario? Oh, my God, how could he not like Mario! Mario took us everywhere, he told funny stories, he was the nicest taxi driver I've ever met!"

Again Betsy consulted her notes. "He was short and pudgy, he wore double-knit fabrics, and his cab smelled of cigarette smoke. In a word, he was tacky."

For just two seconds Godwin's face twisted in anger. "That *beast*! Mario was sweet and he worked very hard for us! I *liked* him, I don't *care* what John says, he was *sweet*!" Godwin paused to take several calming breaths. "All right, I won't deny his English wasn't the best. And he tended to scratch where it itched." He giggled, then shrugged sadly. "Actually, I thought John hardly noticed him; he is a bit that way around servants. Oh, Betsy, here I was comforting myself thinking I gave John some of his happiest days there at the end." He dropped the receiver, put his head down on the little shelf on his side and wept.

She couldn't reach him, she could only let him have all the time for that he needed, and it was several minutes before he pulled himself back together and sat up.

"I'm sorry, wasting time with this. Now I wonder if he didn't like that one night club we went to."

"What happened there?"

"Well, we'd gone to a couple of loud party-night ones and we both were a little tired, so I talked to the concierge and he gave me a list of three quieter places. Mario said we'd like this one only a couple of blocks away. 'There is a guitar player who is so *marvelous*!' he said. So we went. It was a small place, with this little, little stage, and a man came out in shirt-sleeves with an acoustic guitar, sat down, and played—what's it called? Flamenco, that's it. I'm not a flamenco fan, but it was interesting just to watch him. His fingers were flying up and down the neck and he played with all the fingers of his other hand, but his face was very still. And after awhile—" Godwin's voice dropped and he half-covered the receiver with his hand—"it was like he was making love to the guitar. His face got—oh, I can't describe it, but I've seen it often enough. You know, the upper lip, and the eyes . . . And later,

John—" He cut himself off with a gesture. "*Anyway,* I liked it, and I still think John liked it, too."

"You should write for a travel magazine," said Betsy. "That was a beautiful description, Goddy, I almost feel like I was there with you."

"Really?" He brightened at that. "Thank you!"

"Now, on another topic entirely, I'm having trouble with the entrelac pattern I'm knitting."

"What kind of trouble?"

She tried to explain it, but soon he was lost in its complexities. "That's all right, I'll call Rosemary today, she can tell me what I'm doing wrong."

He looked sad again, so she said, "If they won't let you knit for real, try visualizing knitting."

"Visualizing?"

"Yes, when you get back to that quad, lie down and close your eyes. Think about holding your needles—"

"What size?" he said, eyes already closed.

"Fives. You're making me a pair of socks. You want to put beads in the cuffs."

"What color?"

"Oh, I don't know—yes, I do, purple yarn and iridescent pink beads. You want them kind of lacy around the edges. Do you do scallop edges on the cuffs, or little hanging rows of beads?"

His hands began to move. "Scallop edges, they're more fun. With a row of beads above the scallops, and then another row, offset, above that." His head cocked sideways. "*Lacy* scallops, that would be nice." His fingers moved for awhile, then his eyes opened and he smiled at her. "Thanks, boss, that really helped. I'll make you those socks when I get out of here."

"Deal," she said.

On the drive back to her shop, she wondered what she would find there. Though she tried hard not to be superstitious, she tended to look for omens. The water exercise hadn't been great—though that glimpse of the fox looking over his shoulder in the pre-dawn light had been nice. Or was it mysterious? Was mystery to be her portion today? Godwin had started out glum, then had turned bitter and sad, even angry, on learning how John had not enjoyed the trip he'd been so proud to take him on—the cheesy bastard!—but then had been cheered by her suggestion that he imagine knitting in lieu of the real thing. By all that, she was going to have a very mixed day.

She hoped Godwin wouldn't actually knit her a pair of purple socks. If he did, he'd expect her to wear them, and she'd have to buy some purple slacks—and then everyone would be asking her where her red hat was. Gray, now, with pink beads, that would be nice. She'd only said purple because it was easier to imagine purple yarn.

Lacy scallops, hmmmm . . .

A horn brought her back to herself. The light at Route Seven and 101 was green. She drove through and continued up Seven. Maybe dark green if he didn't want to work in gray. Or white with red and blue beads, for the Fourth of July.

The shop was in good order. Two Monday Bunch volunteers were helping Peggy, who was retired and only worked enough hours in the shop to pay for her needlework materials, and Nikki.

"Now, you go right on upstairs and draw some deductions," Peggy ordered, and the others seconded that heartily.

She went up to find her cat weaving impatiently by the door. Betsy had not come back from aerobics, and so the cat had not been taken down to the shop. Denied her opportunity to cadge snacks from chance customers, the cat was in no mood to be placated by a stroke or two.

"I don't suppose you'd believe me if I said it was Sunday, old girl," said Betsy. Sunday in Excelsior was observed by all the shops, and was the one day when Sophie stuck to—or was stuck on—her diet. Betsy took her downstairs, where she was greeted with glad cries and immediately given a small piece of cookie. Betsy pretended not to see that, and went back upstairs.

It was close enough to lunchtime that Betsy went into the kitchen—and discovered there was nothing to be eaten but a dry-looking orange and some wilted lettuce.

She grabbed her purse and went out.

Not directly to the grocery store, but first up to the Waterfront Café. Buying groceries while hungry was a sure recipe for excess spending, especially on cookies, doughnuts, jams, cheesecake, and frozen waffles, none of which Betsy wanted in her apartment. She had too many moments of weakness to allow temptation to take up residence.

The Waterfront Café was an old institution in Excelsior, though not its only restaurant. There was a new and elegant Italian place a couple of blocks away, and a good Chinese place even nearer. The Waterfront, small and shaggy, was more nearly like a greasy spoon, except its spoons were not at all greasy. The food was very basic, on the order of ham and cheese or tuna sandwiches on white or whole wheat with chips and a pickle on the side, homemade soups, pie a la mode. Like The Polonaise, its menu invoked an earlier, simpler time.

The Waterfront Café was also where people came to hear the latest. Even the Internet was not as efficient at spreading the news as The Waterfront—though there was a single station in the back where you could go on-line. It created an interesting anachronistic *frisson,* eating a tuna melt and reading the *National Review Online.*

Betsy decided on a hot dog with relish and mustard, no chips, and a Diet Coke. She had no more than given her order when Sergeant Mike Malloy sat down across from her. "What's new?" he asked.

"Nothing much," she replied, and watched as a slow smile grew on him, lighting up his whole face. She yearned to smack it off for him. Instead she said, "But I'm not finished looking yet."

That was almost as effective as a smack. "Well, look away, look away. You won't find anything to disprove my case." He rose in one swift move and went out.

When her lunch came, she was too angry to eat. She paid her bill and left.

By the time she got out to the big grocery store on Highway 101, she had cooled off enough to wheel her cart around without running into anyone. Godwin would be home soon—somehow, somehow—and she wanted the kitchen stocked for some of his great cooking. It was too early for even the earliest fresh local produce to be showing at a farmers market, so she went to the produce section and did her best among items imported from Texas, Florida, Mexico, and California.

She filled five grocery bags and came home with a hunger headache.

She built a quick sandwich, ate it while putting things away, and after finishing was still putting things away—had she really meant to buy an apple pie?—when the phone rang.

It was Susan Lavery. "Hi, I've got some news," she burbled happily.

"Well, great! What is it?"

"David Shaker has no alibi. In fact, he left work early last Thursday, and called in sick on Friday."

Betsy felt a hot stab of pleasure. "Gotcha!" she muttered under her breath.

"What was that?"

"Nothing. What else?"

"D'Agnosto—"

"I don't care about Mr. D'Agnosto!" interrupted Betsy.

"Well, listen to me and you won't have to read it in day-after-tomorrow's news. This is big, Betsy, seriously big. The man is going to prison."

"Are you sure?"

"I am now. I'd try to explain in detail, but that might take awhile. Here's the brief—the real brief, not a lawyer's brief. D'Agnosto's specialty is arranging settlements between clients of the firm and dissatisfied or injured litigants. Recently a client was pleased to pay a hundred thousand dollars to avoid a trial, but D'Agnosto, the dirty rat, persuaded the litigant to settle for sixty-five thousand."

"Well, good for D'Agnosto, working hard for his client. Right?"

"Wrong. The client wrote a check for a hundred grand and sent it to the firm, to be deposited. The firm wrote a check on another account for sixty-five thousand and sent it to the litigant. And a third check for the difference went into a special account only he knows about."

"Oh, but didn't the people who wrote the checks notice what's going on?"

"D'Agnosto is our chief finance officer. *He* writes the checks."

"Oh, *Susan*! Have you told anyone about this?"

"Not yet. I'm going to make some photocopies of documents first. Gotta run."

She hung up before Betsy could ask her more about David Shaker. Betsy wanted to call her back, but didn't in case someone at Susan's end was paying attention. Instead, she worried all afternoon about Susan.

A little before seven she tried Susan at home. After six rings Susan's answering machine picked up. Betsy waited for the beep and said, "Susan? Susan, are you there? It's Betsy Devonshire! Please pick up if you're there." She waited a few seconds, then concluded, "Please call me as soon as you get home. Thank you."

At eight she called again. Still no answer. Nor at eight-thirty, or nine.

So she called Mike Malloy at home. "I wouldn't bother you, but I think this may be an emergency. I've been talking with an attorney named Susan Lavery, who works at Hanson, Wellborn, and Smith, John Nye's firm. She hasn't come home from work, and I'm terribly worried."

"Why's that?" he asked.

"Because she called me today and told me two things: one, that David Shaker, who was John's superior, has no alibi for the night John was killed and called in sick the next day. John and David had a very serious confrontation the day before John was murdered. Two, she has collected evidence that a partner in the firm, one Walter D'Agnosto, has been stealing thousands of dollars in settlements he arranged for clients of the firm. If either of those people found out she's been snooping . . . I'm scared for her, Mike."

"Jesus H. Christ, you damned amateurs!"

Fright made her flare, "Oh, yeah? If it weren't for us 'damned amateurs,' you professionals would send innocent people to prison for crimes they didn't commit!"

"All right, all right, calm down. What's this female attorney's name again?"

"Susan Lavery. She has a child, Mike, a little boy."

"The two of you should've thought of that before you got her involved in this." The phone slammed down.

Betsy went to the couch in her living room, fell into it, and wept bitter tears.

In a few minutes, she felt a gentle tap on her elbow. It was Sophie, who looked up into her face with concern. Betsy touched her on top of her head, and the cat climbed heavily into her lap, curled herself into place, and began to purr. Whenever Betsy stopped stroking, she would gently tap her arm again.

Half an hour later, the phone rang. Betsy jumped up, spilling the cat onto the floor, and ran to pick up the receiver.

"It's Sergeant Malloy," he said, his voice tight. "She's at County General. All I know is what I was told, and I was told she fell out of a car. Not her car, apparently. She's not able to tell anyone right now how that happened."

Betsy thrust the fingers of one hand into her hair. "Are you there now?"

"Yeah. And I need to talk to you."

"Can you stay til I get there?"

"Yeah."

Betsy grabbed her purse and started for the door—then

turned back. In her experience, going to the hospital meant a lot of sitting and waiting. Betsy had a hard time just sitting. She ran to her easy chair, grabbed her knitting bag from beside it, and then went out.

Twenty-three

❊ ❊ ❊

BETSY found a parking place on the street near the Hennepin County Medical Center, and hurried into the Emergency Room reception area.

Mike Malloy, thin and grim, was waiting for her in front of the long, tall counter. He took her by the elbow, not gently, and steered her into a small office. "What do you know about this?" he demanded in a low, firm voice, shutting the door behind them.

"How is she?" Betsy replied.

"I said—"

"No. You first. How is she? What happened to her? Can I talk to her?"

"She's still unconscious, but she has a very thick skull, and she'll likely wake up in a little while, none the worse except for a bad headache. She's got a pretty good case of road rash on her arms and legs, along with assorted bumps and bruises, from falling out of a moving car. No broken bones. How did she come to be in the trunk of a car?"

"You're asking me?"

"Who called me away from a terrific basketball game with a complaint that she might be in danger?"

"Um."

"Right. Your turn. How did she come to be in the trunk of a car?"

"Someone put her there, of course. I don't *know* who!" she burst out, forestalling his next question. "I called you to say there were two people she was suspicious of, for two completely different and unrelated reasons." She turned around and saw a metal chair with an imitation leather seat and sat down.

"I went to Hanson Wellborn to see if someone there had a grudge against John. I talked with John's secretary, but she couldn't tell me anything useful. Then I met Susan Lavery, just by chance. I know her, she's a customer. I was surprised to learn she's an attorney. Anyway, we talked and she volunteered to look into various people at the firm. First, she told me about David Shaker, how John had shown him up in an important meeting, and how David had come down to John's office and . . . and there was some kind of confrontation. Tasha, John's secretary, doesn't seem to know anything about it, but Susan is sure it happened. David has a reputation as the enforcer of the firm. I only talked to him briefly, but he seemed perfectly nice right up until he gave Susan a look that should have frozen her marrow." Betsy choked and wiped her eyes. "She told me she expected she would hear from him before the week was out. Oh, I feel just so *terrible*!"

"How did you persuade her to do something so stupid and dangerous?"

"Persuade her? She volunteered! Every time I tried to warn her, she just raved about how much fun she was having! She was digging up dirt on everyone. I asked her just to find out who was angry with John, but then she got this bee in her bonnet about Walter D'Agnosto, who is a very senior partner, and who runs the money end of things. She is very sure he's been stealing funds that are routed through him. She said she had printouts that would prove it. I tried again to warn her, but she just laughed and hung up on me, and I was scared to call her back at work for fear someone might figure out what she was up to—I made no secret of it that I went there to find another suspect in John's murder. Mike, I want to talk to her, can I talk to her?"

"Sure, you can chat away all you like, but she won't hear a word you're saying. She's unconscious, remember?"

"Are you sure she's going to be all right? How long has she been here? When did you check on her last? I want to go ask at the desk, all right?"

"No, stay in that chair. I'm not done with you yet. She hasn't been here two hours yet. I'll go see if she's awake. Now listen to me, you stay put, you hear?" He pointed a finger at her as if it were a pistol.

"All right, yes."

He went out, closing the door sharply, as if to remind her that she was not to open it. She rubbed her upper lip, trying to get her whirling brain to settle down and think.

Maybe it one of those chance things, some rapist picking a victim at random? Where did he wait for Susan? Parking ramps had a reputation as places criminals lurked.

Wait a minute. It had been nearly ten when Mike called,

and nearly ten thirty before she came in here. Mike said Susan had been here "not two hours yet." That meant she'd been picked up off the street some time after eight. She worked until five. Where had she been for three hours? No matter who had grabbed her and thrust her into the trunk of his car, he hadn't been driving around the Twin Cities for three hours. He could have been in Duluth in three hours, or halfway to Chicago in that amount of time. Why hang around here, when there's a person you want to lose? Even if the purpose had been rape, it wouldn't take three hours to find a place to take her.

Maybe David Shaker and Walter D'Agnosto were in an illegal partnership, and one had to wait for the other to show up.

Maybe the grab had been an impulse and now the grabber had to think up a complex plan.

No, neither of those sounded right. If you wanted to get rid of someone, the idea was to get rid of them, not drive around with them in the trunk. That was even more dangerous than leaving them alone. Attorneys could always think up excuses for anything short of being actually caught with a body in the trunk.

Betsy had, for awhile, been a fan of the television show *Cops,* and had been greatly amused at how people reacted when drugs were found in their cars. "That's not mine," they'd universally say. Even when a cop would reach into a pocket and find drugs. "That's not mine." One had gone so far as to insist the underwear the drugs were found in were not his, either.

Not my car—was that going to be the defense?

Where was the car? Had it been stopped? Was the driver in custody?

Suddenly Betsy had more questions for Mike.

The door opened, and he was back, the answer to her prayer. She stood.

He raised a hand against her questions. "She's still unconscious, though they think she may start waking up soon. They're pretty sure she has a concussion, and you know what that means."

"I do? No, I don't."

"People who wake up with concussions don't remember how they got them. They lose at least a few minutes and more often several hours of memory."

"So even if she saw her attacker, she may not be able to remember him?"

"Very likely she won't remember him."

She sat down again. "Mike, do they have the car she fell out of?"

"No. Someone was driving behind when she came out, she almost ran over your friend. She had a cell phone, and called for help."

"Susan must have been conscious to have opened the trunk. Did she tell the woman who stopped anything?"

"Nothing useful. She just said, 'Help me.' The witness said the car Ms. Lavery fell out of was silver, that's all she remembers about it."

"Mike, I was thinking—"

"Always a dangerous thing." He grimaced and turned his face away, then back. "No, that's not true. I apologize. What were you thinking?"

"She gets off work at five. She fell out of that trunk at what, eight? After eight? Where was she taken from? Did she work late? Was she in the parking ramp? Her driveway at home? Oh, and where's her little boy?"

There was a special note of urgency in that last question, so Mike answered it first. "He's with a neighbor, he's fine. She's taken him in before. She'll get him off to school in the morning with her own kids—they go to the same school."

Betsy gave a little sigh of relief. "Good," she said.

"Now, about the other questions. We have retrieved tapes from cameras in the parking ramps near where Ms. Lavery works—I don't suppose you know where she normally parks? Or what kind of car she drives?"

"No," said Betsy, unhappy that she couldn't be helpful.

"That's all right," said Mike genially, glad to prove his side superior in this matter. "We have other sources. One will be able to tell us so we can look for her car when we run the tapes."

"Yes. Yes, that's good. But it's odd that someone thought to drive around for hours with her in the trunk, isn't it? And not going somewhere—or is that true? Where was the car when she fell out?"

"On Cedar Avenue near Lake Street. Only a block from a police station, as it happens."

"Going toward or away from the freeway?" asked Betsy. Cedar Avenue going north ran directly into—your choice—35W going north or 94 West.

"North." Mike nodded. "I'd say he was headed out of town."

"I think that means he'd picked her up shortly before that," said Betsy. "I don't know where Susan lives. Is it any-where near Cedar Avenue?"

"Not really. It would be much quicker to go from her house to 494 than to take city streets all the way over to Cedar."

"What's in the area where she was taken?"

"Now, we don't know where she was taken from. Could be miles from where she fell out."

"But not from downtown, surely. I mean, you can get from Cedar Avenue going north to a quick exit back downtown. If he was coming *from* downtown, he'd be going south."

A twinkling sound came from Mike's suitcoat pocket, and he pulled out a cell phone. "Malloy here," he said into it. He listened for awhile. "Fine, that's good," he said at last. "Right, I'll keep you posted."

He folded the phone up and put it back in his pocket. "Susan Lavery drove a two-year-old Nissan, dark blue. She always parked it on level three or four of the Marquette Avenue Ramp. We have videotape of her getting into her car and driving away at five-fifteen this evening. So she wasn't taken from work. I think that points away from either of the two people you think might be suspects in this kidnapping."

"Possibly. It also might show he has the brains not to take her from a place that could put suspicion on him."

"Or," said Mike, "it could mean she was taken by chance, by a stranger."

"True. But does either David Shaker or Walter D'Agnosto have a silver car?"

Mike smiled tightly. "As it happens, they both do. Shaker has a silver BMW, and D'Agnosto has a silver Audi."

Betsy smiled admiringly back, acknowledging that Mike was, after all, a professional police investigator, not some low-IQ jerk. He also had the resources of several law-enforcement jurisdictions behind him. That could get things done in a hurry. "Well done," she said.

"Now, what we need to do next—"

The door opened, interrupting him. A man in white scrubs stuck his head in. "Sergeant Malloy?"

He turned. "Yes."

"We think Ms. Lavery is about to regain consciousness."

"I'm coming, too," announced Betsy.

Mike sighed, but shallowly. "All right." As they started out the door, he asked, "What's in the bag?"

"My knitting."

This time the sigh was deeper.

Susan lay perfectly flat on her hospital bed, a heart monitor beeping on one side, something clear drip-dripping from a plastic bag down a tube that led to a needle taped to the back of her left hand. Her head was wrapped in cloth with strands of that uncommonly-red hair poking over and under it. Her eyes were closed—the lids looked swollen, somehow—and there were scrapes on her left cheek and forehead. Her left elbow was bandaged, with a betadine stain visible a little above it. A thin woman, it was hard to see the shape of her under the sheet and coverlet; she might just have been a chance set of rumples.

"Ooooh," said Betsy softly, coming up to the bedside.

Mike went to the other side, and the doctor went to stand beside him. "Speak to her," said the doctor to Mike, but Mike looked at Betsy.

"Susan, can you hear me?" There was no response, and Betsy reached under the coverlet for her right hand. "Susan? Susan, if you can hear me, squeeze my hand."

Was there the merest movement in those long fingers?

"Susan, it's Betsy Devonshire. You're in the hospital, but you're going to be all right. You're safe here. Can you open your eyes?"

Betsy bent over the still form. Susan's eyes fluttered, but didn't open, and her lips moved as she appeared to be trying to say something. Betsy leaned closer.

"I believe she's singing!" said Betsy. She turned her ear toward Susan's mouth and listened hard. "She is singing, it's . . . I don't know."

"Uh, *uh*, uh-uh-uh uh uh," sang Susan very quietly.

Mike Malloy, his head near Betsy's, chuckled, startling her. "It sounds like the theme they play at the Olympics," he said.

"You're right, that's what it is!" said Betsy. "Susan, are you singing the Olympic theme?"

The song stopped, and Susan's eyes opened. Betsy found herself staring into those big green depths from a distance of about four inches and hastily straightened. "Hello, Susan," she said. "I'm here, and a police sergeant named Mike Malloy, and Doctor er—"

"Dr. Behr," said the doctor.

"Dr. Behr," finished Betsy.

Mike stepped aside while the doctor became professional with Susan, looking into each of her eyes with a little flashlight, taking her pulse, asking her to wiggle her toes.

"Hi," murmured Susan at him, wiggling obediently.

"Glad to have you with us," he replied, smiling at her.

When he was finished, Betsy asked, "Do you remember what happened?"

Susan thought briefly. "I guess not," she said. She was speaking quietly, not at all like her normal ebullient self. "Last thing I remember, I was exercising." She frowned. "My head hurts. Did I fall? Did someone drop a weight on my head?"

"No, nothing like that," said Mike.

She moved her head slightly so she could look at him. "Who are you?" she asked.

"My name is Sergeant Mike Malloy, I'm with the Excelsior Police. I'd like to ask you a few questions."

Susan looked at Betsy. "Are we in Excelsior?"

"No, HCMC in Minneapolis."

Susan nodded and winced. "Good, I didn't think Excelsior had a hospital. I am in a hospital, right?"

"Yes, Hennepin County Medical Center."

"Good. Otherwise, you have very peculiar taste in bedroom furnishings." She looked over at Dr. Behr. "Who's he?"

"Doctor Behr. He works here at the hospital."

"All right. What happened to me? My head hurts."

"That's what we're trying to figure out," said Betsy. "You were riding around in the trunk of a car, and somehow opened it, and fell out."

"I was not—" she began indignantly. "Oh, wait a minute, the handle glows in the dark, but I had to use my toes." She moved the hand Betsy was holding. "How'd that happen?"

"How did what happen?"

"My hands were fastened together. Behind me." She moved slightly, but as if to replace them behind her back.

"Lie still," said Dr. Behr.

"Who are you?" she asked, frowning at him.

"My name is Dr. Behr," he explained, just as if he hadn't already answered that question. He looked at Mike and then Betsy. "Short-term memory problems, common in concussion." He leaned toward Susan and said, "You were injured when you fell out of a car. You are at the Hennepin County Medical Center, and you are going to be just fine."

"Well, I'm glad to hear that," said Susan. "Where did he go?"

"Where did who go?" asked Betsy.

"The man who put me in the trunk. Where did he go?"

"Do you know who it was who put you in the trunk?"

Susan frowned. "No." Then she smiled. "But . . ."

"But what?"

"I forget." She said this sadly, looking slightly ashamed for forgetting. Her eyes closed. "Tired," she explained, and fell asleep.

Twenty-four

❖ ❖ ❖

Betsy sat in the chair with the cushioned plastic seat and back, knitting. She was on the second sleeve of the entrelac sweater, decreasing every three rows as she neared the end. All she had to do after this was the knit two, purl two ribbing around the neck, sleeves and bottom. It was then she realized she hadn't brought along the gray silk yarn she'd selected for the ribbing. Well, never mind. She put it away. The sweater had been fine, except for all those picked-up stitches. She disliked picking up stitches, there didn't seem to be any rule for doing it properly, you just reached in there and grabbed.

Malloy had gone down the hall for more vending-machine coffee. How he could drink that stuff was beyond Betsy.

On the bed, Susan sighed deeply and opened her eyes. She saw Betsy, blinked once or twice and said, in a rusty voice, "Well, hello there."

"Hi, how are you feeling?"

"Terrible. I have a headache." She started to move her left hand, winced, tried again and saw the big bandage over the needle. "What's this?"

"You're in Hennepin County Medical Center," Betsy replied, trying not to sound as if this were the fourth time she'd explained this to Susan.

"What happened? Was I in some kind of car accident? I hurt all over."

"Not exactly. You were being taken away by someone who had put you in the trunk of his car. But you opened the trunk and fell out. Fortunately the person behind you managed to stop before she ran over you."

Susan was staring at Betsy wide-eyed. "When did this happen?"

"This evening—well, yesterday evening. It's Thursday morning. Very early morning." Betsy looked at her watch. "Four-twenty in the morning."

"I was tied up," said Susan. "I think I remember ropes around me. Thin ropes. They hurt." She frowned with the effort of trying to remember. "But that's all I remember."

"Do you remember going to the health club?"

Susan stared at Betsy. "Wow, you *are* a detective, how did you know about that?"

"I have my methods." Including being already told twice about the health club—the third time Susan hadn't mentioned it.

Susan looked skeptical, but said, "Three nights a week I go to my health club. I went tonight—okay, last night—and it was crowded. I had to park way in the back. I had a massage afterwards, an indulgence I allow myself once a week, so by the time I showered and dressed . . ." She stopped frowning. "I *think* it was dark out. It should have been, it was after seven." She frowned and thought some more. "Then I was curled up in a dark place on some kind of itchy fabric that smelled of fish." She wrinkled her nose. "That must be the trunk you told me about."

"Yes," agreed Betsy. This was more coherent than Susan had been the other times she'd come awake and talked. "How did you get out of the trunk?"

"I don't know. I must have, because I'm here, and all too often women who get stuffed into the trunks of cars don't live to tell about it." Her expression tightened, and she asked fearfully, "Was I raped?"

"Apparently not. You had your work clothes on when you were brought in, and the only damage to them appears to have happened when you came out of that trunk."

"Trunk. Came out of a trunk." Susan's mouth twisted and the line between her eyebrows became a cleft as she tried to remember. "Nope, sorry." She moved on the bed, winced, and closed her eyes. "I feel like he beat me up."

"You were struck on the head, and you hit it again when you came out onto the street. You're also suffering from what Mike calls 'road rash,' which is scrapes and bruises from skidding and rolling on the street."

Susan nodded. "Yep, that's what it feels like. Especially my left elbow." She smiled, still without opening her eyes. "Why is the human left elbow funny?"

"I don't know."

The door opened, and Mike was back. "How's she doing?"

Susan opened her eyes. "Are you Mike?"

He stopped short, staring at her. "Awake for real, I believe," he said. "Yes, I'm Sergeant Mike Malloy, Excelsior Police."

"Why Excelsior? Did I fall out of the trunk in Excelsior?"

"No, I'm here because I'm in charge of the investigation into John Nye's murder."

"What does—oh." Her eyes closed again. "You think maybe David Shaker did this to me."

"Maybe he did," said Betsy.

"It's also possible that this was a random kidnapping, someone looking for a woman to take away, assault, and possibly even murder," said Mike.

"He's saying that because he wants the murderer of John Nye to be Godwin." Betsy felt her fingers clench angrily around her knitting, and immediately released them. This was not the time to pick a fight with Mike.

"I'm looking at everything, trying to figure out what happened," said Mike, also lightening his tone, and Betsy looked up at him in surprise.

It was then she saw he had a brown paper bag, grocery-store sized, in one hand. "What's in there?" she asked, thinking it might be something to eat, or a six-pack of Diet Pepsi. She could use some of either. Maybe it was both.

Mike came to the bedside table and put the bag on it. The way he lifted it, the way it sounded being put down, there were no weighty containers of soft drinks in it.

"Evidence," he pronounced, and opened the bag. From it he lifted numerous tangled lengths of thin rope of a shiny white nylon.

"Is this what was used to tie Susan up?" Betsy asked, reaching to take a length of the stuff from Mike's hand.

"Yes," he said, holding a piece himself and shaking the rest off it into the bag.

He held it out to Susan, who stared at it, then at him,

shrugging and shaking her head. It set off no memories in her mind.

Betsy looked closer at her own piece. It wasn't tangled, it was knotted. Whoever had cut it off Susan had the intelligence to cut it between the knots, so they were preserved. The long knot she was looking at was a sheepshank, an arrangement used to shorten a length of rope that was already tied at either end.

"What, you see something there?" asked Mike, alerted by the way she was looking at the rope.

"Give me another piece," Betsy ordered.

"Sure. Here." This was two ends tied together in a sheet-bend, a version of the square knot.

"He must have been going to untie you," said Betsy to Susan. "Probably after you were dead."

Susan stared at the knot in Betsy's hand. "How do you know?"

"Because this can come undone fairly easily. Just—" She was reaching for the place in the knot to pull to make it come apart.

"Don't!" barked Mike. "That's evidence, remember?"

"Oh, yes. Of course. Sorry." She handed it back. "But now I know who did this to you, Susan."

"You do?" She stared at Betsy.

"Certainly. Of Shaker and D'Agnosto, which one is a sailor, familiar with knots?"

"D'Agnosto!" said Susan.

"That's why his trunk smelled of fish." Betsy chuckled. "And that's why you woke up the first time singing the Olympic theme song."

"I did? Why?"

"Because he drives an Audi, and the emblem of an Audi is four interlocked rings, not unlike the Olympic symbol." She held out her hand to Mike. "Show me all those knots, I'll bet not one is a granny."

Mike did. And not one was.

"I'll grant you that if these are sailor knots, and one of your suspects is a sailor," said Mike, "then you've got something. What I want to know is how come *you* know so much about knots."

"Back in my youth, I was a Navy WAVE. For about six months, I dated a bosun's mate. He taught me a lot of sea lore, like white work and the rules of encounter at sea—and knots." Betsy's eyes went distant for a few moments. "And other things."

She came back to the present with a bump when Mike said, "I suppose you think this proves Mr. D'Agnosto murdered John Nye."

"Oh, no," said Betsy, surprised at him. "I think Mr. D'Agnosto tried to kill Susan because she found out he was stealing money from Hanson, Wellborn, and Smith. John Nye's and Walter D'Agnosto's paths never crossed."

"Not never," said Susan sleepily.

Betsy had the familiar feeling of her ears growing big points that swiveled around. "What do you mean, 'not never'?"

"Well, they knew each other. D'Agnosto was the chief financial officer. Any time money entered the equation, D'Agnosto had to be notified. And you know lawyers, money is *always* part of the equation."

Betsy thought about that. "There was that deal John dreamed up to give an executive a lucrative compensation plan. Did D'Agnosto have anything to do with that?"

"No, no, no. That had nothing to do with money coming to the firm, except the fee, of course." She sighed, and her eyes closed. "Want to sleep now."

"Hold on," said Mike, reaching for the call button. He said to Betsy, "People with concussions aren't supposed to sleep."

"Well, what has she been doing up til now?" asked Betsy crossly.

"That was being unconscious. This is sleep."

"Oh." Betsy sat down and began to put her knitting away. She was pretty sure they were going to be sent away so Susan could rest, if not sleep.

"So what do you think, Susan," asked Mike, "is Betsy right or wrong to say D'Agnosto had nothing to do with John Nye's death?"

"I dunno," murmured Susan.

"Come on, talk to us," he persisted. "Did you get a look at the man who pushed you into the trunk?"

"I don't remember," said Susan even more softly.

Betsy asked, "Susan, tell me about that executive compensation plan John figured out. You did help with the research on it, didn't you?"

"Mm hm," said Susan, barely audible now.

"I think it may be important," said Betsy.

Mike looked at her, puzzled. Betsy shook her head no, and waggled her eyebrows at him. She was trying to keep Susan awake until the nurse came, that was all. He nodded comprehension.

"Important? Not important," Susan said. "Can't be important." She sounded more awake, if somewhat more fuddled. She blinked at the ceiling.

"Why not?" asked Betsy.

"The executive remun—remumeration—renumeration—wasn' for a member of the firm. Partners share in the profits, ever'one else gets a 401-K plan. We don' do pensions." Her eyes had closed again.

"Golden parachute! Oh my! Um, how much did the firm charge to come up with the plan?"

The door to the room opened and a nurse came in. "Yes?" she said, going to the bed and touching Susan's forehead.

"Well, hi, there!" said Susan, smiling up at her.

"Welcome back, Ms. Lavery," said the nurse. "How do you feel?"

"Sleepy. Can you send these two away so I can sleep?" She moved her head to indicate Betsy and Mike.

Mike said, "I seem to remember being taught that you don't let people with concussions fall asleep."

"Nowadays we do let them sleep, we just wake them up every fifteen minutes to see how they're doing."

"So go away," said Susan. "Let me have my fifteen-minute nap."

"All right," said Betsy, turning around, bending down, to make sure nothing had fallen out of her purse or knitting bag to roll away. "Mike?"

"Yes, all right." He said to Susan, "I'll check back on you later today."

"Me, too," said Betsy, impatient now to be gone. "Come on, we'll ride down in the elevator together. There's something I want to ask you."

"Jesus sufferin' Christ," sighed Mike, following her out.

Twenty-five

❖ ❖ ❖

"WELL?" growled Mike in the elevator, but Betsy waited until a nurse—a far cry from the stiffly starched, all-in-white women of Betsy's youth; this one wore clean but rumpled crayon-blue scrubs with a pattern of goldfish printed on it—got off one floor down.

"I want to come with you while you arrest Walter D'Agnosto."

He looked at her, pale eyebrows raised high on his freckled face. "Why should I let you do that?"

"Because he murdered John Nye, too."

"Wait a second, you told me not three minutes ago that David Shaker was the murderer."

"That was before Susan mentioned the golden parachute."

"No, no, you were the one who said 'golden parachute.'"

"Now don't get technical. She was talking about the same thing, a method of putting aside money for an executive in case he quits before retirement."

"All right. So?"

"Well, John Nye invented a false identity and used it to open a bank account over in Wisconsin."

"How do you know this?" interrupted Mike, his tone sharp.

"Didn't Charlie Nye tell you? He showed me the driver's license, and it's got John's photograph on it. Anyway, John's been stuffing the account with money, tens of thousands of dollars, deposited in irregular amounts at irregular intervals. His brother, executor of John's estate, says he has accounted for all of John's income—and that he definitely did not have tens of thousands of dollars to spare for a savings account in Wisconsin, so this money is coming from some secret source."

He frowned at her. "So what are you thinking? Theft?"

"Actually, I think it's blackmail. I think John was claiming a share of the money Walter was stealing from Hanson Wellborn."

"How sure are you about this?" The elevator stopped at the ground floor and they got off.

"Almost positive." Betsy looked around, got her bearings, and headed for the lobby. "I think, if he was directly involved in stealing money from the law firm, Susan would have said something—she's been rooting into everyone's computer accounts. He was doing something illegal; why else set up a bank account in another state under a false name? I will bet you an airline ticket to anywhere in the world you want to go that the printouts Susan had of the settlements Walter was stealing will match within days of the date, the deposits John made into that account. Come on, hurry! D'Agnosto must be in a terrible panic about now—Oh, rats!" She came to a halt so sudden Mike nearly ran into her.

"Now what?"

"I don't know where he lives."

"Who, Charlie?"

"Walter D'Agnosto, of course."

"Well, for—"

"Can you find out?"

"Certainly."

"Then do it." Betsy hurried off again, this time to the information desk in the lobby. She stopped in front of the very young woman sitting at a computer and phone console. Betsy said to her, "Pardon me, but can you tell me if someone specific called to ask about a patient here?"

The woman behind the counter looked at Betsy with bored and tired eyes. "I doubt it."

"It's terribly important."

"Who's the patient?"

"Susan Lavery. I want to know if someone from her place of employment—Hanson, Wellborn, and Smith—called to see how she's doing."

The woman studied Betsy warily. "Why do you want to know?"

"Because someone from her place of employment is responsible for her being here. He tried to kill her."

The woman's eyes widened, and she didn't look sleepy anymore. She clattered her fingers on her keyboard. "Susan Lavery, you said?"

"Yes, room 714B."

"I can confirm that Ms. Lavery is a patient here."

"Yes, I know, we were just up talking to her. Sergeant Malloy and I." Betsy looked around and nodded at Mike, ambling toward her. "Mike, show her your badge, please."

He complied. "What's up?"

The woman said, "Yes, there was an inquiry about an hour ago. He didn't ask to speak to her. I'm sure I told him that she's conscious and talking to the police."

"Whoa!" said Betsy. "I bet he didn't like that!"

Now the woman looked frightened. "I didn't know I wasn't supposed to say that."

"Who called?" demanded Mike.

"Walter D'Agnosto," said Betsy, willing the woman behind the counter to hold her tongue long enough to get Mike out of earshot. "Come on!" Betsy turned and ran out the double set of doors into the chill spring air, pleased to hear the slap of his feet behind her. A wind had sprung up, young trees—why weren't there ever any old trees in a downtown, she wondered irrelevantly—waved their barely clothed branches at them, as if to hurry them along, as she ran down to the corner, looking for her car. "Where are you parked?" she asked, raising her voice over the wind. "I'll follow you!"

"No, you'll ride with me," he said, and took her by the elbow, not any more gently than he had when she first walked into the hospital. He hustled her to a big Chevrolet pickup truck, probably blue, it was hard to tell under the orange street lights. "Get in."

She went around to the other side. She had to climb up into the truck and tried not to grunt with the effort. Mike had his cell phone in his hand by the time she got herself seated. He was using very cryptic language, by which she understood he was talking to police officials. One term she knew: backup. Jill had told her that the cowboy cop, running into danger all by himself, was a myth. "Nobody wants to go home with more holes in his body than he started out with," she'd noted, and one way to avoid that was to bring along enough help so the person to be arrested didn't even think to resist—or if he did, he was easily taken down.

So Mike wasn't going to go after Walter D'Agnosto with only a short, plump civilian—noncops were civilians, in cop talk—for backup. Betsy was far more relieved about that than Mike was.

Mike pulled away from the curb and raced up Seventh. "Where are we going? I mean, I know to get Mr. D'Agnosto, but where does he live?"

"Riverplace, on Hennepin." He made the corner, turning so sharply the big tires on his truck squealed, and raced across the suspension bridge. Immediately on the other side were two very modern condominium buildings facing one another across Hennepin, made as if of big gray blocks irregularly stacked. A shallow curved driveway led up to the entrance on one side; a glassed bridge over the street connected the two; a sidewheeler boat in neon ornamented the bridge. Because she was frightened, her attention was painfully sharp, aware of every detail. Two squad cars were waiting in the driveway. As Mike pulled up, another joined them.

As Mike shut off his engine and opened the door he said to her, "You stay put. I mean it."

"Yes, sir," she said, having no desire to go see if this was going to turn dangerous.

It seemed to take forever, but was probably about fifteen minutes later that two men in uniform came out of the building with a third man between them. The man's hands were fastened behind his back. He wore khaki trousers, a brown sweater, brown loafers. His head was down, his gray hair gleaming in the street lights: D'Agnosto. They led him to a squad car with a heavy metal screen separating the back seat from the front. One of the uniforms had to open the front door to unlock the back door. As he did, D'Agnosto looked up and around, and saw Betsy sitting in Mike's truck. If he recognized her, he gave no sign, but bent his head again and climbed into the back of the squad car. The two cops climbed into the front seat and, lights blinking but no siren whining, they headed back up Hennepin, across the bridge.

Betsy looked down the river, at the buildings on the other side. There was the clock tower on the red-granite City Hall, a Victorian castle. A block from it, she knew, was the Adult Detention Center, invisible from here. Soon, and for just the next little while, he and Godwin would both be in there, breathing the same air, wearing the same color in jumpsuits.

Then Godwin would come home.

The door on the driver's side of the pickup opened, making her jump.

"Satisfied?" he asked.

"What did he say?" she returned.

Mike smiled a thin smile. " 'The bitch identified me, didn't she?' I said, 'No, we have other ways of finding things out.' He was packing to leave town; you were right that we had to move fast. He also said, 'Some day someone is going to sue Audi about that handle in the trunk.' " Mike laughed.

Betsy smiled. "It glows in the dark. She used her toes to open it. Remember? I thought she was talking nonsense until I remembered seeing a handle in my Buick's trunk. Funny how when she woke up for real she couldn't remember that part, isn't it?"

"The human brain never fails to amaze me." Mike started the engine. "I'm going to take you over to your car, so you can go home. It's been a long night." As he pulled out of the driveway, he began to whistle the Olympic theme.

Twenty-six

❖ ❖ ❖

THE Fourth of July that year was a scorcher. Betsy sat on the folding chair on top of the big hill at the Common, Excelsior's main park. The hill was above and behind the band shell, and from there the various bands could only entertain, not deafen. There were mature trees up on top, so she was able to sit in the shade. She wore low-heeled sandals, a loose-fitting white cotton dress with lace trim on the scoop collar, and a white straw hat with a curved brim and a lot of openings woven into its crown. She was sipping a genteel lemonade from a real glass.

"Isn't this *civilized?*" sighed Godwin, resplendent in white duck shoes, white linen slacks, and a pale blue sleeveless shirt. He, too, was sitting in one of those canvas and aluminum chairs that unfold like an umbrella, and sipping lemonade. A breeze off the lake made the heat tolerable.

On a blanket in front of them was an old-fashioned wicker picnic basket, and in the basket were silverware and plates, wine- and drinking-glasses, cloth napkins, two loaves of French bread, a mystery novel, and two stitching projects. Beside the basket was an ice chest, and in it were roast chicken, Betsy's Great-Aunt Velva's bean salad, a dozen chocolate chip cookies, three bottles of wine, and more lemonade. It was about ten minutes to high noon.

"There you are!" said a new voice and they looked around to see Susan Lavery coming up the hill holding hands with a handsome little boy, very blond, wearing blue shorts and a red tank top with a badge pinned to it. His mother was carrying an ice chest in the other hand. "I brought potato salad. It's not a picnic without potato salad." She put the ice chest down on the blanket. "Whew, it's a hot one!" A long-fingered hand brushed her flaming red hair back from her pale forehead.

"How's the private eye business?" asked Betsy.

"Things are going swimmingly! Thanks so much for introducing me to Mr. Lebowski."

"You said swimming, can we go swimming?" asked the boy.

"*May* we go swimming. Do you want to eat first or swim first?" Susan asked him.

"Swim! Swim!" he demanded, and began a little dance on sandaled feet.

"His majesty commands, I obey," said Susan.

He gazed up at her, a surprised golden angel. "I'm not a majesty! I'm a *policeman*!" He rubbed his badge with his fingers, as if to make its shine more obvious.

"Even more must his orders be obeyed," said Susan to Godwin and Betsy. "We probably won't be long. Which way to the swimming hole?"

"That way," said Betsy, pointing down the other side of the hill. "Nice sandy beach."

After the two of them left, Godwin said, "She looks well."

Betsy nodded, "Nothing like a hit on the head to boost one's health." She looked over at her shop manager. "Or a stay in jail," she added meditatively.

He hooted with amusement, then asked anxiously, "Seriously, do you think I still look good?"

She sighed. He'd asked this question about three times a week for over a month, and she'd hoped to forestall another inquiry with her remark. "You look wonderful, very rested."

"Do I look as good as I did before I went to jail?"

"Absolutely. Better. You're one of those people for whom a little adversity only smooths the brow."

"Hmmm. Maybe if I had some adversity before, John wouldn't have been so mean to me."

"Just living with John was plenty of adversity, I would think. Come on, Goddy, he wasn't exactly Prince Charming, was he?"

"Yes, he was!" Godwin said heatedly. "Well, most of the time."

"Goddy, think about this: Every time you took a step toward independence, he tried to block it."

"But it was because he loved me. He wanted me to stay with him and be his sweet little boy."

Betsy nodded. "I remember a friend from my first marriage. Do you know, her husband actually touched her on top of her head one evening when we were talking politics and said, 'Now don't you worry your pretty little head about these things, baby.' "

"What did she do?" Godwin asked, looking afraid of the answer.

"She giggled and said, 'Okay, honey.'" Betsy quoted the woman in a sweet little voice.

Godwin laughed, surprised and pleased.

Betsy continued, wickedly, "He left her for a mid-level executive less than a year later."

"So he didn't want a sweet little baby after all," said Godwin. "He was lying to her."

"I don't think so. He liked taking care of his silly little ignoramus when she really was one. But just before he said that to her, she'd made one or two sharp remarks that showed her cute dumb blond act was, in fact, an act."

"Oh, well, I can understand that, then." Godwin sat back and lifted his chin to welcome a cooling breeze that rustled the leaves overhead.

Betsy waited for the penny to drop.

It did, after a minute, and Godwin sat up straight. "Hold on! Are you saying there's a *parallel* here? That John was mad at me because I was only *pretending* to be his sweet little boy anymore?"

"*Were* you only pretending?"

"No, of course not! Mostly not! Only sometimes!" He sniffed and rubbed his nose, then touched it with the fingers of both hands. "Is it growing?" he asked in mock alarm. Then he sighed and said, "And John knew, didn't he?"

"Yes, he told me a long time ago that it was more like a game the two of you played, you being silly and him being indulgent."

"And he was getting tired of it."

"I don't think he knew for sure how he felt. On the one hand, he told his brother Charlie that for the first time in his life he'd found someone who never bored him."

Godwin smiled in delight. "Are you making that up? Or are you telling me what he really said?"

"I'm telling you what Charlie told me he said. After hearing all the different stories surrounding John's death, I'm going to take what anyone tells me with a whole teaspoon of salt. But if Charlie was telling the truth, it seems to me that the quarrel you and John had was just another quarrel. What made it serious was that, I believe, John was fighting with all his might against his own growing maturity, against his realization that he had found someone who satisfied his need for youth and energy—but also his adult need for complexity and intelligence.

"On the other hand, we found evidence on his computer that he was surfing the 'Net for naïve young men. I think he was like most of us, a bundle of contradictions. Oh, Goddy, I'm so sorry his life got cut off before you two had a chance to resolve this!"

He waved off her sympathy. "It would have been worse, I think, if I'd lost him while we were swimming in warm feelings." He frowned, then very consciously smoothed the furrows with a forefinger. "This morning I thought I saw that I'm getting this line, right here."

"A little botox will clean that right up."

He started to agree, then shook his head, then, chin up, announced bravely, "I'm not going to do that anymore. I'm out of my teens now, and there's no reason to be ashamed of that fact. I don't mind looking twenty-five—especially if it's a *young* twenty-five." He presented a profile to Betsy. "What do you think?"

"You don't look that far into your twenties," she prevaricated—Godwin was, in fact, twenty-eight—but she was surprised at this sudden willingness to be perceived as older than nineteen.

"I've also decided to start dating."

"Well, good for you!"

"But I don't want to go looking for an older man. I mean, you can do that only so long before you're going out on the town with someone from the wheelchair set. Right?"

Betsy didn't dare laugh, or cheer, for fear of hurting his feelings. Bound up with those restrictions, she could only nod for a few seconds before she trusted her voice. "That's right."

"And I don't want to be like John, taking them out of the sandbox."

"No, of course not." She was sure of that; she could not imagine Godwin turning predator.

"So that leaves people my own age. I think . . ." He started to frown but again thought better of it, and instead closed his eyes as his expression turned dreamy. "I'm thinking of looking for someone dark. Hispanic, maybe. There was this *gorgeous* young man selling jewelry at Teotihuacan. I bought this bracelet from him." Eyes still closed, he held up a wrist ornmented with heavy silver links. "*Such* shoulders! And his *eyes!* Like big drops of melted dark chocolate, you know what I mean?"

Betsy smiled. "Yes. Very romantic."

Godwin sighed, nodding. "We'd make a beautiful couple, him so dark and me so blond." He sighed again, and after a few moments more of reflection, his eyes opened and he put his lemonade down. "I think I'll take a little walk, okay?"

"All right. Lunch in half an hour?"

"Right."

She watched him walk away, pleased to see this rekindling of his blood. He was heading downhill, in the direction of the band shell, where young people had gathered to listen and dance to a rock group. His movements were as lithe and youthful as he could possibly wish—at least judging from her end of the calendar. Those youngsters down there wouldn't be fooled, Betsy knew. She remembered from her own youth, how anyone over twenty-five was instantly detected—and thought to be over the hill. She hoped it was true that Godwin was going to accept his age—or at least something a little closer to it.

It was nice to be very young, but even nicer to be grown up. Then, of course, there was real maturity. What would those youngsters think of her—for that matter, what must Godwin think of her, trundling inescapably down her fifties?

She was saved from further consideration by a voice talking cheerfully, coming up behind her.

"It's the assistant superintendent of education standards, the cultural integration liaison, the curriculum instruction specialist, the management program specialist for math, and for fine arts, language arts, physical education, science—for every subject. There are pages and pages of these people, you'll see. Every one of them has a secretary and at least one support person. They're the ones who soak up all the money, they're the reason I have to make every student bring me boxes of Kleenex every fall. I tell you, it's discouraging. Whew, it's hot! Hi, Betsy!"

Shelly was looking very attractive in a fluttery dress, her hair up on top of her head with tendrils falling in front of her ears. With her was a woman in her twenties, comfortable in denim shorts and a T-shirt advertising the Children's Museum of St. Paul. Between them was slung an ice chest. The young woman looked at Betsy, then Shelly. "I didn't believe you, I'm sorry," she said.

Shelly explained, "I tried to tell her we were dressing for the picnic, but she said no one dresses for a picnic."

"You look very comfortable," Betsy said to the woman. "Would you like a glass of lemonade?"

"Thank you, yes. I'm Alison March."

"She'll be teaching second grade this fall," said Shelly, who would herself have third graders. "Where is everyone?"

"Susan Lavery and Liam are swimming, Goddy's down the hill dancing, and the others haven't arrived yet."

As if on cue, Nikki and three other part-time employees of Crewel World came panting up the hill with folding chairs and ice chests and wicker baskets. They were wearing sun dresses and straw hats. There were high-pitched cries of greeting and compliments on the costumes, then lemonade was poured and everyone sat for five minutes of rehydration. Then chairs were set out, another blanket was spread, and Rennie brought out the silver and china picnic set she'd inherited from her grandmother. Linen napkins her great-grandmother had embroidered were an added touch.

Everything was just about ready when Susan came back with Liam, who was wrapped and shivering in a towel. Betsy stood to look for Godwin, who was just coming up from the band shell, an odd look on his face.

"They're all so *young*," he said.

"And so are you, Goddy!" said Susan, coming to kiss him on the chin. "Funny how it took so long to finally meet you, because now I see you all the time."

Everyone sat down, either on blankets or on folding

chairs, handed around bowls of salad or plates of chicken, draping linen napkins across laps, trying not to look too superior to the people across the way ducking the smoke from their grills as they prepared a hot meal while the temperature climbed to ninety-three.

"T'woooooooooo! T'woooooooooo!" breathed the low-pitched steam whistle of the antique steamship Minnehaha as the streetcar-shaped boat pulled away from the dock, taking passengers on a one-hour tour. Sailboats dotted the bay, and powerboats cruised among them.

On land, it was a Norman Rockwell day in the park. The parade up Water Street had been this morning, but children with decorated bicycles cruised the park, still showing off. A high school band began rocking Sousa in the bandshell. Distant squeals of children playing in the water down by the beach could be heard. Down at the baseball diamond, a dad was showing his son how to throw a sinker, his daughter smacking her hand into her glove as she waited to catch it. A woman was laughing with her infant as they watched a kite shaped like a butterfly climb into the cloudless sky.

Lars and Jill came by. Jill was wearing one of Lars's shirts over her shorts to disguise the bulge just starting to show in her tummy. They didn't stay long; they were so wrapped up in one another, they didn't have much to say to anyone else. All the Crewel World people sighed and smiled after them when they walked away.

Soon after, the women gathered up the remnants and dishes and put them away. Then, one by one, they visited the rest room down by the baseball diamond to wash their hands. Back under the big, old trees, stitching projects were brought out.

Shelly said, "Goddy, you're not knitting a sock," her tone indicating surprise.

"No, I thought I'd try a little printed needlepoint canvas I found when I was rearranging a rack of them." He handed it to her.

Shelly looked at it and put a hand vertically over her mouth, as if suppressing tears.

"What?" asked Betsy, and Shelly handed it on to her.

It was a bird perched in the open door of a cage set before an open window. Half finished as it was, Betsy could see Godwin had changed the colors; the bird had been green and was now white and silver, the cage had been gray, but was being stitched in metallic gold.

Betsy looked over at Godwin, who smiled at her. Walter D'Agnosto had denied any knowledge of what had happened in John's house that evening; there seemed no chance to recover any of Godwin's good jewelry, most especially his little diamond bird in its ormulu cage.

But with this piece, Godwin was saying it was all right; it was time to let the little bird go free.

"Do you miss him?" asked Shelly.

"Sometimes," admitted Godwin. "But what I'm coming to understand is that it was so important to John that he be the boss that nobody else could take him on vacation and make him have a good time." He looked at Betsy. "Right?"

Betsy nodded. "I'm sure that's true. That's why, even though it really was a wonderful vacation in one of the biggest cities in North America, where you visited a world-famous museum, an ancient Aztec pyramid complex, he whined and complained about it. It couldn't be any good; it wasn't his idea and he didn't get to buy it for you."

"Why, that's despicable!" said Shelly.

"On the other hand, I don't think he would actually have signed that new will," said Betsy.

Bershada said, "Well, since he didn't, does that mean you're now independently wealthy, and too good to be consorting with the likes of us?"

"The will hasn't finished probate yet," said Godwin, "so I'm not rich yet. Nor," he sighed sadly, "will I be when it is all done with."

Shelly asked baldly, "How much did he leave you?"

"A lump sum of eight thousand," said Godwin, "*plus* the interest from a trust fund that will bring me a few thousand a month for the rest of my life. The lump sum is supposed to be for me to move somewhere else, like San Francisco. He specifically mentioned San Francisco." He looked around the blankets, at the smiling faces looking back. "As *if!*" he shouted, and fell back in his chair, laughing.

Later, as the long summer twilight turned to night and everyone began focusing on the lake in anticipation of fireworks, Betsy leaned toward Godwin and murmured, "You're not even tempted to try San Francisco?"

"No," he murmured back. "Too expensive. Besides, out there, I'd just be one of several thousand brilliantly gay men. Here, in this little pond, I'm the shiny big frog."

Out on the lake, two long barges were anchored. Small figures could be seen hurrying about on them. Down in front of the bandshell, someone had set off a big fountain and children could be seen dancing around its golden sparks.

"Betsy," Godwin said, his tone just a trifle too studied, "do you think I'll ever fall in love again?"

"Of course you will. You'll find a nice young man with a future. A doctor fresh out of medical school, perhaps." She nodded. "Yes, I can see you settling down with a doctor."

"You sound like a Jewish mother," said Bershada with a deep chuckle.

"Or an Italian one," said Shelly.

"She sounds like Mrs. Everymother," said Nikki, "including my own."

"Oh, look!" said Godwin, pointing. From somewhere across the lake, Wayzata perhaps, a big skyrocket was spewing stars. Then, farther south, another.

A minute later, something out on the barge went, *"Phoomp!"* A silver-white rocket painted a squiggly line up the sky, and with a multitude of stars and a rattle of little explosions the Excelsior display began.

"Aaaahhhhh," sighed everyone, happily.

Directions for
Tlatolli Pattern

There are two ways to approach this pattern.

First way: Using the DMC 321 red floss (or any red floss), two strands, make a single cross for every black square on the pattern. Outline the design in backstitch using a single strand of DMC 310 black, or any black floss.

Second way: Do the back stitching in DMC 310 or any black floss. Use a single strand. Then fill in with DMC 321 red, or any red floss, using two strands. You may wish to use half or other partial stitches.

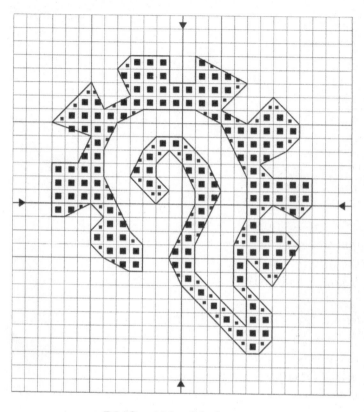

o DMC 310 Black
■ DMC 321 Christmas Red

Fabric: Aida, White
Design Count: 26w x 28h
Design Size: 1.9 x 2.0 in, 14 Count